THATCHER

LOCP

TARA LEE
DL GALLIE

Proofread by **Karen Hrdlicka**, Barren Acres Editing

Edited by **Lisa Edwards, More Than Words Proofreading** and **Margaret Neal**

Cover Designed by **Tara Lee**

Interior formatting by **DL Gallie**

The Lords rule supreme, they're cruel, reckless, and
crave the power their status brings.
Their world is corrupt—filled with lies and secrets.
They rule Crestwood Prep like their fathers before them, but
nothing lasts forever.
Secrets are about to spill free, lies uncovered,
The Lords aren't as invincible as they once thought.

Let The Games Begin.

This is my school, my kingdom.

My brother's and I rule, we are The Lords.

Our secrets have always been just that, ours. Until *her*—

Remington Hearst.

She hates me, but I despise her and what her family did.

She needs to learn her place because she doesn't want to cross me.

I'll make them pay.

I'll make her pay.

This is a game she isn't prepared for. Turns out, neither was I.

THATCHER

My jaw ticks as my gaze follows her. She walks through *my* school like she belongs here. Breathing the same air as us. Her long brunette locks, blowing in the slight breeze.

My heart races, it feels like a tornado rippling through my chest, but lust isn't what provokes it, it's hatred. Pure, everlasting hatred flows through my veins as I watch *her*.

Seeing her here after what happened has my blood boiling. My body vibrates as anger pumps through my system. I never thought she would ever face coming here. But I guess she has a death wish, just like *them*.

My fists clench tightly. My body tightens with each step

she takes. Like a hawk, I watch her every move. She has not a care in the world but not for long, she's in our world now.

Her gaze filters across the grass, taking everything in and finally it lands on me. From where I am, I see her breath hitch and her eyes blink rapidly as we continue to stare at one another. From all the way over here, I feel the air change around us. From the blank look on her face, she has no idea who the hell I am, but I know who she is. I know everything about Remington Hearst and her family. I know everything. But soon, she will know who I am.

I've been waiting for the perfect moment to make my move and as if she's been presented to me on a silver platter, finally, the time has come. The time has come to make them pay. Nothing will stop me from seeking out my revenge, and since she's the Hearst that's here, she gets to feel my wrath. *Lucky her.*

When I heard she was coming to Crestwood, I didn't believe it. She was enrolled here, just like her brothers, but I still wasn't convinced I'd actually see her here on school grounds with my own two eyes, which makes this all the more delicious.

She'll pay for their sins.

Pay for *her* mistakes.

She.

Will.

Pay.

I'll delight in toying with her. Taunting her. I'll show her just who rules these halls. Her eyes hold immense pain, but seeing how she's nothing to me, what do I care?

I know her story. I know why she's here. As I said, I know everything about *her*. I'd have to be an idiot not to. But nothing passes through these walls without my knowledge. After all, I'm one of The Lords.

Our name holds everything.

Power.

Wealth.

Respect.

And my favorite—fear.

I take small, measured steps as I make my way toward my brothers, Hendrix, Saint, and Reign. Hendrix, Saint, and I are triplets and Reign is a year younger than us but he's a super genius and they skipped him a grade, allowing him to be in the same grade as us. Poor Mom had four kids under two, Dad knocked her up again when she was breastfeeding us triplets. We like to tease Reign that he's adopted or a stork dropped him off because he's blond whereas us triplets and our parents are brunettes.

As I get closer to them, I know they're aware of her too because just like me, they're watching. Taking note of every move she makes. There's a glint in my eye because finally, the time has come to seek revenge for what her whore of a mother did to my family.

Hendrix moves the toothpick around in his mouth, his eyes locked on her just like mine. "She's actually here?" His tone is clipped, his anger vibrates off him and it shocks me a little because he's the laid-back one of the four of us. I'm a hothead, the bad boy if you want to call me that. Reign is the quiet nerd who wears his heart on his sleeve and Saint, he's broody and sensitive. But underneath it all, we have each other's backs, no questions asked and we will do anything for those we love.

"Certainly looks like it, to be honest, I didn't think she would. Girl's got some big fuckin brass lady balls, I'll give her that," Reign boasts, running his fingers through his shaggy blond hair.

The one thing we can all agree on, her coming here was her first mistake. I need to know why. And if she came here to find answers, she won't like what she finds.

Turning my attention to Reign, I stare intently. "You know what to do," I order. He nods and takes off toward his room.

"Think he'll find anything we don't already know?" Hendrix questions me, his eyes still locked on *her*.

I click my tongue and nod. "If anyone can find shit, it's Reign," I tell him. He chuckles because Reign is a straight-up fucking genius, too smart for his own good, probably why they skipped him a grade and he's in the same grade as us. His hacking abilities are straight-up FBI level, and his skills are going to come in handy now that *she* is here. Looking at my youngest triplet, Saint—I love lording that I'm older than Hendrix and Saint, even if there are only twenty-six minutes between the three of us—I point at him. "You, follow her. Keep an eye on her. Fuck, even befriend her, maybe it will get us insight we don't have or can't find online."

With a nod, he hitches his bag over his shoulder. Slapping me on mine, he strides across the grass and follows her inside Crestwood Hall.

"Can we trust Saint to get the job done? He's not in a good headspace right now." Hendrix's concern over our brother matches my own. Saint is troubled, something is going on with him, but just like the rest of us, his secrets are behind lock and key. Our secrets are locked up tighter than a nun's cunt, and unless we are ready to share, that's how they will remain.

"I trust him with my life. He won't let whatever's going on impact this. He wants this just as much as we do, and I cannot wait to see how it all plays out."

"What are you going to do?" Hendrix spits out his tooth-pick, rubbing his tongue over his teeth.

Lifting my gaze to him, a sinister smirk lifts my lips. "I'm going to have some fun." He returns my smirk and for the first time ever, I can't wait for class to start.

Making our way through the front doors, it's chaos as we head toward our lockers but the chaos parts and allows us through. That's the thing about being top fucking shit, every day is met with new adventures, endless possibilities, and respect. Unlike most of the students here, we belong. This is our school, like our father before us and his father and his father's father, nothing happens unless *we* give the go-ahead.

I linger in the halls as our cousin Rian hands me a piece of paper. Nodding at him, I slip it into my pocket to read later. He slaps my back and pulls a blonde into his side. He licks the side of her neck making her giggle before he sticks his tongue into her mouth. Being a Lord gives us endless access to pussy, there's always some girl willing to spread her legs or suck dick. It's tough being a Lord, not!

My phone vibrates in my pocket, but I ignore it knowing full well it's only my father. The old man has things to answer for as well, but first things first, I have to deal with *her*.

I don't simply want to break her. No, I want to destroy Remington Hearst for what her family did.

After all, an eye for an eye, right?

REMY

STANDING in front of the gates of Crestwood Prep, I feel nothing. I hate every second of being here. This wasn't my life, nor is it supposed to be. I was happy at Alton Academy, I had friends, and no one knew of our family and our ... dramas. Yes, let's go with dramas. But what Mother wants, Mother gets. Even if it means uprooting my life and moving me across the country mid-semester.

My mother, Rochelle Hearst, is the lord of our manner, and when she says jump, you jump. Daddy couldn't even stop her from doing this but then again, what could an absent father do to stop this from happening? Nothing ... just like usual.

Taking a deep breath, I put one foot in front of the other, and I enter hell aka the school grounds of Crestwood Prep. Home to the elite of the elite and those whose parents don't want them around twenty-four seven. The school itself dates back to the dawn of time, well maybe not that far back but it feels like it. The building reminds me of something out of a movie. The gothic-style structure looms high above with its medieval aesthetic and ivy-covered walls, characterized by arches, vaulted ceilings, and small stained-glass windows. All that's missing are the gargoyles watching over everything like the creepy lil' mofos they are and the ominous black clouds, complete with rumbles of thunder and flashes of lightning.

My eyes dart here and there, taking it all in. I'm only halfway along the path when I feel like I'm being watched. Looking around, I don't see anyone paying me any attention, that is until I see him. He's across the grounds and staring intently at me. My breath hitches at the intensity of his gaze, his heated and hate-filled gaze. And like the scene of a car crash, I'm powerless to look away.

He turns his attention to someone near him, breaking the invisible thread holding our connection and I take in a breath. A breath I hadn't even realized I was holding in.

Continuing on, I walk up the stairs, and the first thing I notice is a frickin gargoyle door knocker. Shaking my head, I enter the building. Inside is just as opulent and ostentatious as the outside; marble floors, gold trimmings, and a chandelier in the main entrance. A fucking chandelier in a school, how much more cliché can this place be?

I follow the signs toward admin, thankful I'm already in uniform and not standing out like a sore thumb. Pushing open the door, I enter the office.

It's all rich hardwoods, blood-red plush carpet, and sconces with candle-shaped bulbs. This is more like a museum or a house of horrors than an administration room.

Actually, the whole place is over-the-top, but what more can you expect from the elite?

"Can I help you?" an elderly lady from behind the counter asks.

"Hi, I'm Remy Hearst. Today's my—"

"Yes. Yes. Yes, we've been expecting you. Take a seat there." She points to a black plastic chair, the only non-hoity-toity item I've seen since arriving. "I'll let the Dean know you've arrived."

"Thanks," I reply with a smile.

Taking a seat, I look around the room, but no sooner have I sat down and the door beside me opens. "Remington, welcome to Crestwood Academy." A lady in a pinstripe pantsuit and hair pulled back into a tight bun greets me. "I'm Dean Doyle, please come in."

Before I have a chance to reply, she turns on her heel and marches into her office. She points to the seat across from her mahogany desk. "Transferring mid-semester is highly unusual but when I spoke with your mother ..." She doesn't finish that sentence, but I know my mother. I know she would have given Dean Doyle no choice. What mother wants, mother gets.

"I appreciate all you've done for me, Dean Doyle. I just want to finish senior year, get into the Fashion Institute of Technology in New York, and become a fashion designer."

"Glad you have a plan. Feel free to make an appointment with the guidance counselor if you need anything, but from where I'm sitting, you're all set and will be an asset to Crest-wood Academy. Here's your schedule, and Quinn should be here momentarily to escort you around the school. Have you settled into the accommodations?"

Nodding, I smile. "Yes, my room is great." And the smile on my face is genuine because my room literally is the greatest room ever. At Alton Academy, I had a teeny tiny square with a single bed, dresser, and I was lucky and had a window, sure it looked over the staff parking lot, but it was still a window. My room here, well, it's huge. A king-sized bed with thousand thread sheets—yep thousand thread, I'm a total sheet snob so this is everything. A dresser with matching desk, a walk-in closet, and to top it off, a private en suite. The carpet is plush and looks like it was recently replaced but the kicker of the room, the bay window with built-in seat that overlooks the gardens and toward the cliffs

.

"The first bell will be ringing any minute now, run along." With that remark and a wave of her hand, I'm dismissed.

Picking up my bag, I exit the office. "You must be Remington, I'm Quinn."

"Remy," I inform her.

"Whatever, just keep up." She turns on her heel, and I have to run to catch up to her. First impressions of this Quinn? Bitch with a capital B. I'd bet my last hundred bucks she's the queen bee around here.

She's yammering on about this and that, but with the chatter of the other students and trying to take it all in, I don't hear a word of what she says.

We enter a classroom and Quinn ignores me, taking her seat and leaving me standing here alone. All eyes are on me. "You must be Remington," the teacher offers, walking toward me. I look down at my schedule and see I have English first up with Mrs. Plunkett.

"It's Remy, Mrs. Plunkett."

"Remy, okay." She smiles at me. "Take a seat anywhere, we're studying *Romeo and Juliet*. You've arrived halfway through but I'm sure you'll catch up just fine, it is a classic after all." From the dreamy look on her face, she's a romantic. I bet she goes home each evening and after cooking Mr. Plunkett dinner, she loses herself in a romance novel where the hero sweeps the heroine off her feet, shit happens, they fuck like rabbits, and then they live happily ever after. You can probably guess from my tone I'm not a romantic. Don't get me wrong, I like sex but love and romance, total bullshit.

"Thanks," I tell her and take my seat. I remember briefly seeing her when I arrived yesterday.

"Here you go." The girl next to me hands me a book from the shelf next to her. "We're up to act three where Romeo kills Tybalt."

"Spoiler alert," I tease. Her eyes widen in fright that she might have actually spoiled it for me and then she notices the grin on my face.

"You and I are going to be fast friends," she states matter-of-factly. "I'm Rowan Ashford."

"Remy Hearst."

"I know, word travels fast when a new girl arrives mid-semester, and the floor monitor is moved from her room to a closet-sized one." My eyes widen at this information. "Don't worry, that bitch deserved it, AND it means you're closer to me, my room is across the hall from you." I don't miss the eye roll Quinn gives us as Rowan finishes talking.

From the brief chat with Rowan, I feel like we are going to be the bestest of friends. English passes by in a Shakespearean blur and then it's on to history.

After history it's time for lunch. Alani, the girl who sat across from me in history, welcomed me with open arms, literally. She scooped me into a hug, and with that gesture, I could tell she was a sweetheart. Quinn all but abandoned me after escorting me to English earlier this morning but it's no loss, she seems like your typical stuck-up preppy bitch.

Alani and I step into the cafeteria for lunch and my eyes immediately widen as I take in the room. It looks more like a 3-star Michelin restaurant than a prep school lunch area. The tables are covered with white tablecloths. The buffet is immaculate, and the food looks amazing. No sloppy joes for lunch here. There's a window peeking into the kitchen, and my eyes widen again. There's no lunch lady Doris with a grubby hairnet in there, there are chefs. Full-on proper chefs with hats and chef whites. The kitchen is totally a chef's wet dream.

We grab food and my mouth is watering. We make our way to where Rowan is sitting. My eyes keep gravitating toward the table in the back corner. "Who are they?" I ask Alani as we drop into our seats, joining Rowan. They both turn to where I nod toward the back corner.

Lounging about as if they're royalty sit four guys, four guys who exude masculinity and alphaness. Once again, my heart does that skippy beat thing when my gaze connects with the guy from this morning. I can't tell if he's checking me out or planning my demise.

"The Lords of Crestwood Prep," Alani whispers.

"The Lords, really?"

"Really really," Rowan confirms, popping a grape into her mouth. "Thatcher, Hendrix, Saint and Reign Vanderbelt run this school. Nothing happens without their say so."

"Who died and made them king shit?"

She shrugs at me. "The Vanderbelts have reigned over this school and town for eons now." She turns her attention back to food, ending our conversation when from beside me, Alani grabs my arm. She stares intently at me. "Ignore them, Remy. Run if they approach you but whatever you do, stay the fuck away from them."

Nodding, I glance back over at them. They look harmless, maybe a little conceited but with a title like The Lords of Crestwood Prep, I bet they are anything but harmless.

"I'm serious, don't get sucked into their vortex." Her gaze wanders over The Lords—insert eye roll—and when they land on the blond one, something passes between them. There's definitely a story to tell there, but I'll let her tell me in her own time. I mean, I've only known the girl for a few hours. Sure, she's awesome but I need to give her time to open up to me. I mean, I haven't word-vomited my history and I'm not planning on doing that anytime soon, preferably never, but history and secrets always have a way of coming out. She turns her attention back to me, "Remy, they will suck you in, chew you up, and spit you out without blinking an eye."

"Speaking from experience?" I question her, instantly hating myself for probing when I just told myself I'd let her tell me in her own time.

"Kinda sorta, but let's not focus on that, just stay away from them."

She stands up and joins the food line again, leaving me to ponder her words. Looking back over to them, my insides race again when I cast a glance at him. A wicked smile appears on my face, I know without a doubt I'm not going to heed Alani's warning. I'm going to get to know these Lords, consequences be damned. Plus, when someone tells me not to do something, well, let's just say, I'll do the opposite of what they tell me. After all, there's a baaaaad girl hidden under this sweet and innocent exterior.

THATCHER

SHE'S BEEN HERE for less than a day, and I can already tell she's plotting something. She is a Hearst after all. I glare after her as her gaze filters across our table.

My jaw twitches as does another appendage. Hey, I'm a male and I can appreciate a hot as fuck woman when I see one … even if her family is the spawn of the devil.

"That the new girl?" Rian asks from beside me as he shovels his burger into his mouth like a starved man. Idiot needs to learn how to chew his fucking food.

Simply nodding, I don't take my eyes off her. I watch as she places her knife and fork back on her tray and watch as

Alani heads back for seconds, obviously needing energy for when she sneaks away with my brother later. The two of them think I don't know, but I know all.

"Fuck," Theon, Hendrix's best friend breathes. "What I'd do to her," he says.

I can only imagine the depraved and downright freaky things he's conjuring in his mind right now. I give him a murderous look. Only I can be thinking that about her.

"Keep your fucking hands to yourself," I bark at him. A feeling of possessiveness overwhelms me, over a girl I have no right to be possessive of. The only right I have over her is to end her.

Hendrix chuckles beside me knowing just what this means to me, to us. His best friend needs to learn to keep his dick to himself.

Conroy, my best friend outside of my brothers, slaps him up the side of his head. I nod in thanks.

"Ouch, fucker," Theon hisses.

Conroy just chuckles at him.

"So, is it true?" Lennon questions.

"Is what true?" Hendrix lifts his eyebrows and closes his eyes leaning back in his chair, bored by the conversation already.

"That she was locked away like some fucking princess in an ivory tower or some shit?"

We both snap our eyes to him completely taken aback by whatever fucked-up rumor he heard.

Rian chuckles loudly, grabbing the attention of the other students.

Leaning forward he shakes his head.

"You'd believe any-fucking-thing, bro. Nah, she wasn't locked away like Rapunzel, she was just at a school that wasn't here. Now that she's here, she's just become the pawn in our plan to make her mother pay for fucking with our family."

Is taunting her to get even with the woman who destroyed our family wrong? Probably but her evil bitch of a mother ruined something I hold near and dear. One way or another that woman will pay and I'm going to start with her sweet little daughter. As far as I'm concerned, without her brothers here to protect her, Remington Hearst is fair game and I'm a brilliant hunter. I'm going to make her suffer for the cunt her mother is, and I cannot wait for the hunt. That's the thing I love about this place, when someone new comes to a school like ours, their secrets become ours, and those secrets become our weapons in maintaining our position on top.

I know all too well about secrets. After all, I'm a Vanderbelt, secret may as well be our fucking middle name.

With my eyes locked on my prey, a sinister smirk appears on my face, I'm looking forward to introducing Remington-fucking-Hearst to all the delights that Crestwood Prep has to offer.

Our table grows loud once everyone finds their seat. The chatter between the guys is incessant, and the focus is mostly on the newest student at Crestwood Prep.

Reign finally arrives, dropping into the seat across from me and chucking a folder down. He takes a bite of his burger, and his gaze finds Alani across the hall. I smirk knowing he's secretly been trying to get with her for a while. After their first time a few months ago, she sparked something inside him, but Alani hates him. I have a feeling I know why, we Vanderbelts are cursed.

Let's just say my brothers and I aren't the relationship type. We have fun and being at the very fucking top gives us lots of options for fun, if you get my drift. Wink, wink. Nudge, nudge.

We earned the right to our titles.

We are The Lords of Crestwood Prep. We are fucking royalty within these walls. It's an honor to be in our presence. My brothers often say I'm cold, ruthless, and cruel but after everything, I have a right to be. My brothers don't really know me at all, no one does. I hide behind a facade, just like they do. Just like everyone with the last name Vanderbelt does.

We all carry our pain and anger differently.

Silently.

After what happened, we all know our family will never be the same again and someone needs to pay for that. And that someone is currently sitting on the other side of this cafeteria.

I cock my head regarding Remington as she smiles at something Alani says.

"Fuck, she has a lot of nerve laughing like her family hasn't caused us shit," Hendrix spits, glaring toward where they sit.

Hendrix is ruled by his emotions. He's always been a moody son of a bitch. He's filled with conviction. I've heard people call him the evil triplet. But that's just who he is, Hendrix doesn't take shit from anyone, and he doesn't give a flying fuck.

Hendrix is just Hendrix.

You do right by him, and he'll go to the ends of the Earth for you, but fuck him over and it's game over for you. Remington is about to find out just how ruthless we can be.

"Fuck this, I need to find Quinn," he growls. His impatience shows when he stands and heads over to Quinn's table. He yanks her up, and I watch as my brother pulls her toward the hall, going all caveman. He doesn't give her an option, but from the giggle and heated gaze on her face, she's down for whatever Hendrix has in mind.

"How the fuck does she go with whatever he wants? He's a grumpy fucking asshole, and he has the hottest fucking chick at this school follow after him like a damn puppy." Hart isn't wrong, Hendrix has a way with the ladies—just like any guy at this table—but his control over Quinn is like no other.

Those two are on and off more times than in one of those fucking drama shows. Hendrix loves sex, just like any regular guy, but I've heard those two numerous times. Their shit is wild, crazy, and fucked-up. My gaze drifts back to *her*; again.

Fuck, I can't help it. I grind my jaw as an image of her riding my dick while she pants my name flashes in my mind.

My dick twitches behind my pants, loving the idea of being inside her but that's not the goal. Sure, it would be an added bonus, plenty of time for that with all the parties coming up but I need to focus. Maybe I'll show her just how good we could be together then rip it all away when I destroy everything she loves.

Picking up the folder Reign brought over, I leave the table without a word. I don't miss her eyes following me as I walk toward the doors and I smirk, loving I've caught her eye. *In time, little peach. In time.*

I lick my lips and wink in her direction before I push the doors open and leave the cafeteria.

Walking toward my room, I head up to hide the folder. I nod at the students loitering in the hall. I don't know their names, and I don't fucking care to learn them. They're all just faces to me, but they are faces who respect me, and a head nod is the least I can offer them. Hell, a nod from me might even make their week, no, their fucking year.

Unlocking my door and closing it behind me, I shove my fingers through my hair taking a deep breath. I go to open the folder, but the ringing of my phone stops me. Chucking the folder on my bed, I answer.

"What?" I snap.

"You might want to come back," Conroy states.

Sighing in frustration, I shake my head. Can no one deal with shit without me for two fucking minutes?

Hanging up, I fling my door open and slam it behind me. I guess whatever's in that folder will have to wait until tonight.

The second I storm into the cafeteria, I see red. Conroy

was right to call me because Brennan-fucking-Dawson is talking to Remington, *my* Remington.

It looks like he's about to seal the fucking deal.

Over my dead body is that goody-fucking-snot-faced-two-shoes-asshat getting friendly with my fucking girl. *She's not your girl, you fucking idiot!*

Stalking over to the table, I yank Brennan up by his shirt. I don't miss the way Remington gasps as I drag him out into the hall. Shoving him in front of me. He's shaking and so he fucking should. Spinning him to face me, I notice he's scared. He knows he's overstepped.

"Stay the fuck away from Remington Hearst. This is your only fucking warning, Dawson," I sneer at the weasel through clenched teeth.

I don't give him time to reply because he knows the rules. He's bottom scum. He will never get with a girl like Remington. Girls like her are available for guys like me, and I'm going to show her just how fun guys like me can be.

Welcome to Crestwood Prep, Peach. I'm going to fucking devour her like the sweet little peach she is.

REMY

WHAT THE FUCK JUST HAPPENED?

Staring at the doors, I sit here open-mouthed and in disbelief. The hottie with a temper who I now know is Thatcher Vanderbelt—and can I say Vanderbelt is such a pompous surname—drags Brennan—also a pompous jackass name— out of the cafeteria by the collar of his shirt. Not one person stepped in, everyone stood or sat by and watched Thatcher become an animal.

"Case in point as to why you need to steer clear of them," Rowan, who joined us moments ago declares before taking a bite of her pesto gnocchi ... yes, pesto-fucking-gnocchi is on the menu here. She swallows and points her fork at me. "Now that Brennan is on their radar, you need to steer clear of him too, if you want him to live till graduation that is."

That comment has my eyes bugging out of my head. "Wwww ... what do you mean? I was just flirting with him, and he was flirting back."

"And The Lords, specifically Thatcher, have decided you are theirs."

"I'm no ones," I snap.

"Ohh, honey, you have a lot to learn about how Crestwood works. Nothing, and I mean nothing, happens without the A-okay from them."

"But—"

"Nope, no buts," Rowan interrupts me.

"This is like something from *Cruel Intentions*."

"It's worse than that movie ... and minus Ryan Philippe. If he was here, he'd somehow make them much more bearable."

"He is hot," I agree.

"Sooo hot, but I prefer my man to be less broody." Her gaze drifts over to The Lords' table and when her eyes land on Saint, it piques my suspicion about her and him and then I think of Alani and the obvious thing she has going on with the blond dude, Reign. Why is it these girls are warning me off The Lords when, clearly, they both have something going on with Reign and Saint. My inner bitch decides to play a little.

"He's kinda hot," I say, popping a fry into my mouth.

"Who?" she nonchalantly replies, playing dumb but we both know who I'm referring to since her eyes are still locked on his.

"Him," I reply, pointing at Saint with another fry. "I think I'd like to take him for a ride."

"Did you hear nothing Alani said earlier?" she snaps. "Stay away from Saint, I mean them."

Staring at her, I smirk, and she realizes I was goading her.

She shakes her head and pops another gnocchi ball into her mouth. "One of these days you are going to tell me the story of Rowan and Saint."

"That story needs tequila, a pint of Ben and Jerry's, and more tequila."

"That can be arranged."

"Deal, but let's save that story for another day." She takes a sip of her iced tea and proceeds to change the topic. "So, tell me all about Remington Hearst."

"I'm eighteen. A Virgo. I hate peas. My mom is a mega bitch. My dad is absent, probably hiding from the mega bitch. I have, or had two older brothers, one is dead."

"Arlen, right?" she questions.

Nodding, a wave of sadness washes over me when I think about my brothers. They are the best brothers a girl could ask for. Arlen is the complete opposite of Grayson, but when Arlen was alive, I thought the three of us had an unbreakable bond, but just before he died, he started to change. Where Arlen was quiet and caring, Grayson is loud and boisterous, but we always had each other's backs. I may be the youngest, but they treat me as an equal. Life was great but when Arlen killed himself, a part of Grayson died too. He's your typical jock but with a heart of gold once you get to know him. He had the world at his feet, but now, now we're left with this obnoxious asshole who thinks the world owes him. I want the old Grayson back, and maybe now that I've been summoned home, he and I can get that relationship back. Arlen would be disappointed in us both, that much I know.

"Do you—" She doesn't get to finish her question because the doors to the cafeteria slam open suddenly and an enraged Thatcher storms back in and stalks over to us. Resting his hands flat on the table, he stares down at me.

A lesser person would fold back into themselves at this but not me. "Yes?" I offer in way of greeting.

"You're not welcome here," Thatcher snarls between clenched teeth.

"My enrollment paperwork states otherwise, now if you don't mind, I'm eating." To emphasize my point, I pick up a fry and take a bite. Moaning as the fried goodness dances over my tongue.

My nonchalance pisses him off. Raising his hand, he swipes it across the table. My leftover fries, plate, and cutlery fly through the air, crashing to the floor. If all eyes weren't already on us, they all are now. Everyone is staring at the standoff between Thatcher and me.

"I wasn't finished," I taunt him. "You owe me more fries."

"I don't owe you or your family shit," he hisses. "I say you're done, therefore you're done." He leans down and gets into my face. He's that close I can feel his heated breath on my skin. "Keep your head down and watch your back, Hearst."

"Duly noted, now if you'll excuse me." I bend down, pick up my bag and swing it over my shoulder. "It seems my lunch is done, and I have to get to French." Standing up, I step around him and with my chin held high, I walk out of the cafeteria and head to my next class.

My heart is racing at the confrontation with Thatcher just now. As much as he pissed me off with his holier-than-thou persona, I also wanted to throw myself at him and mount him like a bitch in heat. What's up with that?

Before I exit, the silence in the cafeteria is broken and the whispers start. I just know they are talking about me, and I bet by the end of the day, rumors about me, Thatcher, and The Lords will spread like wildfire throughout the school. So much for sneaking in quietly.

The rest of the day passes without any further incidents, and I don't see Thatcher and his gang of merry men again, thankfully. Heading to the library, I grab a table in the back and pull out my books to get to work on my history assignment. History is not my favorite subject, so I really need to focus but my mind keeps drifting back to Thatcher, and I wonder how such an asshole can be so hot.

Giving up on my assignment, I decide to explore the library. I love the smell of old books and a library as old as this one, has the deep and pungent book smell that leaves me feeling all warm and fuzzy. Most girls want chocolate and roses, but me, I'd love nothing more than an old book.

Walking down the stacks, I run my fingers across the spines. A shadow runs by behind me but when I spin around, no one is there. Libraries as old as this also have ghosts, not that I believe an apparition will appear before me, but there's just an eerie feeling associated with the place.

A noise startles me and I peek around the end of the stack, "Hello?" I call out like a dummy. Calling out like this is Scary Movie 101 in 'how to get yourself killed' but clearly, I'm the dumb girl who is going to die because I head closer to where I think the noise came from.

Poking my head into the last row, I don't see anything. I'm so focused on finding the source of the noise that I don't feel someone come up behind me. They wrap their arms around my head, covering my mouth. They breathe heavily in my ear as they drag me backward. My heart races with fear and I kick and thrash about as they drag me away. Whoever it is, is much stronger than me and my fighting is useless. Spinning me around, they shove me into a closet. Stumbling, I turn around just as they slam the door in my face, leaving me in darkness and with no clue who just accosted me.

"Let me out," I scream, banging my fists on the wooden door. "Let me out. Heeeeeelp," I scream again, but I'm met with silence, well, apart from my heavy breathing and rapidly beating heart.

Someone bangs on the door from the other side, scaring me, and I scream in fright. "Please," I cry, "let me out." Then they up the creepiness meter and whisper-sing "Rock a Bye Baby" to me. They emphasize the cradle will fall part and goosebumps spread over my body. That song has always creeped me out and when you're trapped in a dark room, it's really fucking creepy. Who the hell sings to a baby about a cradle falling and dying? Some sick fuck, and said sick fuck is currently taunting me through this door.

Suddenly, I realize it's quiet. There's no more singing, and I don't feel a presence through the door. "Is anyone there?" I shout out again and rather than silence a deep voice replies, "Where are you?"

"In here," I cry out, banging on the door. "I'm in here," I scream. My heart races with hope that I'm going to be freed.

The door swings open and the brightness of the library blinds me. Rapidly blinking, my eyes adjust and I make out Brennan standing before me. "Brennan," I cry out in relief. I throw myself at him, and he envelops me in his arms. Relief at being freed overwhelms me and I begin to cry.

"Shhhh," he whispers, then adds, "I've got you, Cutie." He rubs my back, and it soothes me. My breathing evens out, my heart rate returns to normal, and the tears slowly stop.

Lifting my head and stepping back, I smile at him. Thankful to be comforted but now that I'm fine ... ish, I step back. "Thank you for that, I needed it."

"Anytime, it's what friends do, right?" I nod at him, "Talk to me, Remy, what happened?" He seems genuinely concerned for me and his concern is unexpected since I only met the guy recently.

"I ... I was exploring the ... the library, and then someone covered my mouth and dragged me into that room."

"Who would do that?"

"There's only one asshole I know who would do something like that and when I find him, I'm going to punch him in the dick."

Brennan doesn't say anything to that. "Come on, Cutie, let me walk you back to your room. You're shaking."

"Thanks, Brennan," I tell him, even if the fact he calls me Cutie is kinda weird for only knowing each other for a short period of time. Sliding my arm around his waist, we walk back to my things. Before we reach my stuff, I see Thatcher and my blood boils. He wasn't here before, but now he conveniently is. A growl slips out and I pull away from Brennan and stalk over to him. "You fucking asswipe dickwad," I shout, poking him in the chest.

"Excuse me," he sneers.

"Were you dropped on your head as a baby and think it's okay to terrorize people?"

"Huh?" he replies, confusion all over his face.

"Don't play dumb, asshat. You just accosted me and shoved me in a closet."

"Nope, nah, not me, Peach."

"I'm not stupid, it was you. It had to have been you. Just … just stay the fuck away from me."

Stalking back over to my things, I pack everything up, and then Brennan escorts me back to my room. I'm thankful not to be alone, but at the same time, I want to be alone. It's such a weird feeling.

"Thanks, Brennan," I say again when we reach my room. "Thank you for rescuing me and comforting me."

"Anytime, Cutie, friends help each other."

"Yeah, they do." Leaning forward, I press a kiss to his cheek and if I'm not mistaken, his cheeks darken. Taking my bag from him, I unlock my door and step inside. Smiling at Brennan, I murmur, "Night," and close the door. Making sure to lock it behind me.

Dumping my bag on my bed, I kick off my shoes, walk

over to the window bench, and take a seat. That's when I notice a flower sitting by my feet. I must have an admirer, picking it up, I bring it to my nose and sniff. I smile as the scent of the rose infiltrates my nostrils. "Who left you here?" I whisper. Placing the flower next to me, I pull my knees up, rest my head on them, and stare out the window. My room has a view looking over the gardens and toward the cliffs and the urge to head out there washes over me. I know I was just stuffed into a closet and should hide away in my room but the pull to go toward the cliffs is strong.

Standing up, I strip out of my school uniform and change into a pair of skinny jeans and a black tank top. Slipping on a pair of purple Chucks, I slide my phone into my back pocket and grab my hoodie. Pulling it over my head, I exit my room and make my way to the cliff top.

Staring out into the black abyss, I think of Arlen. This is where he supposedly killed himself. I don't for one minute believe he did that to himself, regardless of what Dad says happened.

...I'm in my room getting ready to head to a party when my phone rings. It's Dad, he and I haven't been on good terms since he left. He refused to take me with him so I'm stuck here with Mom, alone. Arlen is away at Crestwood Prep and Grayson has just started at Duke, he's going to be a lawyer.

"Hey, Dad," I say when I answer, "I can't chat long, I have somewhere to be in an hour."

"Sweetie." His voice is soft and very undad like.

"Dad, what's going on?"

"It's, it's Arlen."

"What about him?"

"He ... he's gone, sweetie."

"What?" I hiss, my eyes welling with tears.

"He left me a voicemail saying, 'I'm sorry I wasn't more.' I called the school and they can't find him. A witness confirms seeing

him at the cliffs. With my message and his disappearance, the police say he killed himself."

"But there's no body?" I say, hope in my voice.

"Sweetie, the current there is strong, his body would be miles out to sea by now."

"No," I shout. "No. No. No. He ... he's not gone."

Collapsing to my knees in the center of my bedroom, I cry for my brother, even if I don't believe it. Sure, Arlen was different but my brother was no coward, he would never do that and leave us to deal with his loss, and if he did, he certainly would not tell Dad and not Gray or me.

"I miss you, Arlen," I whisper into the night sky as the memory of that shitty day a few months ago fades. I still don't think he committed suicide, there's more to his disappearance. The biggest red flag for me, well, apart from their being no body, why didn't he reach out to Dad and not Grayson or me? It just doesn't make sense.

"I miss him too," a voice from behind says, startling me. Turning around, all I see is a dark figure, hidden in the shadows. "He loved you so much," they inform me.

"And I loved him dearly," I tell this mystery person.

"Me too," he whispers back.

A silence falls between us, the only sound is the waves crashing into the rocks below. "Who are you?" I ask, curiosity eating at me.

"I'm your worst nightmare," comes the reply, and before I can ask a question, a noise to my left takes my attention from the man in the shadows. I can't see anything, and when I turn back around, he's gone. I begin to wonder if maybe I dreamed him being here.

Turning back around, I drop to the ground and pull my legs up. I know there's a perfectly good bench to my left but the need to sit here is strong. Hugging my legs, I rest my head on my knees, and for the first time since arriving here, I feel content and at ease. It's almost as if Arlen is with me.

Watching over me in that brotherly way he did when we were growing up. That thought comforts me and for some reason, I know I'll be fine here at Crestwood Prep.

Not wanting a repeat of lunch, after returning from the cliffs, I grab a sandwich, drink, and chips from the cafeteria and head back up to my room. I'm not hiding per se, but I'm mentally drained. I keep playing the incident in the cafeteria, library, and up at the cliffs just now over and over again. What's Thatcher's fascination with me? Who locked me in the closet? And who the fuck is the mystery person who also loves Arlen?

I've been here all of five minutes, and already it's a mess. I've clearly pissed in Thatcher's cornflakes, and if he thinks I'm going to bow down to him, he has another thing coming. I bow to no one.

THATCHER

Adrenaline still flows through my veins after my run-in with Remington earlier in the library. Fuck. The way she bit back at me had my cock twitching but fucking her, that's not in the plan. Fucking WITH her mentally however, that's definitely in the plan. I smirk knowing how much fun it's going to be to break her. To destroy that sass, but I do want to know who locked her in the closet. My brothers assure me it wasn't them so if it wasn't one of us, who the fuck was it? Because they need to know no one but us fucks with her and hopefully she won't last long. And with my brothers and me on the case, it's a certainty.

Stripping out of my uniform, since I can't fight or fuck tonight, I opt for a shower instead. Once the water rains down on me, my body relaxes. I know fighting isn't the smartest move, but my body screams at me for a release, and it's either that or I strangle my father and orange isn't a color I ever see myself wearing.

We may be The Lords here but my father, Thornton-fuck-ing-Vanderbelt, is more powerful than we'll ever be. My grandfather was one of the original Lords. So, naturally my father was the second generation. His word is final, it's the law. We know all too well not to test him.

But after what he's done, after what they did, I'm going to make them pay because Mom deserves better and if she won't stand up for herself, my brother and I will. We are going to look after her when *he* couldn't. My father can only be on top for so long before everything will come crashing down under him and mark my word, once we're finished, there will be nothing left of him and that bitch.

Excitement is brewing because it's almost time to play 'Ready or Not.' The thrill of catching my prey. Of catching what will be mine to do with as I please is a feeling like no other. Smirking, I know just who I'll be picking this year.

Being a Lord has its perks, and of course, we always choose our ladies first. They have special markings that match ours, so everyone knows they are off-limits to anyone but us. And the best part, the girls never know who picks them. It's a game that has been a tradition here for many years now, and it's one my brothers and I love to uphold.

To some, the curfew would be a hindrance, but there are ways around it, but even so, we have to be careful. We can't let Father down, the last thing we want is for our antics to get back to our father. And sneaking out past curfew and throwing disrepute on the Vanderbelt name is forbidden. If we're caught, he'll ship us off to military school quicker than you can say ROTC.

Wiping the towel through my hair, a single piece of paper slides under my door catching my attention.

What the fuck.

Wrapping my towel around my waist, I yank the door open. Poking my head out, I look left and right, but I don't see anyone. No one is there. The halls are empty, as they should be at this time of night, but someone was here, evident by the piece of paper at my feet. My chest rises and falls with heavy breaths. Bending down, I pick up the note and close my door. Turning the paper over, I read it.

Vengeance is mine!
After I'm done, you'll all fall to your knees.
Tick tock Vanderbelt, watch your back.

The handwriting is messy and not one I recognize. Screwing the paper up, I toss it in the bin. Someone is playing games, and this isn't one I need to be involved in, so I choose to ignore whoever it is. They clearly want my attention but they won't get it. I'm the games master here, not them.

My head has just hit the pillow when a text from Hendrix comes through. Knowing my brother, he'll be awake for hours before he finally crashes and if I don't reply, he'll keep messaging me until I do, needy fucker that he is.

HENDRIX

You're so going to fuck her, aren't you?

THATCHER

At first no but now...

A soft chuckle escapes me as I type my reply. I know I said fucking her wasn't the plan but maybe having a little fun along the way might be, well, fun.

I fucking knew it.

Did *you expect anything else?*

Chuckling again, I stare at the screen, waiting for his reply. When it finally comes through, a sudden burst of anger flies through my system, his words anger me more than I'd like to admit.

Share!

She's off-limits.

My simple reply should speak volumes.

Okay. She's all yours. I've got Quinn's sweet mouth and cunt anyway ;)

Replying will just make his ego bigger than it already is, so I ignore him. We may be alike in so many ways, but what he has in ego, I make up for in anger. Something I seem to lose control of more so these days; I guess not everyone can be fixed with pills.

Sure, we've shared girls in the past, that's nothing new between my brothers and our friends. We fuck, have a good time, and then send them on their merry, freshly fucked way. So why does the thought of sharing Remington make me want to annihilate my brother's face?

She's mine.

All fucking mine.

The sight of Remy on her knees with that sweet ass up in the air first thing in the morning is a sight any guy could get used to. I may hate her and everything about her last name, but it doesn't mean I can't appreciate the fine art of her body. Her button nose. Gorgeous smile. Eyes that shine brightly. Golden blond locks that would look great wrapped around my fist as I slam into her from behind. *Fuck*, I'm hard just picturing it. Maybe I just need to fuck her, get it out of my system and then we can get back to the task at hand—avenging our mother for *her* mother's cunty ways.

Coming to a stop beside her as she searches her bag, I decide to mess with her. "I think I like you better on your knees, Peach."

Her head snaps up, and she cuts me with a deathly glare. She stands to full height, only coming up to my chest, towering over her like the demi-god I am. Lifting my hand, my fingers find their way into the soft curl of her hair. Twisting slightly, she flinches at the pull, and I can't help but smirk.

Swatting my hand away, she stares daggers at me, but if she thinks I'm going to cower at that, she has another thing coming. My cock twitches at the hatred in her gaze.

"Don't touch me," she hisses. "I wouldn't want to catch whatever it is you have," she sneers, turning to leave.

Gripping her arm, I force her back and slam her against the lockers with a crash. She gasps, eyeing my hand while it snakes tightly around her arm, gaining some attention from the students around us. Leaning in close, I'm inches from her face, I can smell her minty breath mixed with her perfume that reminds me of a crisp fall morning.

My gaze never leaves hers.

Hers never leaves mine.

The air around us begins to buzz, I'm not sure if it's buzzing with hatred or desire. Maybe both.

"Why are you here, Peach?" I whisper the question

through clenched teeth. "Are you wanting to see what rich cock tastes like?" I taunt. "I can show you if you're really that eager." I push my groin into her, giving her a sample of exactly what she'd get. I don't miss the way her eyes widen or how her breath hitches when I do. She shoves me off her, putting a small sliver of distance between us, for a wee thing, she sure is strong. I love a good sexually filled fight, fuck.

"You might want to get a vaccine," she huffs.

"Why's that, Peach?" My breath blows over her face, I don't miss the way her body reacts.

"Who knows what you've caught? I'm surprised your dick hasn't fallen off."

I chuckle as she ducks under my arm resting beside her. She drops down, picks up her bag, and turns to walk away. Standing here, I watch as she saunters away from me, and yeah, her ass is something I can't wait to sink my teeth into.

The longer I watch her, the more I fume. The way she walks with such confidence, like she owns this goddamn school, fires me up. She has no right being here.

Clenching my teeth to the point my jaw hurts, I'm ready to explode. I'm so close to proving to my little peach just where she belongs, underneath me, and I don't mean in a naked way. If she thinks she's going to work herself into our inner circle, she has another thing coming.

It still amazes me after what happened she would face coming here, but I guess she has a death wish.

I feel my brothers behind me, and reluctantly, I turn to face them. We silently stare at one another and without uttering a word, from the looks on their faces, they know what I'm thinking. We all know what needs to be done. What has to be done but there's no harm in having a little fun along the way, right?

The Hearsts and our father are about to be destroyed, we will finally avenge what they did to Mom and the first person to face our wrath will be dear old dad. He's keeping secrets.

He's hidden things from us, and he'll regret the day he used us for his own pathetic agenda. But most of all, he disrespected our mother. He will pay for his sins. He won't get away with this. I'll make sure Thornton Vanderbelt suffers for his actions. And Remy, well, she's going to pay for *all* their sins.

I won't stop until they all suffer my wrath.

REMY

THATCHER VANDERBELT IS A FUCKING PSYCHOPATH, end of story. The encounter with him just now was unnerving, but at the same time, I was turned on. What the fuck is wrong with me? My body has never reacted to a guy like that before. One minute I wanted to throat-punch him, and the next, I wanted him to fuck me harder than I've ever been fucked before.

I'm seriously messed up.

I hoped I was immune to his charms. That I was safe from Thatcher Vanderbelt but how wrong I was. *Damn you, traitorous vagina.*

My phone rings and I smile when I hear the ringtone. Sliding to answer, I greet my brother, "What up, douceface?"

"Douceface, really?" he replies with a laugh.

"I could have gone with asshat or butthead."

"Okay, stick with douceface. Just checking to see how you've settled in?"

"Fine," I tell him through clenched teeth.

"An ass is fine. Tits are fine but you, my big fat liar, liar, pants on fire, littler sister, are anything but fine."

A laugh escapes me because no one knows me like Grayson. "Nothing gets past you, does it?"

"Not when it comes to my baby sister." Ever since we lost Arlen, the bond between Grayson and I changed, it became stronger. He blames himself for not realizing our brother was struggling, he thinks my theory of Arlen actually being murdered, or even alive is ludicrous but I know, knew, my brother. He never would have killed himself, but who's going to listen to little old me? If Grayson doesn't believe me, there's no way the authorities or our parents would, especially since Arl reached out to Dad, which I still find suspect because Dad and Arlen didn't get along. He was so angry to have a 'fairy as a son.' "Are you going to spill the beans, or do I need to drive out and visit you?"

"I wouldn't say no to a visit."

"What's up?" he asks again, his voice laced with concern.

"There's this guy—"

"Do I need to kill him?"

"No, not yet. Anyway, as I was saying, there's this guy and his brothers, the Vanderbelts and—"

"Did you say Vanderbelts? As in Thornton Vanderbelt's kids?"

"Ummm, no clue what their dad's name is but the dicks I'm referring to are Thatcher, Hendrix, Reign, and Saint Vanderbelt."

"Stay away from them, Rem. The Vanderbelts are bad news. Stay the fuck away from them."

"You're scaring me, Gray."

"I don't mean to scare you but if you're at school with them," he snarls the word them, "that means you might be in danger."

"What? Why? What do you mean?"

"Just steer clear of them, Rem. I'm on my way, and I'll explain everything I found out about Mom and them when I get there. If I only stop for piss breaks and gas, I can be by your side in fifteen hours. After class, I want you to go straight to your room and lock the door. Don't let anyone but me in. I'll call you when I arrive."

"Please tell me what's going on?" I plead with him, but the line goes silent, and I pull the phone from my ear to see if it's still connected. "Grayson, you there?"

"Yeah, I'm here. Look, Mom isn't who we think she is and what I have to say, shouldn't be said over the phone. Please just do as I said, I'll explain everything I know when I get there."

"Please be safe, Gray. I'll see you soon."

Grayson doesn't even say goodbye before hanging up and that leaves me feeling anxious. I'm worried now, especially when I overhear the Vanderbelt dicks talking about Grayson coming to visit me on my way to class. *How the fuck do they know that?*

What does Grayson know? And why do I have a feeling something bad, something really bad is going to happen soon?

REMY

WHEN I WAKE the next morning, I grab my phone to check for a message from Grayson, but there's nothing. If he'd stuck to his drive and didn't unnecessarily stop as planned, he should be here by now. Dialing his number, it goes straight to voice-mail and that feeling of unease I felt yesterday intensifies tenfold. I hang up, not bothering to leave a message.

Yesterday after my classes finished, I did as Grayson asked and retreated to my room. As soon as I left English, I stopped by the cafeteria, grabbed some food, and then headed straight for my room.

Stepping over the threshold, I locked the door and leaned

against it, my heart racing. When I heard that lock click, I let out the breath I didn't realize I was holding.

It was a quiet evening, but I was safe. However, in the dawn of the new day, I don't feel safe anymore. Especially since I can't get a hold of Grayson. I call again and again and again, and each time I get his voicemail. On the fourth try, I leave a message. "Hey, Gray, it's me. Just checking on your travels. I'm about to head to class, I'll check in again between classes. Call me."

Throwing my phone onto the bed, I walk into my closet and grab my uniform. Why do these pretentious preppy schools insist we dress like this? It just gives fodder to the porn industry about naughty schoolgirls ... don't get me wrong, dressing up like a slutty naughty schoolgirl only for him to rip off your shirt, buttons flying everywhere, exposing your tits before he ravages you is hot, but I don't want to be dressed like that all day every day.

With my non-slutty schoolgirl uniform on, I grab my backpack and head out for the day and of course, the first person I run into—literally—is Thatcher. "Watch where you're going," he snarls.

"Fuck me," I mumble under my breath. "Why are you everywhere I am?" I snap at him.

"We go to the same school, it's bound to happen, but you know what?"

"What?" I snap, crossing my arms across my chest. I notice his eyes drop to my chest. *Typical fucking male* but what surprises me is the heated look that appears in his eyes but as quick as it appears, it's gone again.

He steps into my personal space. "You can always leave."

"You can take that up with my mother," I inform him, but at the mention of my mother, his eyes fill with anger, and his jaw clenches. Seems Rochelle Hearst is also on his shit list, but why? That's a question for another day, or never. I really don't care to involve myself in the inner workings of Thatcher-I'm-an-asshole-Vanderbelt.

Our silent stare-off is interrupted by the ringing of the first period bell. Not wanting to show weakness, I stand my ground, waiting for him to make the first move. He's the first to break—score one, Remy—but that win soon goes to him because when he steps around me, he shoulder-barges me and my bag spills open. My books, pencils, and emergency tampons go flying.

"Asshole," I mutter to myself as I bend down to pick up my things.

"Here," a feminine voice says and when I look up, I see Alani, holding out my sunglasses case.

"Thanks," I reply with a smile and take the case from her, popping it back into my bag. "He's such a ..." I don't finish because I don't want to say the wrong thing to the wrong person and paint an even bigger target on my back.

"Asshole?" she offers, and I nod, smirking at her. "Why are all the assholes hot?"

"Hot and asshole go together like Ben and Jerry or marga and rita."

She laughs and links her arm through mine. "You and I are going to be the bestest of friends, Remington Hearst, the bestest of friends."

"Not if you call me Remington we won't. It's Remy."

"Noted. Now let's get to English."

"How—"

"You showed me your schedule yesterday in history, remember? We have quite a few of the same classes and now, we have English together too."

"Stalker much?"

"Only if they're hot." She winks and drags me down the hall and into our English class.

"How are we in English together now?"

"I had to swap classes around so I can get into the college

course I want. Mom and Dad will be pissed I've done this but fuck them, this is my life."

Does everyone in this school have parental issues? I think as we walk into class. Clearly, Mrs. Plunkett wants a lazy day because we are to pair up and continue to read *Romeo and Juliet* and discuss—that's code for 'do what the fuck you want, just leave me alone.' Alani drags her chair over to my desk. "I wish we could just watch the movie instead of reading it and when I say watch the movie, I mean the one with Leo and Claire, not any of the old-school ones."

"I don't know, I kinda love reading it. Sure, they talk all fancy and shit, but the love between the two of them is pretty epic."

"But aren't they like thirteen?"

"Can't thirteen-year-olds love?" I throw back at her.

"Well, yeah, I guess, but I couldn't see thirteen-year-old me going all 'I will die without' and killing myself. Mind you, thirteen-year-old me was in love with Tom Harvey." She nods her head toward the back of the classroom, and I see an emo-looking twat. "So, no killing myself in the name of love there."

"He seems, umm, nice."

"He wasn't emo back then, or gay for that matter."

"You turned him gay?"

"No, he was definitely gay before I came along. He only dated me so he could get to know my brother, Raven. He and my big bro have been a couple for a few years now."

"Is that not awkward?"

"Nah, I'm happy Raven has Tom and I like to tease Rave that I'm a better kisser than Tom."

We both crack up laughing, and from the corner of my eye, I see Thatcher staring at me. He's throwing daggers my way. "What the fuck is his problem?" I whisper-snarl. I don't want him to know I'm talking about him, that will only add to his ego.

"Who?" she asks, looking around and I know when it clicks as to who I'm referring to, but then again, it's not hard to deduce since he's the only one staring, well glaring, at me.

"What did you do to piss in his cornflakes?"

"Breathe," I reply with a shrug. "I have no clue who he is. I mean, I've been here for less than two days, and prior to yesterday, I'd never met him or heard of The Lords or the Vanderbelts."

"When it comes to The Lords," she emphasizes 'The Lords' and rolls her eyes, "it's best to just roll with the punches."

"Who died and made them boss?"

"Girl, that conversation needs wine ... and tequila. Over the weekend, I'll fill you in on all that is The Lords and this place. And since you have a kick-ass room which I'm totally jealous of by the way, our little soiree slash gossip session will be held in your room."

"It's a date."

"Perfect, I'll bring the tequila."

"And I'll bring the wine and the room."

After what feels like forever, the bell rings and class is over. We all exit and spill into the hallway. Alani and I agree to meet for lunch after the next class.

Heading upstairs, I make my way to art. Along the way, I pull out my phone to try Grayson again, but I have a text from an unknown number.

UNKNOWN

You look pretty today

That's a fucking weird text, I think as I try Grayson again since there was no message from him. And just like earlier it goes straight to voicemail. I leave another message for him and just like this morning, that 'uh-oh' feeling festers in my stomach.

Art is normally my favorite class, but today, I can't concentrate. I keep thinking about Grayson, Thatcher, The Lords, and our connection. The bell rings and I make my way to history, but I stop when I hear my brother's name mentioned.

Peeking around the corner, I see the Vanderbelt brothers huddled together and my curiosity is piqued. Why are they talking about him? "We need to get him to visit." Saint—I think—states, "We get him here, and then we take action."

A gasp escapes my lips, and due to the silence in the hallway it echoes as if I had a megaphone to my lips. Four heads snap toward me, and my fight-or-flight instinct kicks in. I turn on my heel and race away from them. Pushing open the doors, I exit out into the courtyard. My foot has just stepped onto the pavement when a hand wraps around my arm tightly and they spin me around. I come face-to-face with Saint. He gets into my face. "You listen here, and you listen good. You forget anything and everything you just heard. You are not to get involved. Just back away. You hear me?" Nodding, I stare at him, his face is void of any emotion at all. "Answer me?" he snarls, squeezing my arm tighter.

"Yyyyyes," I stammer, "I … I uuuuu … understand."

A sinister smile appears on his face. "Good, and maybe while you're at it, go back to whatever hellhole you crawled out from." He steps into my face and whisper hisses, "You mess with Thatch, and I'll fuck you up. Capiche?"

Nodding in agreement again, he smiles once and shocking the ever-loving fuck out of me, he leans forward and kisses my cheek. He. Kisses. My. Cheek.

Turning around, he walks up the stairs and back into the building, leaving me standing here with a racing heart and fear for my brother coursing through my veins.

Needing to get away, I spin on my heel, but I come face-to-face with Rowan. "Hey, Rowan," I offer with a smile on my face.

"Stay away from them and especially, stay the fuck away from Saint Vanderbelt."

"Ooookay," I reply.

"I'm not messing around, and neither are they. They eat chicks like you for breakfast. I warned you the other day but this is your last warning." She sighs, and I can't read the look on her face right now. Is she checking me out? "I kinda like you, Remy." *Yep, that's exactly what she's doing.* "I'd hate for something unjust to happen to you before ..." She drifts off mid-sentence, and before I can ask her to elaborate, she turns around and walks away from me.

"What the fuck?" I whisper to myself. Standing here in the courtyard confused and slightly turned on by that carnal look.

THATCHER

"THE FUCK you chasing after her for?" I bark at my brother, gripping his shirt in my fists and shoving him into the lockers. The students around us gasp and scuttle away, leaving me and my brother alone to hash this out.

"Just warning your little peach to forget what she heard and to fuck off," he informs me, and his nonchalant tone pisses me off.

"She's off-limits," I snarl through clenched teeth. My blood boils as I remember seeing his lips on her cheek.

Saint shoves past me checking his shoulder into mine as he does. Growling, I go to chase him ready to show him who's in charge, but a hand on my shoulder stops me in my tracks, adding to the fury pumping through my veins.

"Leave him, something's up with him." Hendrix's warning is clear. Our little brother is off-limits but so is my peach.

"We need to deal with whatever he has going on," Reign adds. I was so filled with anger and rage, I didn't even see my other brother standing there with us, but I should have known, the four of us are always together.

"Let's deal with one thing at a time." I nod, and he continues, "But he's right, she heard something."

Both Hendrix and Saint are correct, whatever Remington heard was minimal but most of all, it wasn't for her to hear. She will only hear what she needs as and when I, we, see fit.

"She's lying, T, straight up. I don't trust her," Hendrix snarls.

"She's a Hearst. What do you expect?"

He nods in agreement. I clench my jaw and grind my teeth back and forth.

Both Arlen and Grayson Hearst always got into trouble here, I swear it was their specialty, just a way to piss off their mom but now they're gone, and their sister has taken their place. I'm not sure what her deal is but I know I won't stand for her trying to make us into fools.

"She had to have heard something. What do we do?" Reign questions.

I look over at my brothers, and each has their own expression that tells me everything I need to know.

"We stick to the plan, we keep an eye on her. Reign, you take command, befriend her but don't be too friendly, and whatever you do, don't let her out of your sight." Reign salutes me and takes off toward class.

"You really think she heard what we were talking about?" Hendrix asks again.

Shrugging, I sigh in frustration. "To be honest, I'm not

one-hundred-percent sure but whatever the case, we need to find out all we can about our enemy. Knowledge is power after all, and WE are the power. Looks like it's time to hit the books."

"Huh?"

"I need to reread the stuff Reign put together." Now that I've met the bitch, maybe something I previously read will jump out at me.

"I don't like this, man," Hendrix huffs, "she's bad news. What if she finds out. What if ..." Gripping Hendrix's shoulder, I stare at him.

"We keep our shit locked up. Nothing gets out, understood?"

"Understood." He nods.

"Good." I clap my brother on the back and feel the tension in his body. "I don't like this either, Brother, but we need to show her who's boss around here."

But if the note I got under my door is anything to go by, our shit isn't as airtight as I once thought.

He nods and we go our separate ways. I watch as Hendrix walks down the hall. Once he's out of sight, I head to history. Opening the door to the classroom, I smirk. My smirk grows when I see who's doing her best to hide at the side of the classroom. I whistle as I walk toward my little peach.

"Move," I growl at the guy sitting next to her. He scrambles to grab his stuff and drops it as he moves for me to take his place. "Hello, Peach," I offer in greeting as I drop into my seat. My voice drops to a deep sound I know most girls here throw themselves at me for, but my peach is stubborn. She rolls her eyes and rather than pissing me off like she hopes, I smile and wink. Earning myself another eye roll which makes my cock twitch.

This is going to be fun. So. Much. Fucking. Fun.

I need to fuck someone, and it needs to be hard and rough. Reading the folder Reign put together on Remington, and finally putting a face to the words, has my blood boiling. My entire body shakes with an uncontrollable rage. Mother-fuck-ing-fucker.

Grabbing my phone, I send an urgent SOS to my brothers. It was our signal when we were younger to cope with our father, the constant abuse and pain he inflicted whenever we did even the slightest thing out of place or even just breathes. The only good thing to come from that cunt is the bond I have with my brothers. There's nothing I wouldn't do for those guys, and I know they feel the same way about me.

We all had our ways of dealing with the reminder. Our mother was helpless when it came to him because he'd already beaten her down. At first, he hid it well, making sure the damage he inflicted wasn't seen but as we got older and bigger, so was the damage he caused.

He turned us into this.

A knock on my door snaps me back to the present. Jumping up, I yank my door open, and my brothers enter. One by one they enter and take a seat, getting comfy.

Reign eyes the folder open on my bed, and when he lifts his gaze to mine, I scoff furiously at him for not telling me this. I know I should have picked up on it the first time I read the report, but *he* should have told me.

"So, anything you want to share with the group?" I sneer at him once everyone is seated.

"What, that Remy's dad is MIA? Or he hasn't been seen in years? Or your peach has no fucking clue who she really is?"

"Well, there are those questions but how about the fact Arlen was in a secret relationship with someone here at Crestwood? How the fuck did we not know this? But most of all, who was he fucking?"

Hendrix and Saint stare at me like I've lost my mind.

"Arlen was gay, so fucking what?" Reign says. "Who he was sticking his dick into has nothing to do with this." He sighs, throwing his head back and rolling his eyes. Staring at me, he adds, "Arlen was a good guy."

"You know that doesn't mean shit, right?" I snap. "Who gives a flying fuck if he was a good guy." I air quote those last three words, "He's a fucking Hearst. All Hearsts are cunts. End of fucking story." Reign rolls his eyes again. I know he and Arlen were friends, that was no secret, but this? Fuck.

"But seriously, how did we not know Arlen was into dudes? We know everything, remember?" Hendrix asks the one question that has been plaguing me since I rediscovered this information. Seems people *can* keep secrets around here.

Saint stands ready to leave, clearly us discussing this is boring him.

"Sit the fuck down, Saint," I growl at him. He glares at me but knows not to piss me off right now so he sits back in his chair, folding his arms and scowling like a motherfucker.

"Look, I don't give two shits that he fucked dudes, that's probably the reason why he jumped, didn't want to disappoint Mommy and Daddy." Running my hands through my hair, I sigh in frustration. Nothing is making any fucking sense, and I hate being in the fucking dark.

"Look, man, I doubt Arlen jumped from the cliffs 'cause he likes dick. There's more to it." Hendrix tries to reason with me, and I notice Reign is nodding in agreement.

He's right, he was seen standing on the cliffs then the next moment he wasn't there. So why does it feel like a setup? Someone knows something we don't. Until we find out who he was fucking, we will never know.

"You're just a mere mortal with a god complex." Remington's words are meant to hurt but fuck if they don't turn me on. I caught her in the library a few moments ago and couldn't resist taunting her. The temptation to taunt was strong. "Your last name doesn't scare me," she throws, her voice laced with venom.

Moving closer to her, she steps back, her strength waning with my nearness. It allows me the perfect opportunity to cage her between me and the wall. I move my nose along her jaw, breathing in her scent, and my cock twitches.

"You should be scared, Peach." My lips touch her skin ever so lightly. Her pulse rapidly thrums against my lip. I can't help but smile at her reaction to my touch, and I can't control myself when my lips leave a wet path along her neck.

Tasting her.

Marking her.

Fuck.

My cock aches, needing a release.

Remington whimpers as my hand slides over her hip, my fingers digging into her flesh. My tongue darts out, tasting her more. My lips suck her skin. My teeth nip her flesh. Biting down harder when she doesn't push me away.

Finally I pull back, her neck is red from my attack. Her breathing has escalated. Her face flushed. Her eyes dilated.

Before I lose all control and fuck her right here, I growl and walk away.

Fuck. I nearly gave in. That can never happen again, but there's also a part of me that wants that ... and more.

REMY

WHAT THE FUCK WAS THAT?

One minute I'm looking for a book on Roman history and the next, I'm throwing barbs back and forth with *him* and then next, I'm pressed against the wall. *He's* attacking my neck with his lips and tongue and I'm a wanton mess. My body comes alive, and my vagina sings like she's Julie Andrews in *The Sound of Music* but rather than the hills coming alive, it's my vagina.

Every nerve ending in my body is buzzing.

I nearly come just from him licking my neck. Imagine what we could do together if we were naked? *What the fuck,*

Remington? And yes, I just berated myself with my full name. I'm currently standing in the middle of the Roman history stacks in the school library, thinking about fucking Thatcher Vanderbelt.

No.

No.

No.

No, fucking no.

Bad Remy.

You must not think dirty sexy things about him. Think only bad thoughts ... but his tongue ... and his lips ... and the grip he had on your hip.

No.

A loud audible groan slips out, and the sound echoes through the library stacks. There is no way he didn't hear that, and that's all I need. I don't need *him* to know he's affected me in *that* way.

Grabbing the book I need, I race back to the table where I'd set up and plonk down into my seat. Dropping my head to the desk, I bump it up and down against my books.

I don't need this.

I just need my brother.

Sitting up, I grab my phone and dial Grayson. This time it rings and gets my hopes up that he's going to answer, but it rings out and goes to voicemail. I don't bother leaving a message, he hasn't replied to the other five million messages I've left. Why would this one be any different?

My phone vibrates in my hand and I inwardly groan when I see my mother's name flashing on the screen before me. Not wanting to talk to her right now, I let it ring out and go to voicemail.

Dropping it to the desk, I lean back in my chair. Lifting my hands, I link my fingers behind my head and stare at the ceiling above. My phone vibrates again across the table.

Mother.

Again.

If she's trying desperately to get in touch with me, something must have happened. "Grayson," I mumble. Sighing, I grab my phone and answer. "Hello, Mother."

"Remington, when I call you. I expect you to answer," she sasses down the line, and I can imagine her Botoxed face trying to portray her anger.

"Sorry, I'm at the library ... studying."

"You've been there only a few days. How do you need to study already?"

"Because it's school. That's what you do to learn, you study. Plus, someone," I snarl the word someone, "moved me mid-semester so I have new curriculum to catch up on."

"Don't take that tone with me, young lady ..." Here we go, she's going to rant and rave about being a Hearst and after the tragic death of Arlen, Dad being MIA, and all the other bullshit I've dealt with in my life, I need to step up and be the daughter I was always meant to be. Blah-fucking-blah. But then Mother utters four words that stop me in my tracks. "It's Grayson, he's missing."

Double blinking, I process her words. "What did you say?"

"You know I don't like repeating myself, Remington. Grayson, he's missing. According to his call log, you were the last one to speak to him. What did you discuss?"

Nothing I'll tell you about. "He said he was coming for a visit, but he hasn't arrived yet."

"Well, he went missing along the highway to Crestwood. The local authorities found his car but not him."

"Where is he?"

"If I knew, I wouldn't be talking to you," she snaps, ever the loving and caring mother she isn't.

"What can I do?" I ask her, hope blooming in my chest that I can do something to find Grayson.

"Nothing," she harrumphs. "You're an eighteen-year-old girl. Just study and find a husband."

"Your son is missing," I hiss, "and you want me to find a husband. Really, Mother?"

"Don't take that tone with me, young lady. You're lucky I even called you at all. Would you rather the police turn up at your school and find out that way? Embarrassing you and our name in front of the other students, again."

Yes, cause then I wouldn't need to speak to you. "Okay, fine," I hiss, tensions are high. "If I hear from him, I'll let you know."

"Thank you." And without a goodbye, she hangs up.

"Bye, Mother. Great chatting to you, Mother," I sass, throwing my phone onto the desk. It slides across the surface and onto the carpet.

Someone bends down, picks it back up, and holds it hostage, spinning it around and around in their hand. When I look up, I roll my eyes when I see who is standing there. "Great, can this night get any crappier?" I whine.

"Lovely to see you too, Remington. I'm fine, thank you so fucking much for asking."

"It's Remy," I snap at Reign. I know it's Reign because he's the blond Vanderbelt asshole, but when it comes to the triplets, however, I'm still a little confused as to who is who. One thing I do know, the Vanderbelt triplets, and Saint, are all hot motherfuckers—emphasis on the hot and fuckers parts. I refuse to refer to them as one of The Lords. They can fuck themselves with a pineapple before that happens and even then, I won't ever refer to them as that.

"I'm sorry, my apologies. Let me try again, lovely to see you too, Rem-E. I'm fine, thanks for asking." And for the first time since I arrived at the library, my lips lift in a smile.

Staring at the man across from me, I try my hardest to school my smirk, not wanting to give him the satisfaction of knowing, I'm happyish to be around him. "I'm sorry, Re-EIGN. It's been a crappy afternoon ... day ... week ... year."

He stands across from me, towering above. He drops into the seat across from me and slides my phone back to me. "A problem shared is a problem halved."

"And why do you care about my problems?" I snap. I know I'm being a bitch, but seriously, these assholes have been nothing but, well, assholes since I arrived. Why does this one care all of a sudden?

"I don't," he honestly states, "but just now, you looked like you're really sad and I hate nothing more than seeing a pretty girl crying."

"I'm not crying, see." I point to my eyes. "No tears."

"Sad. Tears. Same shit really but from looking at your face, the tears won't be too far away."

How the fuck does he read me so well? No one except Gray and Arlen can read me like this, well I guess, Arlen used to. Past tense. The three of us have this freaky sixth sense thing when it comes to our emotions, surely Gray will feel I need him and pop up any minute now. I keep telling myself his car just broke down and he'll be walking here, but fuck, what if someone took him?

A single tear falls down my cheek. "Told ya," his deep voice says from beside me, startling me. When the hell did he move over next to me? "Wanna talk about it?"

"Not with you," I spit, wiping at my cheek.

"One question and I'll leave you alone?"

"You can ask, but whether I answer or not, well, that's another thing." I shrug my shoulders and stare at him.

"Why do you hate us?" he asks as if he's asking about the weather.

"I don't hate you," I defensively reply.

"Okay, let me rephrase. Why are you being a bitch to us?"

"Why are you guys being assholes to me?"

"You can ask but whether I answer or not, well ..." He throws my previous words back at me and I find my lips lifting slightly. "Is that a smile I see?"

"No, I was squinting."

"No, it was a smile." He smirks. "You like me, Rem-E."

"I do not, Re-EIGN." This time, I do smile.

"Knew it." He bumps my shoulder with his. "You like me but it's okay, I'll keep it a secret. I'm good at keeping secrets."

"I bet you are." I nod. "Wanna share any of those secrets with the class?"

He shakes his head. "Secrets are secrets for a reason."

"Secrets always get revealed," I throw back at him.

"Not all do."

We silently stare at one another, and something passes between us. It's not sexual, but it's a look of understanding like we get one another. I notice a sadness in him that feels like it's calling to me, but before I can probe him, he beats me to speaking next. "Well, I'll love you and leave you, little lady." He stands and squeezes my shoulder. Instinctively, I lift my hand and squeeze his back.

"Thanks," I quietly murmur.

He nods and turns to exit the library. He passes Alani along the way and a look passes between the two of them, then she looks to me, smiles, turns, and chases after Reign.

"What the fuck is with all the secrets here?" I mumble as I pack up my things. My head isn't in it to study anymore, today has been a mindfuck of epic proportions, and I hope tomorrow is different.

Leaving the library, I walk back to my room, thoughts and theories whirling around my head. There are secrets all around me here at Crestwood, and I hate being kept in the dark. But one thing I know for sure, I'm going to uncover them all and I'll take down anyone who gets in my way.

THATCHER

"THATCH, DUDE, WE HAVE A PROBLEM!" Reign bellows, waltzing into my room. He slams the door behind him, the frame rattling from his anger.

"What's up?"

"Grayson Hearst is missing."

Four words I didn't expect to come out of his mouth. "What? How do you know?"

"After you left your peach, I approached her." A growl forms low in my throat. "Calm the fuck down, man, she's yours. We all know that. Anyway, she got a call from Rochelle and that's when I overheard."

"And?"

"And I approached her to see if I could get any deets."

"And?" I repeat again.

"And I got jack shit but it feels like his disappearance is linked to our vendetta. Don't know why I feel that, but I do." Nodding, I process his words and then with a shit-eating grin he adds, "Remy smiled at me and well, maybe, she now hates me a little less." *Eat shit, fucker, I got an orgasmic groan* I think to myself as I remember her body pressed against mine in the library. My non-reaction pisses him off and now it's my turn to smirk. "Look, T, I think there's more to what I found." Reign looks to me, waiting for if he should voice his theory. Folding my arms across my chest, I lean against the wall and stare at him, waiting for him to share with the class.

"Care to share?" I push him. He remains quiet and nibbles on his lips. Reaching behind him, he pulls something from his backpack and hands me a piece of paper. I see a grainy image of two people, I can just make out who one figure is but the other is too blurry. "Who's the other person?" I question.

Shrugging, Reign shakes his head. "Not sure, he's blocking their view, but knowing him it could be anybody."

Sighing, I shove off the wall in frustration.

"For once I wish we were ahead of him. What the fuck is he hiding?"

"I can do more digging, it might take some time but if there's anything else, I'll find it. You'll have to be patient though. I have a feeling, the more I dig, it's going to open Pandora's Box and secrets fucking galore are going to pour out and not just his. Ours and every fucking one else who attends or has attended Crestwood."

Are we truly ready for everything to be out in the open?

Once it's out, there's no going back.

My brothers are hiding just as much as I am and being exposed, I'm not sure we're ready for the consequences, but it's a risk we need to take. "Whatever you have to do, do it."

He nods and then I ask, "Are you still in contact with that other hacker?"

He nods. "Yeah, of course, I might be able to get him on this too, I mean, two heads are better than one."

"As I said, whatever it takes."

He nods and even though we just agreed, I'm still not one-hundred-percent sure it's the right thing to do, but we need information.

Grabbing my bag, we exit my room and walk side by side down the hall. Alani catches his eye across the quad. She smiles softly at him and from the corner of my eye, I watch him. His gaze doesn't fall from hers, and he smiles slightly at her.

"You still fucking her?" I ask, snapping his attention away from her.

"It's complicated," he replies with a shrug, and I notice he doesn't expand on that, but when it comes to the opposite sex, it's always complicated. Especially when your dick and her vagina are involved.

I laugh, clapping him on the back. "With women, it always is, Brother."

He laughs and nods in agreement. "I need to go. You'll know when I do." He walks backward down the hall saluting me as he does, probably off to chase after Alani.

I make my way down the opposite end of the hall, and if I didn't know this school like the back of my hand, I'd get lost. But of course I know every secret door, every back entrance, every single inch of these halls.

Turning the corner, I see Remy up ahead talking to Lennon. That fucker better not touch what belongs to me. Not without my permission anyway.

Remy's eyes widen when I stop behind Lennon. "Uh … ummm," she stutters.

Lennon chuckles. "He's behind me, right?" She nods

slowly as if I'm about to rip him to shreds. And truth be told, I just might. I haven't decided yet.

"Thatcher, my man." He turns and winks at me before throwing his arm around her shoulders, pulling her into his side. She makes a face and my blood simmers at him touching my peach. "I was just telling Remington here all about the party next weekend."

The fucker knows what he's doing, and he's one step closer to me ripping him apart.

Raising my eyebrows at them, my lip curves when Remy pushes him away and folds into herself. He was inviting her and she was about to answer when I showed up.

"You're welcome to come, Peach," I offer, and from the look on her face, she's shocked at my invitation. "I mean, the whole school will be in attendance but I'm not sure it's your scene."

"Why? It's a party, anything is better than staring at books all weekend." Her sassiness causes my cock to twitch.

Leaning down, my face stops inches from hers. She inhales a shaky breath and utters, "Are you going to tie me up so I won't be able to come to your precious party?" Lifting her head in defiance, my lips ever so gently brush hers as she does, she frantically pulls back.

My voice is gone for a few fleeting seconds. Is she reading my mind?

The back of my fingers stroke her cheek. I love feeling the way her body moves under my touch.

"As fun as that sounds, Peach, and trust me nothing would make me harder than seeing you tied up begging for mercy, but the party is at the cemetery at the back of the woods."

"So?" She shrugs.

"You're not scared?" I smirk, my fingers gliding down her body, leaving a trail over her hip.

"I thought we had an understanding, Thatcher. I'm not scared of you or your posse."

Lennon chuckles, muttering, "Oh, damn." I almost forgot he was still here.

"Well, by all means, Peach, come enjoy the ride." Pausing, I then add, "I know I will." My gaze travels down her body, following every delectable curve, secretly loving the girls here are required to wear skirts—thank you, faculty heads. They're short, another requirement—again, thank you, faculty heads. I lift my gaze to her face, a safe ground because I'm sporting some serious wood right now.

My body still hasn't caught on to the fact we despise Remington Hearst.

Leaving her with Lennon, I walk away from them before I do something stupid like kiss her.

Every party we throw is some sort of endless duty, it always has been. We make an appearance, make someone moan our names then we leave. It's a way for the entire school to see us in our prime. To remind them all this could be taken away with a click of our fingers if we so wish.

As I walk away, I wonder what Remington would do if she had more than just me in bed? Would she be as adventurous as the other girls at Crestwood? Or would she run for the hills while screaming for help?

"Are we going to have some fun?" Lennon asks as he joins me.

My tongue wets my lips, chuckling. "Yeah, we are. Let's show my little peach, what fun at Crestwood really is."

Heels click against the marble floor, echoing around the hall. Every pair of eyes, including mine, lands on her as she walks toward class. The silence, apart from her shoes, is broken by hushed whispers. She almost makes it to the door before I make my move. Raising my chin, my eyes land on hers and I step forward. Planting my hand against the doorframe, she stops as I halt her entrance to the room. I don't miss the rise of her chest as her breathing quickens.

She swallows thickly, keeping her eyes anywhere but directly on mine.

"Going somewhere, Peach?" I question. Ignoring me, she straightens her spine and tries to move around me, but instead, I move farther into her path, causing her to smack directly into my chest.

Laughter echoes around us, after all, I'm putting on a show and they're eating it up.

"Move," she demands.

Chuckling, my fingers brush over her cheek and she smacks my hand away, glaring at me.

"Make me, Peach." I lick my lips.

Her eyes betray her following the movement of my tongue across my flesh. Leaning in, my breath fans over her ear, making her shiver.

"I'll move, Remy," I whisper, "when you've paid your penance."

My hand grips her hip. My fingers tighten, causing her to clench her teeth through the pain. It isn't much, but the need to hurt her has always been clear.

"I'm not going anywhere," she hisses, showing me she's stronger than we've given her credit for. My lips lift in a smirk, leaning in farther, my nose brushes against her slightly. "We'll see, Peach, we'll see."

Removing my arms from blocking her, I wink and let her enter the room.

Following her, I drop into my seat and keep my focus on her. She's going to be a worthy adversary, and I cannot wait to play with her. Break her. Game on, Hearst, game on.

Remy has been avoiding me since our run-in the other day before class, but with the phone call I got this morning, it's probably in her best interest to steer clear of me right now.

Tonight our father has requested—demanded—our presence for a family dinner. If you're thinking it will be like *The Brady Bunch*, think again. That's not how Thornton Vanderbelt rolls, my brothers and I know the drill. Hold our tongues. Don't bait him. Say yes Sir, no Sir, and if we follow these rules, we can safely walk out at the end of the evening.

We only agree to go to dinner to check on our mother. These days she locks herself away in her room or drinks until she passes out. It's her way of coping now, and this is why my brothers and I are out for revenge. Our father's presence upsets her, but he has that effect on everyone. They are toxic for one another but she's too meek and fragile to leave the asshole. Even after he did what he did, she still stays. Says she'll always love him, blah blah blah AND he's too damn selfish and controlling to let her go either. It's one big mess and why my brothers and I are taking action on her behalf.

If I can get through a dinner without strangling him, I consider it a small victory. Tonight could always be the night I let my inner demons out, I guess time will tell.

Right now, I need a drink, actually more than one and possibly a hot pussy to sink myself into. Forget the world and all the shit that exists for a hot minute.

Speaking of pussy to devour, Remington is walking toward me with her head in her phone, frowning at something, not paying attention. Her hair is in a high ponytail like most of the other girls. It sways side to side in time with her hips.

Standing in her way, she'll have no choice but to bump

into me, and I watch on with glee as she finally lifts her head, seconds away from slamming into me.

"Jesus, Thatcher, what the hell?" she snaps. Stepping around me at the last second, she continues down the hall. Turning around, I follow close behind her.

Leaning forward, I breathe into her ear. "Your tongue is going to get you in trouble one of these days, Peach. Maybe we need to put it to better use."

She halts and spins around to face me with a deathly glare. "I don't have time for your crap today, okay," she snaps, "just leave me the fuck alone."

My eyes search hers, and I notice unshed tears fill the corners of her eyes and I know what those tears are for. My lips quirk in amusement, she's almost at breaking point, and it's ohhh so fucking beautiful to see.

I can't wait to see her shatter.

"If I were you, Peach," I sneer as I step around her and walk backward, watching and waiting for her reaction to my next words. "I'd watch your back. Things are about to get fun."

Her eyes widen at my threat. Fear reflects back at me, and it's such a beautiful sight to see. Winking, I spin around and walk away from her.

This game is just getting started, and I for one, cannot wait to see her fall. She may have a thick skin, but it will never be thick enough to thwart us because what The Lords want, The Lords get … and Remington Hearst is about to pay for her mother's and our father's sins.

REMY

THATCHER'S WORDS ring in my ears as he walks away. I don't need this right now. I'm barely keeping it together as it is. My worst nightmare has come true, Grayson isn't coming home, and some creep keeps texting me.

Over the last few days, I've received multiple messages from my stalker.

UNKNOWN

You look pretty today

You look so sad today

Your smile is brighter than the sun

They don't deserve you

Pushing aside the thought of Creeper McCreeperson, I think about my brother. They called off the search for him this morning, Mother informed me over the phone. Apparently, he sent Mom a text saying he's fine and just needs a time-out. I feel she's hiding something from me, but that's nothing new. Mom ignored my pleas that this is shit. Grayson wouldn't just up and disappear, he wouldn't do that to me, but she told me it's done, and I need to accept it. Why are the authorities and Mom giving up so easily? Grayson is missing, not off on an adventure, I feel it deep in my bones. I've already lost one brother. Losing another brother isn't an option. I wouldn't survive.

Thinking about Arlen being gone causes my eyes to well with tears.

"You okay, Rem? You look like someone just died," Alani says, dropping into the seat next to me. At the mention of death, the first tear falls, and it's followed by an avalanche of them. She grabs my arm and drags me out of the classroom. I can feel everyone's eyes on me as I break down. And of course, we run into Reign out in the hallway.

Through my tears, I see Alani shake her head and mouth something to him. Whatever she says works because he continues down the hallway, leaving us alone. We make our way to the bathroom, she pushes open the door, and we step in.

"Out," she bellows to the girl at the sink washing her hands. Even through my tears, I see the girl jump ten feet in the air. She turns off the faucet and makes a beeline for the door. "Thanks," Alani sweetly says and then slams the door closed behind her, flipping the lock, and giving us some privacy. "What's wrong?" she asks, taking my hand in hers and squeezing in the reassuring kind of way.

"Nothing, I'm fine," I mumble and even I don't believe me.

"I call bullshit 'cause if you were in fact fine, you wouldn't be crying in the girls' bathroom right now."

"Can't a girl just cry?" She gives me the 'do I look like a fool' look. "Okay, fine, I'm just having a rough morning. Week. Month. Year. Take your pick."

"Wanna talk about it?"

"Do I look like I want to talk about it?" I snap at her and immediately I feel bad for being a bitch to her. "Sorry for being a bitch, but I wouldn't even know where to begin."

"The start is generally a good spot." Dropping my hand, she jumps up onto the counter and swings her legs back and forth, staring at me. Waiting for me to open up. "A problem shared is a problem halved."

Leaning against the wall, I cross my feet and drop my head against the wall, staring up at the ceiling above. Closing my eyes, I take a deep, cleansing breath and then look over to Alani. "My brother is missing, and no one seems to care. My mom's a bitch and to top off my shittastic list, I can't stop thinking dirty sexy naked things about Thatcher-fucking-Vanderbelt."

"That's quite the list, and if it makes you feel better, my mom's also a raging bitch. I have both a brother and a sister, if either of them went missing, I'd be crying too, and as for Thatch, well, he is kinda hot in that psychopathic sexy way so I can't fault you for that one. Personally, I'd much rather picture ... well, it's not important who I would picture, but—"

"Come on spill, it can't be any worse than Thatcher-fuck-ing-Vanderbelt ... is it a teacher?"

"No ... and I'm not telling."

"Spoilsport." She sticks out her tongue at me, and I laugh. "Thank you."

"For what?"

"This," I reply with a shrug, flipping my hands around the empty bathroom. "You don't know me all that well, but you knew I needed an escape, and may I say, you can be badass when you want to. That chick nearly shit her pants when you went all momma bear growly."

"She did not."

"Ahh yeah, she did." I nod. "Because I too nearly shit myself. You might be petite, but your bite is strong."

"My girl was hurting. I'm sure you'd do the same if the shoe was on the other foot."

"You bet your ass I would." And she's right, I only met her a few days ago but I already feel a connection to her.

"Wanna get out of here for the day?"

"We're already late for class, may as well make a day of it."

"Fantastic, let's blow this popsicle stand." She jumps off the counter and links her arm with mine. She unlocks the door, and we head down the hallway and out to the parking lot. She unlocks her BMW 8 series convertible, and we climb in.

After clicking my belt, I receive another text.

UNKNOWN

Please don't cry. I hate it when you're upset.

"Fuck off," I whisper as I turn my phone off and toss it into my bag. Future Remy can worry about that, current Remy is going to try to enjoy herself with her friend.

Starting the engine, Alani puts the top down and clicks play on the stereo. "Paparazzi" by Lady Gaga blares through the speakers as she throws the car into reverse and screeches out of the parking lot. You'd swear she was an extra in *The Fast and Furious*.

Closing my eyes, I raise my arms up and sing along at the top of my lungs, feeling free for the first time all day. Opening my eyes, that feeling dissipates when my eyes land on *him*. Flipping him the bird, I mumble "Fucker" and then continue to sing along. I refuse to let him get to me, Thatcher-fucking-Vanderbelt is nothing to me ... but why can't I stop thinking about him?

THATCHER

REMY'S FINGER in the air is a taunt as the girls speed off down the driveway and out of the school grounds.

"I think your little peach needs to be taught a lesson." Conroy chuckles as he stands behind me watching Alani drive as if she's auditioning for *The Fast and Furious*.

A grin tugs at my lips because I have just the right lesson in mind. Without saying a word, I turn and reenter the building. Conroy follows me up to my room.

Ditching class isn't anything new and since I'm untouchable at Crestwood, the teachers never say a word. Mr. Clayton tried once, and well, he no longer works in education, anywhere. We're THAT powerful. No one fucks with the Vanderbelts.

Conroy makes himself comfortable as I bring up the group chat.

THATCHER

It's time to show Remington Hearst who's in charge and what we can do.

HENDRIX

This sounds fun.

RIAN

Please tag me in, you know how much I love to play.

REIGN

Oh crap, what did she do to piss you off now?

CONROY

She gave him the finger.

Our boy's royally pissed.

THEON

You know I'm down for fun and teaching the ladies a lesson makes me hard.

LENNON

We don't need to hear about your dick.

At the party?

Yes at the party, I'll slip her away. Conroy, Theon, you guys know what to do.

Conroy waggles his eyebrows at the fun we are going to have. "I don't think little Miss Remy realizes she's about to regret giving you that finger."

"Exactly. I bet she'll be begging me for forgiveness by the

end."

... later that week

Forcing the doors to the library open a little harder than I intended, I watch as everyone jumps and then averts their gaze. The power of being a Lord is intoxicating, I love watching my peers under pressure.

Glancing around the room, I spot her at a table in the back, none the wiser regarding what's about to happen. My fist connects with the table, making her throw the book she was reading to the floor.

"Th ... Thatcher," she stammers, grabbing her chest. It's a little fucking dramatic if you ask me, so I decide to make this fun. Leaning down over her, I stare intently at her. Reaching out, I grab her upper arms and haul her up and out of her seat. Her skirt rises a little, giving me the perfect view of her legs. I corner her between her chair and my body. A murderous gaze appears on her face, and I grin down at her.

"You need to be taught a lesson, little girl. Why don't you bow down like the good little bitch you are?" I say smugly. My grip on her wrist tightens, my fingers dig into her skin.

"Asshole, let go of me." she snaps and out of nowhere, her untethered hand connects hard across my face, I welcome the sting. A growl passes through my lips. I let go of her wrist and my hand wraps around the back of her neck as I drag her body against mine.

Remy fights me for a second. Her fist pounds into my chest as I pull her along with me. I take her to the back corner of the library and slam her hard against the wall. Before she can respond, my lips take hers. My tongue pushes into her mouth as she fights me. My tongue tangles with hers, and she moans into my mouth. She begins to kiss me back, accepting the kiss. Her fingers clutch my shirt as I snake my hands down her side and begin to lift her skirt up just a couple of inches. Feeling her soft skin under my touch causes me to moan into her mouth. Running my hand up the inside of her thigh, I reach the moist fabric of her panties.

"Fuck," I hiss. She's wet, she wants this, and it causes my cock to harden between us. "Are you wet for me, Peach?" I growl against her mouth.

"Fuck you," she spits against my lips. A moan slips through her lips as my fingers circle her pussy. I bury my hand into her hair, tugging her closer to me. I kiss her with frantic need and with each slash of her tongue against mine, my cock strains against my trousers.

"Is this what you want?" I ask, thrusting my hips against her. She shakes her head, biting her lip as I continue to grind against her. Her whimper is all the answer I need. I lift her up, forcing her to wrap her legs around my waist. Sliding her panties to the side, I push two fingers inside her cunt.

She shoves me back, but at the same time she holds me to her. I grind my cock against her again and she whimpers as I continue to thrust my fingers in and out of her hot wet channel.

Pulling my fingers out, she whimpers at the loss. A smirk appears on my face as I slide my zipper down, freeing myself and before she has a chance to protest, I slip the head of my cock just a few inches into her wet heat. She gasps as I thrust, giving her more and more until I'm fully seated inside her.

She swivels her hips, accommodating me. Pulling almost all the way out, I lock my eyes on her, and with one hard thrust, I bury myself deep inside her.

We both groan as she sinks all the way down on my cock.

Losing control, one hand grabs her hip, the other lands above her head and I slam into her, over and over.

Watching her face, her lips widen, and she lets out a breathy sound of pleasure as I continue to fuck her.

"Oh, fuck. Thatcher, right there, oh God, right there," she shrieks. I don't give a fuck who hears us. Her moans encourage me, and I fuck her harder and faster. The feeling of her tight heat around my cock has my balls ready to explode.

She cries out as her orgasm releases, her fingernails dig into my shoulders, marking me as she continues to convulse around my cock. I follow her grunting my release, spilling into her over and over again until I'm breathless.

We are both panting, coming down from the high and I see the moment realization washes over her. She shoves at my chest, and I lower her to her feet and I have to admit, the sight of my cum leaking down her leg is one of the hottest things I've seen.

"I can't believe we did that," she cries as she rushes past me.

Reaching out, I grab her arm, forcing her to look at me. "Doesn't change anything, Peach. You're still a pain in my ass and I still want you gone."

She stares at me, her cheeks still flushed from her release. "You or your last name doesn't scare me, Thatcher," she snaps and even though I just came, my cock begins to harden again at her sass and strength.

"Watch your back, Peach," I warn her with a wink. Tucking my dick back into my pants, I turn and walk away from her. Everyone's eyes are on me as I exit the library and the murmurs start. When Remy comes into sight, leaving her with her mouth agape and daggers flying my way.

I keep watching.

Waiting.

Waiting for her to appear.

The cemetery is packed—as usual—music pumps through the speakers, drinks flow, and everyone is well on the way to being wasted.

Slowly lifting the red Solo cup to my lips, I drink. The liquid catching in my throat when I finally catch sight of her.

Swallowing, my gaze roams over her. She's wearing a short as fuck skirt and it's perfect for my plan. Her tits squish together in the ridiculous piece of fabric she calls a top, but my dick sure appreciates the view before me.

Her gaze catches mine from across the cemetery and I can't help myself, I raise my cup toward her in a silent salute. She nervously looks away, avoiding my hardened stare. Her nonchalance gets my heart racing, it's time to play.

Sneaking into the darkness, I watch Alani hand her a cup before both of them make their way farther into the party. I slip farther into the shadows, watching her. Remy's gaze drifts over the party and I notice the panicked look on her face, I guess she's not as tough as she makes out. A grin appears on my face as I text the boys.

THATCHER

It's showtime, boys

Across from me, I watch as Theon looks at his phone, smirking when he reads the message. He chugs back the rest of his drink, crushing the empty cup in his hand. Dropping it to the grass below, he turns and makes his way through the crowd. Beelining straight for Remy.

He leans in whispering in her ear. At first she freezes and then she smiles, accepting his hand as he holds it out to her.

Perfect, she's taken the bait.

Sipping my drink, I watch as the two of them sway to the beat of the music. Theon grinds against Remy, just as I instructed him to do.

His hand sits on her hip, he spins her, so her back is to his front and ever so slowly, his fingers tighten around her skirt, lifting the side just enough for me to see her G-string. Her head falls back on his shoulder as she moves with him.

It's almost as if she's under his spell, very few women, and men, can thwart his advances. Theon has this way about him that anyone around him gets sucked into his vortex. His lips find her collarbone and he sucks a path to her neck. I swear from where I am, I can hear her moan over the music's bass.

Theon looks up and catches my line of sight. Nodding back at him, he goes back to pushing himself into her from behind. She tugs on her lip, making me adjust my cock. The whole scene is erotic and if it wasn't one of my best friend's grinding up on her as part of our plan, I'd be over there and my fist would be meeting the guy's face.

No one touches my peach without my permission.

I lick my lips and watch her move in Theon's arms. The sway of her hips has affected my dick to the point it hurts. It's torture being this close but not being able to touch her. I want to claim her here in front of everyone, seal her fate to me because the fact remains, Remy is mine. No one else can have her, I'll take out anyone who stands in my way.

Fuck, the way her hips sway as she walks down the halls has my cock constantly at half-mast. The way her ass looks so fucking edible in that tiny fucking skirt right now is pure agony. Keeping my distance is becoming harder—pun intended—the longer I watch them. I know she's enjoying every moment of it because I know I am.

My cock twitches, making me fully aware she has complete control over me. This girl has brought me to my knees. Me. A fucking Vanderbelt, a fucking Lord. This cannot stand, and the need to make her suffer is now stronger than ever.

Tonight, Remington Hearst is going to discover I am THE

Lord and she will bow down to me, not the other way around.

I watch for another moment as Theon and Remy grind all over each other. She's in such a blissed state with him, she doesn't feel him slip away from her and for Conroy to take his place.

She lifts her arms, wrapping them around Conroy's neck. He bends, kissing her skin before he bites down on her ear, making her tremble in his arms.

His fingers reach in front of her skirt, brushing over her pussy. At his touch, she suddenly looks up and jumps back slightly when she realizes Theon has been replaced with Conroy.

Conroy smirks and holds his hand out for her to join him again.

She's frozen and stares at his outstretched hand and just when I think she'll blow him off and walk away, making our plan null and void, she places her hand in his. Not giving her a chance to get away, Conroy tugs her to his chest, lowers his head and begins to kiss her neck again. She's once again putty in his hands.

He whispers in her ear, and she nods. He offers her his hand again and she follows behind him as he brings her through the crowd. *Stage two is about to begin.*

My cock is aching, but he has to wait, tonight is about revenge and showing my little peach just who rules this school. She has no fucking clue what she's got herself into.

Licking my lips, eager for my turn, I follow behind them into the mausoleum. Closing the door behind me, I lock it, placing the key in my pocket. A grin appears, knowing she has no way out. Nowhere to run.

Conroy and Theon cage a frustrated Remy between them, her gaze flicking between them both.

My footsteps echo through the chamber, finally garnering

her attention. She turns her head and when she registers it's me, the scowl on her face says it all.

She shakes her head. "I should have known you'd have something to do with this." She goes to walk past Theon, but he catches her arm, stopping her from moving away.

"Let me go," she snarls, "whatever you have planned, I want no part of it." She breathes, sounding almost breathless.

Her breathlessness is the opposite of the words she just spoke, and I can't help but chuckle. "Oh, Peach, I think you do." I reach into my pocket, pulling out the key, taunting her. "The only way you're leaving here is with this key and if you're a good girl and do as I say, I might just give it to you."

Swallowing, she looks to the ground and fidgets with the hem of her skirt. It's a tic of hers I've noticed she does when she's agitated.

"Show me," I command, breaking the silence.

Remy stares me down, her fists clenching by her sides. Smirking, I take five steps until we're mere inches apart. She glares up at me, even in her heels I tower over her.

Lifting my hand, I caress her cheek before my thumb slides down over her lip. A flush creeps across her face when I touch her skin. She whimpers softly at my touch and doesn't notice when I push her skirt up with my other hand.

Forcing her eyes shut, she swallows deeply but doesn't stop me.

She wants this.

She wants us.

"You need to be taught a lesson, Peach."

A growl slips from me when my fingers brush across her soaked panties. Slipping under the edge of her panties, my fingers feel her wetness.

"Did Theon and Conroy make you wet?" I whisper, leaning into her. She turns her head away as my breath fans over her exposed neck. "Answer me," I demand when she ignores my question.

She shakes her head in defiance, even though she knows I can feel, and smell, her lies.

"You be a good little girl and maybe we'll take care of that." Staring hatred toward me, she moves slightly so my fingers graze over her pussy.

She moans, biting down on her lip.

I smile and then force two fingers inside her, making her cry out. She grabs my shoulders for support as I slide the digits in and out, soaking my fingers in her juices.

Conroy and Theon move in behind her.

"Oh God." Her breathy moans fill the small room.

"Is this what you want, Peach? Your pussy full?"

Brushing my thumb over her clit, she cries out. She's fucking soaked and putty in my hands. Her pussy is so fucking tight. I remember the feel of it clenching around my shaft in the library a few days ago. Closing my eyes, I think of anything but her moans to keep my dick from exploding.

"Damn, baby, those fucking moans." Conroy comes up behind her, pulling her shirt down, exposing her to us. She gasps but doesn't stop us.

Theon leans forward, taking one of her pebbled nipples between his lips. She whimpers as he sucks hard. Conroy kisses her neck, groping and tugging on her other nipple.

My fingers continue to torture her.

In.

Out.

In.

Out.

Her fingernails dig into my shoulders, and I feel her tighten around my fingers. Pulling my hand free, Remy groans when we all stop and step back from her.

"Please," her desperate plea echoes around us.

We each move around her trading places. Conroy licks a trail from her collarbone to her neck while Theon moves in behind her, lifting her skirt exposing the flimsy G-string she wears.

He squeezes her ass cheek while Conroy continues his task on her neck, again she whimpers and holds on to him for support.

I lean down, tasting her nipple for the first time, pulling it between my teeth, I bite down hard forcing a "Oh fuck," from Remy.

Theon's fingers glide through her wetness, the sound making us all groan.

"Please," she begs again and I watch as Theon pushes three fingers inside her.

"Not yet, Peach, you have to be a good girl first," I taunt her.

"Please, I'll be good, please, I just need ...." She trembles slightly, and I know she won't hold out for much longer. *Fuck, I don't think any of us will.*

"Not yet," I whisper in her ear, biting on her lobe, earning a guttural moan from her that echoes around the chamber.

Again we switch, Conroy bends down and his finger plays with her clit while Theon tugs and pinches her nipples.

She clenches her legs together and bites down on her lip. Pleasure firing throughout her body.

"Fuck, baby, your pussy is glistening," Conroy says before licking her from taint to clit through her panties.

She cries out, almost falling between us.

"I can't, I can't," she screams.

Conroy sucks her clit, forcing her to shake uncontrollably between us when he stops before she reaches her release.

A tear rolls down her cheek, and I know she's doing her best to obey us.

I suck her earlobe between my teeth, groping her pussy while I do. Turning her head, her lips are inches from mine. My lips ghost over hers. I want to know what she tastes like, but not yet. I kiss her neck instead, earning a frustrated whimper from her. Remy cries out when Conroy plunges his fingers back inside her.

"Fuck," he hisses.

Remy bucks against us panting hard, her legs wobble. She's so close.

Theon grinds his cock into her from behind. Conroy takes one last taste and moves so I can finally taste what belongs to me.

Dropping to my knees, I grip her hips and pull her to my mouth. My first taste of her is like fucking heaven. I moan as I coat my tongue in her juices.

Remy grips my hair as my tongue plunges inside her. With every last inch of control in my body, I take one last lick before pulling back. The three of us step back from her, and Remy's uncontrollable whimpers continue but turn into growls of frustration when she realizes we've all stopped.

"What? Why did you stop?" she whines.

Shrugging at her, I lick my lip and groan when I taste her nectar for the final time. Stepping back, she grabs my shirt and pleads, "Wait, what are you doing? I'm so close, please I need it."

Conroy and Theon stand behind me as I cup her jaw possessively, I hesitate for one second, savoring the moment. Remy is teetering on the edge, balancing precariously between anger and a sexual high. She's so close to breaking and it pleases me immensely.

"Now you know not to cross me, Peach. Behave and you'll receive pleasure like never before. Misbehave, and well ..." I shrug and stare at her.

Her mouth opens and closes in shock and rage.

Suddenly I'm imagining her choking on my cock, that is until she takes an aggressive step toward me. Lifting my hand, I halt her and my good little peach stops in her tracks. "For next time, remember what pleasure you can receive if you play along nicely." With my final words, we all walk out.

Unlocking the door, we leave Remy screaming after us.

The words bastards, cunts, and fuckers echo around us as we close the door. I chuckle to myself as we walk away from the mausoleum and my angry peach.

As of right now, I own you and your pussy Remington Hearst. My oh my, I cannot wait to play with my new toy.

REMY

WHAT THE FUCK JUST HAPPENED?

What the actual fuck?

One minute I'm on the cusp of the most amazing, exhilarating orgasm of my life and the next, a murderous rage is coursing through me from being left high and dry, well I'm not dry but you get it.

"You fucking asshole bastard cunt face fuckers," I scream. "This isn't fucking funny, assholes."

Stamping my foot in anger I let out a scream that would get me cast as the lead in any horror film. Taking a deep breath, I close my eyes and compose myself. Pulling my shirt back into place, I rearrange my skirt and lean against a marble tomb. "Sorry, dead dude," I mumble, "but if you were alive and in my shoes, you'd be fucking pissed off too."

Taking a few more deep breaths, I calm the erratic racing of my heart and return to normal, well as normal as you can be when you are in dire need of an orgasm. Shaking my head, I push off the tomb and walk toward the exit, a plan forming in my head. "Game on assholes," I mumble but then I groan when I see the door is closed. "If these doors are locked, those fuckers are deader than they already are going to be." Thankfully the door opens, and I really am thankful because I want to mess with these assholes before I take them down.

Pushing the door open farther, I step over the threshold and march back to the party. "Where have you been?" a drunk Alani asks me.

"Don't ask," I growl and the amazing friend that she has become, she hands me the drink in her hand. Chugging back what was clearly vodka with Coke for color, I swallow. "More," I voice as the liquid burns my throat.

"Wanna talk about it?" she asks as she leads us over to the keg.

"Nope, I just want to get drunk and make a plan to take those asshole bastard cunt face fuckers down."

"I'm all for a takedown. Who are we taking down?"

"Thatcher, Theon, and Conroy," I snarl as I fill my cup.

"Umm, on second thought, I might stay out of that."

Shrugging, I chug back my beer and refill my cup.

"You right there, Chuggy McChugerson?"

"Just peachy," I inform her and then flinch at the mention of peachy. "Fuck you, Thatcher," I hiss as I look around the party and then I see the one person I know who will help me. "Don't wait up," I throw over my shoulder as I walk around the bonfire and drop onto the log next to Brennan. "Hi," I sweetly greet him, "what's a girl gotta do to get a drink around here?"

"Well hello, Cutie." His gaze roams over me and just like the other day in the cafeteria before Thatcher went all caveman, I see that glint in his eye. That glint that says, 'I want to fuck you' and right now, I want that. I need to remove the touch of *him* and *them* from my body. To replace that feeling of utter orgasmic pleasure from him with someone else's utter orgasmic pleasure. But even as I sit next to Brennan with his come-fuck-me glint, I know it's going to be hard to replace that feeling because, holy fucking hotness, that was the most erotic and pleasurable feeling I have ever felt before … only for it to be ripped away at the last second by those asshole bastard cunt face fuckers. I need Brennan to fix this itch and I need him to fix it now. I know that makes me sound like a bitchy slut, but horny Remy needs to get off.

It knows it's the vodka talking but also a mixture of horny Remy thanks to those fuckers leaving me on the edge, but I have that same glint in my eye and Brennan sees it clear as day. I know I'm walking a fine line right now, but I'm horny and I hope *he* sees what I'm doing.

Leaning into him, I flutter my eyelashes and bite my bottom lip. His eyes track the movement of my tongue as it darts out and licks over the indent my teeth just left. The two of us are drawing closer together when someone grabs my arm roughly. "She'll be right back," a soft voice laced with anger growls before they drag me away from Brennan.

"Do you want to get him killed?" Rowan spits at me as she drags me away from Brennan and the party. "I don't know why I fucking care, but clearly I'm not thinking," she mumbles to herself as she pulls a bottle of vodka from somewhere and shoves it into my hands. "Drink," she demands and not wanting to piss her off, I unscrew the lid and drink. "Better?"

"No, I fucking hate vodka."

"Ohhh, I'm sorry, Princess, I'll remember to have a bottle of Kristal on hand for next time."

"Beer will suffice, but if you want to drop a grand on a bottle for me, I won't say no."

"You really are an enigma," she says, taking a sip of the vodka.

"How so?" I ask, snatching the bottle from her and taking a sip.

"You're a Hearst, but you don't act like one."

"And how is a Hearst meant to act?"

"Not like you."

"I have no idea what that means but I have a feeling it's a compliment, so thank you."

"It was, and for the record ..." She shakes her head. "Never mind."

"No, tell me," I push. I hate secrets and even though it isn't a secret as such, I want to know.

"What they did to you tonight, that was an asshole thing to do and I'm sorry."

My eyes widen. "You ... you saw what went down?"

Bringing the bottle to my lips, I chug and chug at the mortification of someone seeing what happened back there. I really don't know what came over me. One minute I'm dancing with one guy and then I'm dancing with another guy and then I'm in a mausoleum having the most erotic moment of my life with my mortal enemy and two, yes two of his friends. *What the fuck, Remington?* And, yes, I just third person full first named myself that's how 'what the fuck' this is.

"Not exactly but after the 'You fucking asshole bastard cunt face fuckers' speech, I can guess what went down. And then the way you were eye-fucking Brennan, it was easy to deduce. For the record, you would have finally gotten off and then Brennan would have died because Thatcher doesn't share." She snatches the bottle from me and takes another sip.

"Could have fooled me he doesn't share."

"When it comes to The Lords, they share within, trust me on that, but they don't share outside of that."

"Care to share with the rest of us your Lords sharing story?"

"You want to share yours?"

"Point taken."

Snatching the bottle back, I lift it to my lips and come up empty, literally. There's no more vodka, but that's probably a good thing because I have a slight buzz going on right now. I feel fuzzy and horny, almost as much so as when the guys left me high and dry. Dropping the bottle to the grass, my eyes widen when I remember, I don't drink vodka because it gets me going, it makes me horny as fuck. Sighing, I look up and notice Rowan is now standing next to me. "I need to get out of here so I can relieve my case of lady blue balls."

"I'll come with." Before I can protest, she laces her fingers with mine and the two of us start walking back to school.

We end up at the cliff top where Arlen supposedly jumped. Stopping, I stare out at the night sky. "This is where my brother killed himself."

"I'm sorry," Rowan whispers, then she adds, "This is where I had my first kiss."

"Wanna share?"

She smiles. "This is a story I'm happy to share." We walk over to the bench and sit down next to each other. "It was junior year and a Saturday night. Stacey Macdonald—"

"Your first kiss was with a girl?"

"Yep, she and I snuck out of the dorms and came to this very spot. We sat on the old bench that was here, just like you and I are right now. A breeze picked up and 'cause we were only in our pajamas, we huddled close together for warmth. One thing led to another and we kissed."

As if history wanted to repeat itself, a breeze picks up and because we're both in short skirts and skimpy tops, we lean into each other for warmth. She slides her arm around me, and I snuggle into her side. Her nipple is hard, and it pokes into my arm when she pulls me closer to her. Lifting my head,

I look up into her eyes. She's staring at me intently. She licks her bottom lip and I watch the motion. Raising my hand, I cup her cheek and like a moth to a flame our heads start moving. Her lips press against mine. My eyes close and when her tongue presses against my lips, wanting access to my mouth, I open and let her in. Our tongues caress one another.

One minute she's next to me kissing me and then next, she's straddling me. Holding my face in her palms, she deepens the kiss. Our pussies rub against one another, in sync with our tongues. That feeling begins to develop low in my belly and when she bites my lip, I see stars and I come. I whimper into her mouth as I ride out my unexpected orgasm, it sets her off too and she moans into my mouth.

"Wow," she breathes against my lips.

Pulling back, we stare at one another breathing deeply.

"Wow indeed," I repeat.

We continue to stare at one another until she climbs off me. "I'm umm, ahh, going to go. Goodnight, Remy."

"Night," I utter and watch her walk away. Lifting my hand to my mouth, I whisper, "What the fuck just happened?"

THATCHER

Brennan Dawson has a fucking death wish, one I'll happily oblige to fulfill. Clearly, he didn't learn his lesson the other day about who Remy belongs to.

Watching them together has an animalistic growl releasing from me, enough for Rian to pull me aside smirking.

"Dude, I wouldn't let that slide if I were you. I mean, she's practically in his lap." Growling at him, I punch him in his arm to shut him up.

Holding his hands up in defense, he steps backward, away from me. "Geez, dude, just saying."

Putting one foot in front of the other, I move to handle my

little peach but Rowan beats me to it. She steps over to Remy and drags her far away from Brennan before I even get a chance. I watch them for a while before they disappear from the party.

Quietly following behind them, I stalk them as they head toward the cliffs. I can faintly hear their idle chitchat before they stop, taking a seat on the bench at the cliff top.

I'm ready to confront Remy but before I get a chance to, the situation takes a turn I never saw coming—she locks lips with Rowan. Remington Hearst and Rowan Ashford are kissing and it's not a quick peck on the lips, it's a full-on lip-lock, complete with tongue. I'm watching a live action porn and it's the hottest thing I have ever seen.

My fingers rub roughly over my chin. I'm furious and a lot fucking horny right now. As much as this kiss is pretty damn hot, okay fucking hot, I'm fuming. I'm seriously pissed the fuck off right now. Rowan kissed her, taking a taste of what's mine.

What the actual fuck?

Before my eyes their kiss turns hot and heavy, and I find my hand gripping my dick. Pulling myself free from my jeans, I stroke my shaft until I feel precum leak, my eyes never leaving the girls. Remy gasps, the sound echoing through the night air, and I know she's just climaxed, that sound has been playing on repeat since our encounter in the library.

Fuck, before I can control it, my own climax shoots onto the grass in front of me. Holding in my groan, my head dips back as the tension from my orgasm leaves me, leaving me sated, well for a few moments that is.

Taking a few deep calming breaths, I wait until Rowan walks off, leaving Remy staring off into the distance. From her mumbled 'what the fucks' I think she's just as confused as I am, but it's time for my peach and I to have a chat.

Leaving my hiding place, a branch cracks under my boot. Announcing my presence and startling Remy.

"Wh-wh-who's there?" Remy's voice cracks as she stands, the moonlight shines down on her showing her fear. Seeing the fear etched on her face has my cock once again hardening, even though I just came a few moments ago.

"Didn't your whore of a mother ever tell you it isn't safe to go out alone after dark, Peach?" Venom drips from my voice as I speak of her sorry excuse of a mother.

"T ... Thatcher?" she questions, and then her mind catches up and she processes what I just said. "What did you just say?"

"Did you think you could escape me, Peach?" Arching an eyebrow at her, I move toward her. Her soft delicate pink lips are swollen and puffy from Rowan, making me even more eager to take my own taste. Looking around us, her gaze wanders through the clearing, plotting her escape I'm sure.

"So, tell me, Remington, how did she taste?"

"What?" Her eyes go wide with surprise. And that surprise has my cock hardening further.

Chuckling to control my anger, I'm not amused by her naivety. "Looks like you do follow after Mommy Dearest after all."

Her face scrunches up as she storms toward me, shoving my chest hard. "Take that back, you asshole," she screams, tears filling the corners of her eyes, letting me know I've hit a nerve.

"Or what, Peach? You don't have any power here, or are you forgetting who the fuck I am?" My jaw twitches waiting for her sassy comeback.

"I don't understand what I did to you or your brothers?"

"In due time, Peach, in due time. But don't worry, you'll know soon enough. I mean the Hearst siblings seem to be dropping like flies around this area, so who knows ...." I don't finish that sentence, but my statement leaves no room for doubt I'm alluding to when she'll meet her Maker, just like her brothers have.

Shocking the shit out of me, she laughs. She fucking laughs like a hyena before she nibbles on her lip like she did with Rowan moments ago. She's silently begging for mine to take over.

"If you think for one second, Thatcher Vanderbelt, that you'll scare me away so easily, think again. I may have originally come here against my will but now that I am here, I want answers and until I get them, I'm not going anywhere." She pokes her finger into my chest, hard.

We're face-to-face. Her hurried breaths hit my skin, causing my body to come alive with something other than hatred.

Between amusement and the feeling of being speechless for the first time in my life, the urge to take what's mine overwhelms me. The need to make her see who she belongs to, even if she doesn't accept it yet, is bubbling to the surface. I want to forget all the shit and be selfish just once in my life.

Her hair starts to fly with the sudden gust of wind, making her shiver.

Lifting my hand, I extend my fingers around the base of her neck, holding her firmly in place. Our eyes are locked on one another, neither of us capable of looking away. The connection between us is intense and unlike anything I've ever felt.

I run my thumb over her swollen lips, licking my own.

Her breath hitches as I lean my head down and my lips linger above hers. "How wet are you, Peach?" Breathing in her scent, I hold her helplessly to me.

My other hand slides down her arm, down her hips, across those sexy as fuck curves, and stops on the outside of her thigh. She closes her eyes for just a few seconds and when she opens them again, her hunger-filled gaze lands back on me.

"You're desperate, aren't you?" I whisper.

"I don't need you," she snaps but her voice is just a whimper. That whimper turns into a moan just as my thumb brushes over her pussy.

"You have no idea what you're doing to me," I hiss and before I can talk myself out of this, my lips crash to hers. For the first time in a long fucking time, everything around me goes silent.

The rush as my tongue meets hers is all-consuming. It's intoxicating. It's a new high, one I've never experienced before and it's one I can happily lose myself in forever.

Remy moans into my mouth. Her hands grip my shoulders. Her nails bite into my skin as my fingers squeeze around her throat. I feel her whimper under my touch and it's utter perfection.

The anger I've been feeling disappears as my lips take hers. My tongue plunges in and out of her mouth. My teeth nip at her lips, sending her a message.

You.

Are.

Mine.

Remy starts making needy little noises in the back of her throat, it takes every inch of willpower to not free my dick and plunge deep inside her, right here at the cliffs.

Threading my fingers through her hair, I deepen the kiss, my primal instincts take over and I consume her. Claim her. Mark her as mine as my tongue continues its assault in her mouth.

We both pull away breathless, resting our foreheads against each other Remy is dazed when I free her from my hold around her neck.

Taking a step back, I stare at her. "I own you, Peach, remember that." With that statement the wave of lust that was there seconds ago is gone.

She looks confused for a moment. My words have ruined whatever it was between us just now. That moment long fucking gone, but that kiss. It was worth everything.

"You really are something else, Thatcher Vanderbelt," she snarls before walking away.

Taking a moment to collect myself before heading back to the party, I take a few steps and stop at the cliffs' edge. The waves below crash against the rocks, loud enough to hear over the music in the distance and the erratic beating of my heart.

The moonlight shines above me, taunting me but the moment is over and I need to move on. Curfew is sneaking up upon us. Soon the party will end, and we'll all go back inside and climb in bed. Turning to leave, something shines below me, catching my eye.

Bending down, I reach out to grab it. I'm just in reach without falling to my death when finally my fingers wrap around it. Lifting it up, I hold it up to the moonlight, I can just make out it's a medallion.

Pulling out my phone, I switch on the flashlight to get a better look. My eyes widen because I know I've seen this before. But where?

Staring at the emblem, I search my memory. Swallowing deeply, I know something isn't right. But what? This medallion here has to be a clue, right? But a clue to what?

Dialing Hendrix because I know he'll be the only one to answer, he greets me in his usual gruff way. "T, where the fuck did you disappear to?" I can tell he's wasted, his words are slightly slurred.

"You near them?"

Without another word I hear him move and then his voice sounds much more sober than it did moments ago.

"You're on speaker."

"I'm at the cliffs—"

"Dude, why the fuck you at the cliffs?" Saint snaps.

"Just shut up, I found something."

"What do you mean?" Reign's concern is evident.

Taking a breath, I hold it up again, remembering where I

saw it. "Fuck," I mumble to myself. "I just found something that may disprove everything we think we know and maybe prove Arlen didn't kill himself."

"What?" they all say in unison.

"T, what the fuck are you talking about?" Hendrix snaps.

"I don't think Arlen killed himself."

"What?" Saint growls, his tone is off, and I hate hearing him like this.

"I don't think Arlen jumped."

"Why do you think that?" Reign hisses at me, his reaction to my theory is un-Reign like and now I'm concerned about two of my brothers. Will Hendrix do or say something next and make it a hat trick?

"For starters, there's no body or note, and something Remy said makes me think he didn't do it." Their collective silence says more than any words can right now. "We need to find out what really happened." I don't voice this next part because if he was pushed and he didn't jump, no one is safe.

Hanging up, I walk back through the trees to rejoin my brothers.

Something doesn't add up. Why was this between the rocks?

Is this a coincidence or just a fluke?

One thing is for sure, no one is safe at Crestwood anymore, not even me.

REMY

"WHAT THE FUCK JUST HAPPENED?" I mumble again as I storm back to my room. Stomping up the stairs, I walk toward my room on a mission to lock myself away from the world. Digging my key out of my pocket, I unlock and open my door. Slamming it behind me, I kick off my shoes and take a seat by the window. Bringing my legs up, I hug them to me and rest my head on my knees. "What the fuck happened tonight?" I grumble again.

Tonight has been a whirlwind of emotions, feelings, highs, lows, and everything in between. I need a time out to process the evening, but one thing remains clear, I'm a whore ... just like my mother according to Thatcher. What did he mean by that? Sure, Mom is no saint but a whore? No way.

Sighing, I look out my window and my eyes land on the bench where I kissed Rowan. It was my first time kissing a girl and it was pretty hot, but it doesn't compare to the other kiss I had up there tonight. That kiss with Thatcher was one of the best kisses of my life, actually it's THE best kiss of my life. How can such an arrogant jerk kiss like that? Clearly, he's had a lot of practice, maybe it's him who's the whore and not me, or Mom.

This place just keeps throwing curveball after curveball. I could really do with a Grayson chat right now. Even though it's nearing midnight, I grab my phone and dial my brother. Like the five million other times I've called him, it rings out and goes to voicemail. And like the five million other times, I leave a message. "Hey, Gray, it's me, again. Please call me back, I really need to speak to you. Something happened, nothing bad but I could really use your adv—" It cuts off, informing me the inbox is full. That scares me because it means he hasn't been listening to my messages. "Where are you, Grayson?" I mumble.

My phone pings with a text arrival and I jump in fright when I see who the message is from. I've saved my stalker's number now under 'Creeper McCreeperson'.

CREEPER MCCREEPERSON

You kissing that girl was the hottest thing I've ever seen. I can't wait for the day I get to kiss and touch you like that.

"What the fuck?" I whisper as I reread the message again. A shudder runs through my body and the need to wash tonight off intensifies.

Standing up, I open the top drawer to grab clean underwear and my face scrunches because a pair of panties is sitting askew. I always keep my undergarments organized, but I was running late this morning so maybe I made a mess of things. Rearranging them back into place, I grab a clean pair, followed by my pajamas from the next drawer down. Stepping into my private bath, I strip off and climb in.

After a lukewarm shower, I dry off and change into my sleep shorts and tank. Drying my hair, I hang my wet towel on the back of my door and climb into bed. Pulling the covers up to my neck, I lie back and stare at the ceiling above.

Sleep eludes me. My mind is racing a million miles an hour flitting between Thatcher, Grayson, what happened in the mausoleum, kissing Rowan, and back to Thatcher; again. "Gah," I huff, slapping my hands down on the mattress.

Standing up, I decide to go for a walk. Sure, it's after curfew and I'm likely to get into trouble if I'm caught but when I can't sleep, I walk. Walking seems to calm me.

Pulling on my robe, I slip into the hallway and sneak down the stairs. Reaching the ground level, I walk into the common room but stop mid-step when I see someone sitting on one of the sofas. Their back is to me so I can't see who it is. Turning to leave, I stop with my foot in the air when they say, "You and I need to talk."

Spinning back around, I walk farther into the room. Coming around the sofa my eyes widen when I see it's Reign. He has a three-quarter empty bottle of Jack Daniels in his hand.

"Take a seat." He gestures to the armchair next to him.

Feeling defiant, I flop onto the sofa next to him. Outstretching my hand, I point to the bottle of Jack in his hand. He takes a swig before handing it to me. Bringing the bottle to my lips, I take a sip, wincing as the alcohol burns its way down my throat and into my stomach, leaving a warmth spreading through my body. Taking another sip, I hand it back to Reign.

Silence envelops us. The only sound is the ticking of the grandfather clock in the corner. The silence is deafening so I ask the most obvious question. "What did you want to talk about?"

"You're different."

"Ooookay, different how?"

"No, it's a good different. You're exactly how he described you. You're not at all how Thatcher thinks of you."

"Thanks, I think."

Silence falls over us again and then I wonder who would have been talking about me to him. "Who told you about me?"

"That's not important but what is ... is ..."

"What is important?"

"I'm getting there," he snaps. He snatches the bottle of Jack from me, brings the bottle to his lips, and drinks. He finishes the bottle and slams it onto the coffee table in front of us. "I miss him so fucking much and I can't talk to anyone about it. I thought I'd accepted it and then you came waltzing in and brought it all back up again. I. Fucking. Miss. Him."

"Miss who?" I'm even more confused now than before I came down here.

"He was my everything and—" A noise in the corridor causes both our eyes to widen when we hear someone say, "Whoever I find in here will be in detention for a month."

"Shit, it's the Dean," I whisper.

Reign jumps up, picks up the empty bottle then grabs my upper arm tightly and pulls me up. He drags me toward the bookshelf in the corner, there's nowhere to hide here and I start to panic. Like I'm in some Hitchcock movie, he drops my arm, pulls on a book and the bookcase swings open. "Get in," he whispers.

Standing here frozen, my head swivels back and forth from Reign to the secret door that just opened and back to Reign again. "For fuck's sake," he snarls. He spins me around and pushes me into the opening. Turning around, I see Reign enter behind me just as the lights in the common room flick on. The secret door closes, shrouding the two of us in darkness and away from the wrath of the Dean.

"Follow me," he mutters. Taking my hand in his, he pulls us along the dark secret passageway. I should be freaking the fuck out right now but for some reason, with Reign, I feel safe. Stupid, considering he's a Vanderbelt and Thatcher's brother.

We begin to climb a set of stairs and the higher we climb, apprehension begins to kick in. I'm so disoriented right now. I have no clue where the hell I am or how to even get out of this internal maze I didn't even know existed.

Reign finally stops and feels around and then like downstairs, a secret door opens. He steps to the side and lets me go first. Stepping into the room, I squint at the brightness after being in the dark for so long. Then a voice bellows, "The fuck you doing in here?"

THATCHER

STANDING in my room in just my boxer briefs, I'm about to climb into bed when the secret door opens. I'm expecting one of my brothers to step through but I'm shocked when none other than Remington-fucking-Hearst steps into my room. "The fuck you doing in here?"

Her eyes widen when she sees me, but she doesn't speak. Looking over her shoulder and back through the door she just entered, I see movement and then behind her, Reign comes into sight.

"What the fuck, man?" Glaring after my brother at his audacity to bring Remy here. Into my room.

Remy turns trying to flee back the way she came, but Reign places his hand on her shoulder, forcing her farther into my room.

I don't miss the way her gaze lands on my half-naked form. Reign notices too and chuckles as he helps himself to my secret stash of alcohol.

"I ... I should go." She hitches her thumb toward my door. Shaking my head, I cut her off and stand between her and the exit. Rolling her eyes, she bites on that damn lip, waking my cock up from his slumber.

Her eyes roam my torso, not stopping until her eyes land on my junk. They widen at the outline of my semi-hard cock in my briefs, and I notice her breath hitches.

Adjusting myself, I purposely pull down my briefs just enough to give her a glimpse of me. I grin at her, not missing the gasp that escapes her when she sees my cock as I walk past her.

"God, just fuck already, the tension in here is fucking insane," Reign groans, taking a massive swig from the bottle in his hand.

Giving him a 'shut the fuck up, dude' look, I snatch the bottle from him, taking my own gulp. I hold it out to Remy, hesitantly she steps forward and takes it from me. Bringing it to her lips, she sips and scrunches her face up as it burns its way down.

"Oh, God, that is awful. What is it?" She hands it back to me while Reign and I both laugh.

"Damn, baby, can't you handle the heat?" Reign teases her.

"Don't like scotch, Peach?" I mutter.

"I'd rather drink vodka." The sassy smile on her face is enough to irk me.

"Well, I'm off to find a little midnight snack, if you know what I mean." Reign winks, heading straight for my door leaving Remy alone with me.

Her breathing changes the moment she realizes we're alone in my room. It's just the two of us and I can't help but chuckle to myself. Reign, the fucker, left her here with me—on purpose.

"You wanna watch, Peach?"

"What?"

I smirk, pulling my briefs down letting my hard cock fling free. Remy's eyes widen at my brazenness and she gasps, turning abruptly to face the door.

"God, you couldn't wait until I left?"

"Well, I figured since you're trying to use X-ray vision to look, I may as well help you out. You're not afraid, are you?"

Coming up behind her, my hands brush up her thighs as my cock presses into her back.

Her breathing quickens and her body shudders when I gently rub my fingertips back and forth on her arm.

"Are you thinking of my cock deep inside that pussy, baby?" Grinding my cock into her, she whimpers. My lips touch her ear, kissing her softly. "I bet you're so fucking wet thinking about it."

She jumps when my fingers reach around and brush over her pussy.

"Thatcher, stop," she pleads, but I notice she presses herself into my hand. Her mouth may say no, but her body tells me otherwise.

My cock jumps behind her when she wriggles herself against me. My hand still cups her pussy and my other hand travels up, squeezing her tit.

"I'd give anything to punish you right now, Peach. To give you the cock you so desperately want, but I think I want to make you so needy for me. So desperate you'll be begging me."

With one last brush of my fingers over her clit, I remove my hand and step back.

"You can leave now," I state, dismissing her.

"Fuck you, Thatcher." She huffs out a frustrated groan and storms from my room, slamming the door behind her.

With a satisfied smile, I lie back on my bed. I'm in her head and the sooner Remington understands that, the better things will go for her. With that satisfying thought, I close my eyes and drift off to sleep.

"Wait, shut the fuck up." Conroy raises his hand, stopping me. "You're telling me you had a wanton and needy Remington Hearst in your room, alone last night, and you fucking let her walk out the door?" Conroy questions me in disbelief. "You let her leave without sticking your dick in her?"

Nodding at him, I shove a fry in my mouth.

He shakes his head at me, taking a bite of his burrito.

"You're a fucking idiot," Hart huffs.

And I think I agree because the moment she walked out, all I thought about was claiming her. Of putting that sassy little mouth of hers to good use, but I know in time I will. Of course, the guys don't see it like that, but there are things that don't add up and until all my ducks are in a row, my dick will stay away from Remy's cunt. I already made the fatal mistake of fucking her in the library, that won't happen again. We need clarity before making our move and right now, there are too many questions.

Why is Remy really at Crestwood?

Who really was Arlen Hearst? There's something about him and his death that's bugging me, especially since I found that medallion last night.

Was it all a ruse to keep us off whatever she's really behind? Or should I say what her mother was behind?

There has to be a reason for sending Remy here, what's she up to?

"Hey, man, do you think Grayson is really missing?" Rian asks between a mouthful of meatballs.

Taking a drink of my Coke I have to think because I'm not a hundred percent sure about anything anymore.

"I mean, they found his car, with no sign of him. His belongings were still in it. His cell phone is missing and there are no tracks or clues as to where he went. I mean, if that doesn't scream 'kidnapped' I don't know what else would. Or is it just one hell of a fucking coincidence?" Rian shares. "But none of us believe in coincidences so ..."

My gaze focuses off to the side where Remy is sitting with Alani. Staring at the chick who has invaded my mind, I wonder if she is really capable of deceiving us. To make us think she's the victim. Or is she following her mother's orders?

Hudson joins the girls. Kissing them both on the cheek before he takes a seat.

"Damn, Finley's stepping in on your girl, T. Might want to teach him a lesson." Lennon smirks.

"I think he'd be more interested in what this table is packing," Saint voices without looking up.

"What? No fucking way?" Lennon argues.

Chuckling, I shake my head at his naivety. Everyone, well clearly not Lennon, knows full well Hudson Finley swings both ways and he doesn't give two shits if anyone knows.

"It's all good, Huddy boy, he wouldn't be interested in you anyway Len, I think you better just stick to pussy."

"Shut the fuck up, I'm not into dick." Lennon shoves him.

Hart slaps him on his shoulder as he gets up disposing of his empty tray and when he returns, they start to wrestle, causing everyone's eyes to swing toward our table, including Remington's.

Her gaze collides with mine and she quickly turns away,

averting her eyes but even from where I'm sitting, I can see the lust, and hatred mixing in her gorgeous orbs.

Guess my little peach is a touch sexually frustrated but truthfully, she's not the only one.

Hart and Lennon separate just as Mr. Ashford heads their way. "Boys, please no wrestling in the cafeteria." I don't miss Saint tensing as he hears his voice. I watch him, wondering what the fuck that's all about. I know he doesn't like him, not many of us do, he's a fucking dick but Saint's reaction is more than the usual student hatred for a teacher.

"Come on, Mr. A, we were just having some fun." Lennon passes by him, winking and dropping back into his seat.

Hart just glares at him, not saying a word.

Mr. Ashford sighs, moving his glasses up his nose and back in place before he walks back through the doors.

Saint stands, leaving his tray and follows through the doors. Hendrix stands, sensing the tension too.

Nodding, he follows behind Saint. If anyone can get Saint out of whatever the fuck this is, it's Hendrix. They've always had a bond different than anything any of us share. You'd think I'd be included in that since the three of us shared a womb together for nine months, but nope, and I'm okay with that because the bond I have with them is stronger than that.

Once all the boys have cleared their trays and made their way to their next class, I can't help but wonder what lies ahead for all of us at Crestwood Prep. Something has changed, and I'm not referring to the weather. What's most concerning is even without chatting to my brothers, I know I'm not the only one who can feel it.

That medallion holds answers, but to what?

My phone beeps in my pocket. Pulling it out, I groan when I see Father's name on the screen.

FATHER

Dinner Friday night, don't be late.

THATCHER

See you then, sir.

Don't be a smart-ass, Thatcher, just do as I tell you.

"Fuck off, old man," I mumble. I guess dinner won't be all bad, I have a few questions for dear old dad and for once, he's going to answer me because I need to get to the bottom of this. I don't like the changes that are happening around me and people need to realize, I'm the fucking Lord here and no one takes a Lord's crown—not even his father.

THATCHER

Sitting in debate, listening to people drone on and on about the benefits of a university degree is sucking the life out of me. Moving my neck, trying to release this fucking kink, my gaze catches sight of Remy a table over from me. She's sketching and totally lost in what she's doing, paying no one any attention. Her arm blocks my view of whatever it is she's working on, but I will say she has me intrigued.

Finally, Mr. Bexley dismisses everyone and they all scatter, heading to their next class. Caught in a daze, my little peach hasn't moved a muscle.

When she finally notices the room is all but empty, she

starts to pack away her things. Reaching over, I grab her book before she has a chance to pack it away. She reaches for it. "Thatcher, give me my book."

Throwing it under my arm, I head out with her hot on my heels, her fingers attempt but fail to snatch it back.

"I mean it, give it back," she demands.

Lifting it above my head taunting her, her glare means nothing to me.

Flicking through the book above my head while walking backward, my gaze catches on something familiar.

Remy all but slams into my chest when I stop, flicking until I find the page again.

What the fuck.

Staring back at me is half my face.

She's fucking drawing me.

Holding the book up I demand, "What the fuck, Peach? You drawing me now?"

"Thatcher, give me my book. Please." I know that last word hurt her to say, and I can't hide my smirk. She holds her hand out like the demanding little thing she is.

Flipping more pages, secretly hoping I'm on more than one, I'm circling her while I look through what she's drawn. I hate to admit it, but she's good, really fucking good.

"Thatcher, I have to get to class, now." She tries to snatch it back but I lift the book above me again. "This isn't funny. Stop," she all but pouts.

The hall falls quiet so I know we have the attention of whoever's left.

Taking a step forward, she takes two back. We continue this until her back presses against the wall behind her.

Lifting my arm above her head, her chin lifts and her soft gasps fill my ears. Our chests touch, her tits press against me, her nipples pebble as I slowly run my finger down her cheek, leaning in, I whisper, "I love that I'm in your head, Peach."

She turns away from me to avoid my lips as I move them over the softness of her skin.

"Class, please now," a deep voice rings out, interrupting our standoff.

Turning my glare at Mrs. Devine, she hurries away leaving us alone once again. "Please, move," she tries again. "Unlike you, I want to get to class," Remy snaps, shoving me.

"Nah, follow me, Peach." Not giving her a chance, I take her hand in mine and pull her behind me. She struggles against my grip the entire time. Pushing us into a corner out of sight, I cocoon her with my body. "I think I like you like this, cornered, alone, wet." Licking my lips, I don't miss the way her eyes follow the action.

"Is it because you get hard every time you see me, Thatcher?" Lifting her chin, she smirks at me, pleased with her comeback.

My soft chuckle turns into a loud vibrant laugh all while she rolls her eyes, using her hands to push against my chest, trying to put distance between us.

"Come on, Peach, you know you like what you see. Every time you roll your eyes, my dick gets a little harder."

I nibble on her jaw, feeling the way her body shivers under my touch.

"I'm pretty sure your dick is the last thing on my mind, now move." She shoves me harder this time and it catches me off-guard, allowing her to snatch back her book. She steps around me, and I watch as she walks away, practically running from me.

My gaze falls to her ass and the need to sink my teeth into it intensifies with each step she takes away from me.

My phone dings, drawing my attention from her just as she gets to the door for her class.

Looking down, I fume when I read the screen.

HENDRIX

SOS. Saint's room.

Fuck.

Opening the door to Saint's room, the last thing I expect to see is him pacing back and forth, mumbling incoherently to himself while Hendrix tries to calm him down.

"Saint," I say, closing the door behind me but I get nothing in return. He ignores me or just doesn't hear me as he continues to pace. "What the fuck happened?"

Hendrix shrugs. "Fuck if I know. He called me in a panic and said he couldn't do it anymore, then hung up. I came here. He's been pacing like that, mumbling to himself since I arrived."

Calling his name again, he ignores me. Stepping in his path, I block his way, making him run straight into me. His eyes are bloodshot and glassy, this isn't my brother staring back at me. Gripping his neck, I pull him toward me. "Saint, talk to us." His gaze filters over me then to Hendrix.

"I ... I can't, you ... you won't understand. Just leave me alone," he mumbles, trying to move around me.

Hendrix forces him to stop this time by gripping his arm. "You think I'm fucking leaving you when you're like this?"

Saint tries to shrug him off, but Hendrix stands his ground.

Like he's giving up, Saint sinks to the floor in a heap at Hendrix's feet, making us both move faster than we ever have before.

Wrapping our arms around him, we hold Saint while he

breaks down. Trying to hurt himself he pulls at his hair, mumbling incoherently to himself again.

"Is it Dad?" Hendrix asks the obvious question.

Shaking his head, Saint tries to break free from our hold, but we hold him tighter.

The smell of alcohol is putrid, it's like he bathed in it.

"How much did you drink?" I try to force the answer out of him. I'd like to know because I left him less than an hour ago and he's drunk as a skunk now. We won't be getting any answers because he's passing out before our eyes.

"Fuck," Hendrix curses, gripping Saint as his weight goes slack.

"Why did you mainline vodka like it was water?" I ask his almost passed out form, my answer is a jumbled slur and a few seconds later, he's snoring heavily, his intoxication finally setting in.

"Help me." I nod at Hendrix, both of us lift his dead weight ass until he's firmly on his bed, ready to sleep whatever he drank out of his system.

"Go, I'll watch over him," Hendrix volunteers.

"Update me, he's going to have a killer headache when he wakes, but whatever you do, we need to find out what caused him to drink himself into a stupor and we need to do it fast. I know we all drink to cope but this is the worst I've ever seen him." Nodding in agreement, Hendrix pulls a chair up beside Saint's bed and watches over our brother as he sleeps like he didn't just succumb to whatever pain he's hiding.

Everything is spiraling and I don't like it. I'm not sure why Saint felt the need to drown his sorrows at ten a.m. on a Friday, but whatever it is, I'd bet my left nut it has to do with our father. Because what else would drive Saint to block everything out with alcohol?

Fuck, this is the last thing we need.

When my phone dings I expect it to be Hendrix with an

update but keeping in the 'this day is shit' traditions, it's from an unknown number.

UNKNOWN

> I bet you thought you were untouchable, guess what Vanderbelt, NO ONE FUCKING IS!

REMY

AFTER BREAKFAST, I decide to head to the library, I need to do some research into the Vanderbelt family. There's something going on here and I'm determined to discover what. The fact my parents seem to know them doesn't sit right with me but then again, nothing regarding Mr. and Mrs. Vanderbelt sits right. Why they had kids I will never know, but it does give an insight into why those brothers are fucked up like they are.

I'm about to exit the hall when from the shadows a deep voice says, "You remind me so much of him."

It scares the shit out of me, causing me to jump and gasp

in fright. Covering my chest with my hand, it feels like my heart is about to beat out of my chest.

"Sorry, didn't mean to scare you but just now, you looked so much like him."

"Like who?" I'm not expecting Reign to answer but when he does, he says the last name I ever expected to hear come from his lips.

"Arlen."

"You knew my brother?" I scrunch my eyes in confusion at this revelation.

"You could say that. He and I, we ... we were ... friends." I get the feeling he's hiding something else, but I know he won't tell me anything unless he wants to. Seems keeping secrets is a running trait amongst the Vanderbelt brothers.

This is the second time he's chatted with me without any taunting, but is he just leading me into a false sense of security? Wouldn't put it past him, he is a Vanderbelt after all. Wanting to see where this goes, I walk closer. He's leaning against the wall, one leg bent at the knee, resting against the wood paneling. He looks me up and down, I can't read his face, but I don't feel scared. "Seems not all Hearsts are fucking cunts. Some of you have hearts." Again, it feels like he wants to say more, and again, he doesn't.

A silence falls between us. I think about what he just said and wonder if he's referring to Arlen or Grayson. Knowing I can't come right out and ask, I put my detective hat on. I'm leaning toward him referring to Arl, so I ask a question a 'friend' would know the answer to. "Did you know he was ... into men?"

He looks at me for a few beats and then nods. "Yeah, I knew." He pauses and looks to his feet, then he looks back at me sadly. "You're the first person I've admitted that to."

"Did you know I was the first person he told too?"

He nods again and smiles, it's a sad smile but it is a smile. It's almost like discussing Arlen is hard for him, but why?

"Yeah, he told me not long after he confessed to you. I kinda already suspected, but it wasn't my place to push him." He falls silent and grips the back of his neck. "He really was something," and then he shocks the ever-loving shit out of me when he says, "I miss him every-fucking-day."

"Me too." I pause and then add on, "I miss Grayson too."

"Grayson's a dick," he sneers, his voice laced with venom. "Sorry to burst your bubble there, Princess."

"And your brothers are saints?"

"Technically one is," he teases with a shrug. "Well, in name, not so much in the holy sense."

"No shit," I chortle, causing him to laugh. "Why are you being nice to me?"

He shrugs. "Who said this is me being nice?"

"Reign, this is the most you've spoken to me since I arrived, and it's actually been civil. I'm waiting for your inner Thatcher to come out and for the taunts to begin."

"I may be a Vanderbelt, Princess, but I'm my own person. I have my own secrets and demons but it doesn't mean ..." He once again looks to the ground. He looks like he has the weight of the world on his shoulders, and I have a sudden inclination to hug him and comfort him.

"Mean what?" I ask, stepping closer to him.

"Nothing. Forget it." He shakes his head. Lifting his gaze back to mine, I see the walls are back up and dickwad Reign is back. "Watch your back, Princess. You never know what monsters are lurking."

And with that, he pushes off the wall and walks away from me, leaving me confused about this entire conversation. I stand here and watch him until he turns the corner out of sight.

Arlen told me he was seeing someone and it was amazing, but they were keeping it a secret. Could Reign be who he was seeing? Nah, he and Alani are hooking up so it can't be him. Guess I will never know who was making my brother so blissfully happy before he died. Shaking that thought away, I continue on to the library.

My phone pings with a text just as I reach the library.

CREEPER MCCREEPERSON

Red lingerie looks good on you

"What the hell?" I hiss as I find a table in the back, I drop my things and head into the stacks to find a history book on Crestwood. With a few books in hand, I make my way back to my table. When I pass a few students, they start to whisper, and I swear I hear someone whisper-cough "whore" and "skank."

Not wanting to get involved in any more drama, I ignore them and walk back to my desk. I freeze because sitting on the desk is a bunch of pink peonies, it's stunning and the smell is subtle but refreshing. There's no note but I can't help smiling at my surprise gift.

Taking a seat, I open up one of the books and begin to read but my stomach growls and then I realize I skipped breakfast this morning. Deciding to head to the cafeteria, I can read and eat there. Walking over to the front desk I place my delivery on the counter before I grab my library card from my purse. I check the book out and place it in my bag. Picking up my flowers, I exit the library and head toward my room to drop off my gift before heading to get some food, but a ruckus up ahead snares my attention.

"More fucking drama," I mumble to myself but when I turn the corner, my eyes widen when I see what's on the wall before me.

THATCHER

I'M YET to show my brothers the text I'd been sent. I'm not really sure why I'm keeping it to myself, we don't keep secrets from each other. We're brothers, best friends, but lately that bond we share feels like it's changing. Everything seems to be falling apart and it all started the moment *she* arrived at Crestwood. It was all fine until Remington-fucking-Hearst stepped foot on Crestwood soil. I had a plan to destroy her, but I didn't count on her getting under my skin the way she has. I need to get control of whatever this is. I was hoping fucking her would get her out of my system, but her pussy is like crack, one hit and I'm addicted, and I want more.

Ruining her needs to jump back to the top of my list. Along with finding out who the fuck is taunting us. They are delusional to think playing games with The Lords will get them far.

But is there really any harm in having a little fun with my peach along the way? Suck her into a false sense of security and then BAM, we bring her to her knees for her family's actions.

"Yo, Thatch, you have to see this?" Rian shouts, coming toward me with his face full of panic.

Nodding, I follow him toward the cafeteria, and it doesn't take long to see what has everyone's attention.

The words **'PAYBACK IS A BITCH'** are written in bold capitals above the girls' locker room door. Whispers and murmurs can be heard throughout the halls. Coming closer, that's when I see image after image littering the walls of Arlen with someone, and although you can't see the other person's face, there's no doubt they are not female. Each image is a little more indecent than the next.

Who the fuck else knew Arlen was gay?

Reign stops beside me, anger seeping from him. He snarls angrily and begins to furiously pull them down.

"Seriously. He's fucking dead and this bullshit is happening." He turns, glaring at the circle of people who have come to see what all the fuss is about. It doesn't take them long to back off just enough to give him space to pull the images down.

From the corner of my eye, I see Remy coming toward us. Someone coughs "whore" but she ignores it and storms toward the wall of pictures. Her eyes are locked on the images, and she snatches one of the photos from Reign's hands and gasps in shock. She looks at the intimate picture of her brother and his secret lover and tears build in her eyes.

"Who did this?" she shouts, turning to face the crowd. Her voice is laced with anger, and I kinda feel sorry for the person who did that if she finds them. Her gaze darts around, looking at everyone. "Who the fuck did this?" she bellows again, throwing the flowers in her arms onto the floor in anger. Her loud and angry voice, paired with the murderous look on her face, causes people to back away.

Taking a step toward her, she turns her head my way and if looks could kill, I'd be hanging in hell with Luci right now. She slams the photo into my chest. "Is this a joke to you?" I stumble back from the force of her shove. "He's dead," her voice breaks saying this, "and you have to go and ruin his name again."

"Sorry to disappoint you, Peach, but it wasn't me," I hiss through clenched teeth, warning her to back the fuck up.

"Who then, huh?" she venomously sneers at me. "Because I know this is the type of shit you'd pull just because you could. My brother is dead, no need to tarnish his name any more than it already has been." She wipes at her cheeks, brushing away her tears. "Does the thought of me being here anger you that much?" she murmurs.

"Yes, Peach, I'm fucking pissed you're here. The thought of you here acting like you don't have a fucking clue, pisses me off more than anything but I didn't fucking do this," I snap, making her step back, putting distance between us. "I'm not that much of a cunt to run a dead guy's name through the mud. If I have an issue, I face up to it. I'm not a fucking coward."

Her mouth opens and closes. I've left her speechless but seeing the hurt on her face over her brother, it cuts me to see her upset and that feeling of remorse for her is fucking with my head. She's the enemy, but why do I want to protect the enemy right now? To defend her brother?

"Remy, it wasn't us." Reign defends me. Us. He reaches out to her and places his hand on her arm to reaffirm his words.

She looks up at him, staring at him intently and in the

blink of an eye, her eyes soften and her anger begins to dissipate. The sight of the two of them together in their intimate-ish moment, makes me want to smash my own brother's face in.

She nods and swallows back a sob, but she can't hold them back. She falls into his chest and breaks down. I stand here and watch as Reign wraps his arms around her, comforting her. I'm man enough to admit, it fucking stings to watch. It stings knowing my brother and her are becoming friends.

Rage builds at that revelation and I know if I don't walk away I'm going to attack my brother, so I leave, not caring if they follow me or not.

Storming up to my room, I shove open the door with a little more force than necessary, it bounces off the wall before clicking shut again. I head straight for the bottle of Jack I have sitting on my shelf.

Unscrewing the cap, I take a swig before I climb through the secret door in my room. I squeeze down the narrow hallway, sipping the bottle as I go. Relishing the burn.

My phone vibrates multiple times in my pocket, but I ignore each and every one of them. The need to ignore the world is strong but with the never-ending shit that keeps happening, I know I have to check in.

Stopping to pull it out, I stare down at the screen and see five new messages.

REIGN

Where are you?

HENDRIX

Bro, I think Saint's in trouble

RIAN

T, your dad is here and he's looking for you.

UNKNOWN

Like the little show? Don't worry, your turn's coming, Vanderbelt. Soon everyone will know your dirty little secret.

FATHER

Where are you?

"Fuck," I hiss as I read through each one of them. I totally forgot about dinner with Dad and if he's here, and texting me, it must have been about something important. I'll face the consequences of that later.

Ignoring them all, I slide down the wall and continue to drink, the bourbon burns my throat as I take huge gulps.

Before long, the bottle is half-empty and I'm cramped from squeezing my huge frame into such a tiny space. Pushing myself up, I stumble down the secret passageway, eventually I find myself in the library. My legs feel slightly uneven, and my vision is blurry. Knocking some books off a nearby table as I walk past, I murmur to myself, "I'm drunker than I thought."

Even though my vision is blurry, I don't miss *her* sitting there staring at me. "You," I sneer, a little more brusquely than intended and I stumble toward her.

"Are you drunk?" she asks, ignoring my rude ass.

"Maybe. A little," I slur. Bringing the bottle to my lips, I gulp down three huge mouthfuls before she rips the bottle from my hand. "Hey, what the fuck," I protest, reaching for the bottle, but my reflexes are a little slow and she pulls it away from me.

"Everyone's been looking for you for hours. Where have you been?" Her tone sounds worried.

"Aww, were you worried about me, Peach?" I taunt, throwing her a wink that nearly causes me to trip over my own feet.

Remy sighs, shoving her books back in her backpack

before coming to my side. "Come on, drunky, put your weight on me. I'll help you back to your room."

"Help me, with what?"

"Getting you into bed, Thatcher."

"Oh, I could use some company in bed, Peaches." Wiggling my eyebrows at her suggestively, she ignores me, grabs my arm, and drags me toward the exit.

"Ooh feisty," I snigger, chuckling to myself until I notice her glaring at me.

I let Remington lead me through the halls back to my room, silently liking the way her touch makes me feel. My phone vibrates in my pocket, my sudden halt makes Remy look up at me. Taking my phone out, I see my father's name across the screen. "Fuck," I hiss. I really don't want to speak to him right now and meeting him for dinner is the last thing on my fucking mind. Running my hand over my face, I swipe to accept the call, slowly raising my phone to my ear. "Yes?" I say in greeting.

"Thatcher, you better be on your way?" His angry voice bellows loudly through the phone.

"I'm not feeling well, Dad. I'm giving dinner a pass." Not waiting for whatever backlash he's ready to hand out, I hang up.

Remy doesn't say a word, and silently continues alongside me up to my room. Digging my key out, I try to slip it into the lock but my hands are shaking. After missing the lock several times, Remy snatches them from me and standing aside, I let her open the door.

Grabbing my hand, she tugs me in behind her. The moment the door closes behind us, my hand moves to the back of her head, and I fist her hair in my palm, yanking her back into me. Pushing her locks to the side, I expose the column of her neck and I suck and bruise her, leaving my mark on her creamy smooth skin. Spinning her to face me, I crash my lips to hers in a bruising kiss. Wrapping my left arm around her waist, I step her backward and pin her between me and the door.

My lips claim hers in a brutal way that finally has my dick joining in. I'm hit with an intensity to fuck her I can't explain.

I hate her but the more time I spend with her, the reason why is becoming blurred. Originally I wanted her to suffer because of her mother's indiscretions with our father. I thought if I punished her, it would make the hurt of what they did to our mother go away and maybe, just fucking maybe, everything would feel somewhat okay again. What had started with a fiery hatred has turned into a fiery passion instead. I want to imprint myself on her so deeply that she never wants to leave me.

Our tongues start a war for control and our kiss turns hungry, desperate, and the heady combination makes me groan out loud.

Remy finally pulls back, breaking our connection. I'm breathless and horny, so fucking horny, but she pushes on my chest, and I stumble backward, putting some distance between us.

"You're drunk and this is wrong," she snarls at me.

"Wrong? I promise, sweetheart, I'm not that drunk." I almost stumble again, making her raise her eyebrows at me.

"I'll get you into bed then let Reign know where you are."

Realizing she's serious and I won't be getting laid tonight; the thought of my bed becomes very appealing. Toeing my boots off, I struggle with my shirt, getting it stuck when I lift it over my shoulders and head.

Remy's soft laughter echoes around the room until she's helping me remove my shirt. Unzipping my jeans, I slide them down, not missing Remy's gasp seeing my erection poking through my briefs.

"Told you, I'm not that drunk."

"Mmmhmpf," she replies, shaking her head, but I notice her gaze is still on my dick.

Shaking her head again, she ignores me and walks into the bathroom. I hear the faucet running, the cupboard open and shut, and then she returns. "Here." She hands me some painkillers and a glass of water. She watches me as I swallow the little white tablets and drink all the water. Placing the empty glass on my bedside table, I fall into bed.

"The offer still stands, Peach," I tell her with a smile, but my eyelids are suddenly heavy and my eyes droop closed.

The last thing I hear before my drunkenness takes me into slumber is the door clicking shut as Remy leaves my room.

REMY

"Anyone else think Mr. Ashford is a creepy fuck?" I ask when he walks past our table and out of the cafeteria.

"Yesss," Alani replies, adding a few extra s's for emphasis. "I'm so glad I'm a chick, he seems to be extra creepy with the guys but FYI..." She leans into me and whispers, "He's Rowan's dad."

My eyes widen at that revelation, and I thank my lucky stars she's currently in line for food, but I notice her eyes are locked on Saint's as he exits through the doors that Mr. Creepy, aka her dad, just went through.

"I heard ..." But Alani drifts off, turning my attention to

her, I prod her with my eyes to continue but she's currently eye-fucking Reign and, of course, because I looked where she was looking, my eyes land on *him*.

Averting my gaze, I look down at my food, stab a carrot with my fork, and then someone's kissing my cheek. Looking up, I scrunch my eyes in confusion when I see it's Hudson. After kissing me, he leans over and kisses Alani, and I notice two things. One, his lips lingered a lot longer on her than they did when he kissed me. And two, after he drops into the seat next to me, I realize he's very close to Alani. I thought she liked Reign? And three, she seems very comfortable with him.

The two of them are currently eye-fucking each other, but I need to know what she was going to say before I press her on who she actually likes.

Snapping my fingers in her face, I finally get her attention away from Hudson. "Heard what?" I ask. I need a distraction from Thatcher, the drama that is Crestwood Prep, The Lords, and the pulsating between my thighs. I've been a fucking horny mess since I left Thatcher's room last night. If he wasn't so drunk, I probably would have ridden him hard because right now, I have the equivalent of blue balls. "What's the girl's equivalent of blue balls?" I suddenly ask. Both Alani and Hudson turn their heads toward me.

"Huh?" they both say at the same time. Both clearly confused by my out of the blue—ha blue—comment.

"Guys get blue balls when they're cockblocked, what's the equivalent for girls?"

"It's blue bean," Quinn says, dropping into the seat Rowan was in and, speak of the devil, she returns with a tray of food.

"That's my seat," Rowan snaps. Quinn shuffles into the seat next to me and steals a carrot from my plate. Then she snarls at Quinn, "What are you doing here?" Clearly there's some angst between those two.

"Just being helpful," Quinn sweetly replies, then turns to

face me. "As I was saying, it's called blue bean. The bean refers to the clitoris. When a woman becomes sexually aroused, her clitoris will harden and swell with blood. The vaginal walls and labia will also get pumped with blood. If she doesn't reach orgasm, the remaining blood will stay in the clitoris. This will cause blue bean."

"Thaaaaanks," I reply. "That was very scientific."

"The vagina is fascinating if you ask me," she nonchalantly says, and I shake my head. Apart from the occasional hello, Quinn Ellis and I have never spoken more than two words and now, she's giving me a lesson in blue clit.

"I too think vaginas are fascinating," Hudson adds. "And if you ask me, vaginas and penises together are extremely fascinating."

"You would know," Alani teases him.

"As do you, babe. As do you." He winks at her and then steals a carrot from my plate.

"Everyone, back off my carrots," I snap.

Hudson leans into Alani and not-so-quietly whispers, "Yep, she's blue beaning."

This causes her to shake her head and I notice she slightly smirks at him in that 'you can ease my blue bean' kind of way. Her and I will definitely be discussing this later and while this is happening, Hudson steals a fry from my plate. Carrot stealing I can handle, but no one touches my fries. Picking up a carrot, I throw it at him. It hits him in the face and falls to the table.

Without missing a beat, he picks it up and takes a bite. "You know, I'm happy to help relieve your blue bean anytime, Rem. As I said before, vaginas and penises are very fascinating. I have a penis. You have a vagina. Fascinating."

"And if you don't want your dick ripped off and shoved down your throat, I suggest you forget all about Remington's vagina," Thatcher growls as he grips Hudson's shoulder, squeezing, and going by the whiteness of his knuckles and the clenched teeth of Hudson, it's not a friendly squeeze.

"You have no say over my vagina," I snap at Thatcher. "I can show, fuck, and do whatever the hell I want with MY vagina."

"Is that right, Peach?" He shoves Hudson off his chair and with a sinister look on his face, climbs up on it and whistles loudly, gaining the focus of the room. "Attention, Crestwood Prep, Remington Hearst's vagina is off-limits. If I find out anyone has touched, seen, or smelled it, you will deal with my wrath." He nods. "Now, go forth and learn." He claps his hands and jumps down.

Smiling at me, he leans over and steals a fry. Biting it in half, he rests one hand on the table and gets up in my face. I can feel his breath on my face and my fucking traitorous body comes alive at his proximity. "You are mine, Peach. I thought I made myself clear?"

"I'm ... I'm no ones. I'm not a piece of property you can claim."

"No, you're so much more than that but regardless of what you are..." He leans into me, his nose brushing my ear. "You are mine, Peach." He bites my earlobe and I shit you not, I nearly come right there in the middle of the cafeteria. Before I can come up with a retort or tell him to fuck me— right here, right now—he stalks away, leaving me turned on and confused.

"If she wasn't blue beaning before, she's totally blue beaning right now," Hudson says, breaking the silence.

"I totally am too," Rowan says, she wriggles in her seat. "You and Thatch just need to hate fuck and get it over with. A good fuck will break that animosity and then you can both get on with senior year ... Or you'll possibly fuck each other to death, but death by fucking would be a fucking amazing way to go."

"I'd rather fuck a pineapple," I snap. "Thatcher Vander-belt is never, N E V E R coming near my vagina again."

A chorus of "again?" echoes around the table.

"Fuck," I whisper-hiss, "I … I didn't mean that." But everyone at the table is giving me 'that look' because every-one, me included, knows I'm a big fat liar. Given the chance, I'd mount him like a cowboy mounts a bull and I'll ride him —for a lot longer than eight seconds—again.

Biting into a carrot, I sigh and inwardly groan because I'm so screwed. I want Thatcher to fuck me into the next millen-nium, but how can I want to fuck someone who hates me?

THATCHER

WHEN I HEARD Hudson talking about Remy's vagina and his penis, I wanted to rip the fucker's head off. I was already in a foul mood because I distinctly remember offering myself to Remy in my drunken state last night with no success, and to top it off, tonight is dinner with my father. The thought of being in the same room as him is pure torture.

Slamming my locker shut, the sound echoes through the corridor from the force. Heading to art class is the last thing I care about because right now, I just want to make trouble and right now seems like the perfect moment to strike.

It's time to send Remington Hearst packing. Yes, my dick

wants to argue the fact he wants her to stay but for once, I'm thinking with my other head.

The longer she's here, the more I despise her presence and the more I fucking want her. She needs to pay for what her mother did to our family. Regardless, I want to fuck her seven ways to Sunday.

As if the gods are finally on my side, the perfect moment is presented to me when I see Remy making her way down the corridor.

After she passes by me without so much as a glance, I increase my pace and sneak up behind her. Grabbing her wrist, I pull her into a nearby alcove—thank you, old school and random hallways—hiding us from the main thoroughfare.

She gasps, ready to throw down, and when she realizes it's me who has hold of her, she becomes enraged. "Thatcher, what the hell?" she snarls through clenched teeth.

Gripping the back of her neck, I pull her closer, crowding her. I lean down, my breath fans her ear and I don't miss the way she shivers under my touch. I whisper, "You're mine, Remy. You can run but you can't hide, I'll always find you." She swallows, taking a deep breath as I continue, "I've claimed you, Peach, but just know, it won't be me bowing, it'll be you." Nipping her earlobe, she shivers at my bite. "In time you'll be sinking to those pretty little knees of yours and you'll willingly surrender yourself to me. And when that time finally comes, I'll cherish every fucking moment. Do you know why?"

Hesitantly she shakes her head.

"Because I'm Thatcher-fucking-Vanderbelt, one of The Lords of Crestwood Prep and nobody will take my fucking title away, not even you."

"I don't want your fucking title," she hisses back at me.

Tangling my fingers through her hair, she whimpers and I love hearing that sound pass through her lips. I grip her hip with my other hand and I lower her backward, bending us over. She reaches out and grips my arms, holding on to me to stop herself from falling.

Her eyes flutter when I brush my lips over hers. Her mouth begging to be kissed.

Fuck, no! I berate myself.

I need to stay focused, she is the enemy.

But I can't control this pull she has over me, she weakens me. She's my kryptonite but no matter what happens, I can't let her know what she does to me. How deeply I want to bury myself inside her.

Shaking my head, my lips hover over hers as I clench my teeth and issue a warning.

"I'm the fucking Lord here, not you, don't forget who runs this fucking school."

"Like I said, I don't want your fucking title. I don't want anything to do with you." The look in her eyes contradicts what she's saying. Her tongue darts out and wets her lip, brushing mine in the process and that contact causes me to crash my lips to hers, relentless and uncontrolled. I bite down on hers, making her cry out. The sound is music to my cock.

My tongue swipes at hers, tasting her one last time.

Bringing her upright, she crashes into my chest in a daze. Her footing off-kilter, I catch her before shoving her away from me. She glares at me in anger and confusion.

Throwing her a wink, I step around her, turn, and leave her in the alcove. A smile graces my face when I hear her sigh and mutter, "What the ever-loving fuck?" to herself. *Check-mate, Thatcher!*

Walking into class, I take my seat, smirking to myself knowing the effect I have over her.

My little peach has no clue what she's a part of and after that just now, I'm going to have so much fun teaching her. After all, I'm Thatcher Vanderbelt. Nobody will stand in my way, not even the sexy minx who is Remington Hearst.

Heading back to my room, I reluctantly begin to get ready for dinner with my father. These dinners are sporadic, thankfully, but when he calls, we come running.

As I approach my room, I see something taped to my door. Anger builds, I'm furious someone has the audacity to tape something to *my* door.

Ripping the envelope off, I tear it open. There's a note attached to what looks like a newspaper article. I read the note first and scrunch my face in anger and confusion.

`Daddy can't make everything go away.`

Then I look at the attached article and my eyes widen.

It's an article my father made disappear, it's an article that could have ruined my life if it saw the light of day.

It's also a day I never want to repeat.

It's the day I got a DUI and lost my license for a year.

It's the day I almost killed someone.

It's the day I almost killed *Hannah* ...

...*"Come on, babe, it'll be fine, I'm not that drunk."* And I'm not, I feel okay enough to drive. Sure, I'm over the legal limit, but I'm not smashed off my face like Reign is.

"Thatcher, you're drunk enough, maybe we should just stay here," Hannah pleads, her hand cocked on her hip and her 'I mean business' look on her face.

"Nah, come on, babe, I wanna do dirty things to you and I can't do that here, let me take you back to school." To reiterate what I want to do to her, I grab Hannah's hand and pull her into me. I

slam my mouth to hers, taking her lips roughly for a passionate kiss.

While she's distracted by my tongue in her mouth, I open the passenger door and quickly push her inside before she can argue with me anymore.

Stumbling around the hood, I realize I'm a little drunker than I thought, but I'll be fine. It's not the first time I've been a little buzzed while driving.

Speeding down the highway back to Crestwood, the music is blaring, and Hannah's hand is on my thigh. It's so fucking close to my dick and the minx that she is, she's taunting me. I can't take it anymore. Letting out a groan, I reach over, fist her hair, and bring her mouth over to mine. I only take my eyes off the road for a second but it's too late. I don't see the deer until I'm right on top of it. Barreling through it, the car spins and spins before we're flying through the air. It comes to a stop with a loud bang and then I black out.

Groaning when I come to, I realize everything hurts. Reaching for my head, I feel a wet patch just over my eye, blood trickles down my face.

"Hannah," I croak and see the passenger seat next to me is empty.

Crawling from the wreckage, my legs give out, sending me to the pavement near my car. "Fuck," I hiss as I take in my car, it's fucking totaled. Dad's going to kill me.

Finally, I'm able to stand and that's when I hear sirens in the distance and my fight-or-flight instinct kicks in. "Fuck," I hiss. I need to get out of here, I'm totally fucked, but that's when I spot Hannah. She's facedown and unmoving in the middle of the road ...

Pulling myself from the memory, I look down at the article and note that it's now in a ball in my fist.

My father lost his shit that day and the beating I received was one of the worst. Hannah was in a coma for four months, four long fucking torturous months. When she finally woke up her memory was gone. She had no recollection of the accident, that night ... or me.

My father called it a win because he'd paid off her family to keep the events of the accident quiet and in the process, saving me from a prison sentence.

That event changed my life. I saw my father in a new light after he did what he did, and that was when everything changed for the worse when it came to my father.

Sitting in my car, I wait for my brothers to get their asses here. I've been waiting—hiding—in my car, thinking of what I'll be making Remy do once I catch her in 'Ready or Not' next weekend. The possibilities are endless, and I can't fucking wait. Shaking my head in frustration, I look out the windshield, wishing the assholes would hurry the fuck up and get here so we can get in and get out.

Hearing Hendrix's Bugatti Chiron pull up beside me, the sigh I'd been holding escapes. Thank fuck someone's here, the last thing I want to do is walk in alone.

Hendrix knocks on my window and as I lower it, he smirks. "Hiding?"

"Just buying time, you fuckers are fucking late," I hiss, my tone giving way to how pissed I am.

He chuckles, popping some gum in his mouth. "Nah, bro, you're just fucking eager to get in and out."

He's right. The thought of tonight has caused me to almost grind my teeth to the point of needing dentures as there's no tooth left, and in the process, I've given myself a headache.

Reign and Saint finally pull up beside us, their engines making as much noise as my heart right now. I'm determined to get answers about the medallion tonight, but I know it won't be easy.

Nothing ever is when it comes to Thornton Vanderbelt.

He's difficult at the best of times, and when it comes to the secrets he holds, it's far worse for my brothers and me. We've discovered some of his secrets, but we've always known they were just the beginning.

What is our father really hiding?

Hendrix and I nod toward Reign and Saint as they step out of their cars.

"I don't understand why we can't just carpool, we're all going to the same fucking place." Saint grunts as he storms up the front stairs, seems I'm not the only one in a mood tonight.

Furiously he rings the doorbell and just as the rest of us make it behind him, the door swings open and my parents' long-time butler, Alfred—yep, our butler's name is Alfred, but we don't have a Batcave ... well I don't think we do, but who fucking knows with this family—smiles and greets us.

"Boys, welcome home."

We all cringe at those words, welcome and home are two words we do not associate with this place. This was never a home, it was hell on Earth.

Stepping aside, he ushers us inside. Like lambs to the slaughter, we head in and past him. He closes the door behind us and beckons for us to follow him into the dining room. No wandering unaccompanied around our 'home.' I'm the first to enter and upon seeing our mother, I know tonight is going to end in disaster.

"My babies are home," she singsongs.

Rising to stand, she stretches her arms out to us and cradles each of us like she used to when we were kids.

Something is off, she seems too joyful. Extremely so.

"Are you taking your meds, Mom?" Saint asks her as he pulls away from her.

She waves him off like it's the stupidest thing she's ever heard. "Oh hush, Saint. I'm perfectly fine and I do not need my youngest child telling me what I should be doing." She grips his cheek lovingly and smiles brightly at him.

"Mom," I say just as Father walks in, killing any chance of us finding out what the fuck is going on with her. She scurries away from us, kissing our father on the cheek before she sits, letting him push her chair in.

We all follow suit, not offering any chance for our father to reprimand us for our lack of respect for his time.

Lisette, the housemaid we've had since we were little, places a plate in front of each of us but minutes after we sit, my appetite is gone. From my spot, I watch Mother as she smiles away to herself like she's fucking high.

Hendrix leans in whispering, "What's he got her on now?" I shrug, having no fucking clue.

"Is Crestwood still tip-top?" Father's voice booms across at us, breaking Hendrix and I apart like it used to when we were kids. We give each other a wide-eyed look waiting for him to berate us for whispering at the table, but nothing comes.

Reign eyes us and then looks down at his lap.

Fuck, Remy, father will want to know. Swallowing the thick lump in my throat I pick at my dinner with my fork.

"Is there something you want to tell me?" he murmurs.

My eyes cut across at my brothers, each of us having the same confused look on our face.

Father leans his elbows on the table and steeples his fingers, his expression severe. His gaze filters across us all. Saint keeps his head down, his gaze lifting slowly toward Hendrix. Sharing a look, Saint goes back to playing with the food on his plate.

"You know exactly what I'm talking about, Thatcher. Care to share?"

My heart is beating like a fucking madman waiting to

break free. I clear my throat and utter two words. "Remington Hearst."

Father glares at me, waiting for me to continue. "I can't believe she actually thinks she can fuck with me." His assumed tone confuses the four of us, me especially. "First her son and now this." He shakes his head in disbelief. He licks his lips and leans back in his chair. Mother's gaze is now fixed on him, along with ours. "After that lil' shit killed himself, Rochelle became desperate. That bitch would do just about anything, and I mean anything, to make sure her children have it all. Manipulation is a running trait in the Hearst family." I share a look with Hendrix, he's grinding his jaw back and forth, just like me. I can't believe he's talking about the bitch who ruined his marriage, in front of his wife ... his wife who once again seems off in fucking la-la land.

"She's a whore, just like her mother, and no doubt a cunt like her brothers and father." He pauses and steeples his fingers once again, sitting there like the pompous jackass he is.

Reign straightens his back, even Saint's ears perk up at that. All of a sudden Dad hates Rochelle? What are the Hearsts hiding now?

Guess my little peach has her own deep dark secrets and not just her family's. I intend to find each and every one and then I will reveal all, tarnishing the Hearst name once and for all.

"It'd be in your best interest to keep your distance from that girl. I wouldn't want anything to happen to her ... or you for that matter." Did he just threaten us? His own sons? And what's he alluding to?

Throwing his napkin on the table, he stands abruptly.

"I think I've had enough for one night." He turns to leave, but I finally find my voice.

"Do you know what this is?" I hold out my phone to the

picture I took of the medallion, I wasn't stupid enough to have it on my person.

He stalks over to me and looks at the screen, his eyes widen and his face turns red with anger the longer he stares at the screen. The veins on his neck protrude, pulsing rapidly.

"Where did you get that?" he demands

"Found it." My curt and dry answer angers him further.

"If I were you, Son, I'd forget ever finding that medallion. It'll only lead to bad things."

Shaking his head, he storms out of the room and like a programmed robot, Mother stands, comes around the table and kisses each of us on the top of our heads before she walks from the dining room, following Father.

"We need to find out the significance of that fucking medallion," Hendrix hisses, munching on a bean ... how he can still be eating is beyond me. "It might hold some answers."

Saint shrugs, throwing his napkin on top of his empty plate. "Or leave us with more questions."

"I say we do some digging, and in the meantime, we keep our eyes on Remington," I murmur.

Reign swallows, his demeanor changes slightly, he's nervous. "I ... I think I have some answers regarding what Father was talking about."

"What?" I snap.

Grabbing his phone, he swipes at the screen and stares at it, lifting his gaze, he murmurs, "I just got sent a link."

"A link to what?" Hendrix asks.

Sighing he straightens up, shaking his head. Dinner is over. He pushes back from the table and walks away from us and heads toward the door.

Silently, we all follow behind.

Fury boils in my blood with each step we take. What the fuck isn't he sharing with us?

Standing on the front porch, I reach out and grab his arm,

I force him to stop just before he goes down the stairs. "What the fuck are you hiding?"

"This." He bites his lip looking between all of us. "Just look." He holds his phone out toward us and I take in what's on the screen.

"Fuck," Hendrix curses beside me.

She lied to us. She came to Crestwood for a reason. And it wasn't to find out about her brothers or because Mommy transferred her.

She's here for us.

Remy needs to confess but how the fuck do we get her to do that?

Maybe getting her drunk at 'Ready or Not' on the weekend is the key.

And with that we head back to Crestwood. Along the drive back, I come up with a plan and I'm willing to bet I can get Remy to talk. I just need her compliance. Easy, right?

REMY

Lying on my bed, I stare up at the ceiling. Sleep eludes me right now. I keep thinking about the e-mail I received earlier from Grayson, when I saw his name as the sender it pissed me off. He can e-mail me from wherever the fuck he is, but he can't call? And with his e-mail he managed to morph my anger into confusion and hurt for Arlen. Even in death my brother can't rest, and now, I'm even more convinced he didn't kill himself.

Grabbing my phone, I log into my e-mails and reopen the one from him. There's no 'hey, how you doin'?' it's just an attachment. Clicking the link, I open it and reread it.

It's an e-mail Arlen sent to Grayson. I read it for the millionth time this evening and like the other million times, I can hear his voice reading it out to me.

```
FROM: Arlen@hearst.com
TO: Grayson@hearst.com,
SUBJECT: ...

This secret and affair need to be
shared but there will be repercussions
once it's exposed.
Mom. Dad. The Hearsts. The Vanderbelts
... too many people could get hurt but
it needs to come out ... I wish it
could be different.
I wish I could be different.
I wish it was out in the open.
I wish ...
```

You wish what, Arl? And what secret? What affair? But most of all, why did Grayson forward me this now? He got this before you died, why now? And why can't the asshole pick up the phone and tell me he's okay.

My anger boils over so I sit up, cross my legs, and send him an e-mail since he no longer seems to know how to use a phone or text.

```
FROM: Remington@hearst.com
TO: Grayson@hearst.com
SUBJECT: answer me ...
```

So you can forward me an e-mail from
Arlen but you can't tell me you're
alive or fucking say hello? I've been
worried sick about you and now I also
have to worry about a secret
affair too?
As if my life isn't complicated
enough.
Please call or e-mail me, we need to
talk and more importantly, who's
having an affair?
Please Gray, e-mail me back ... I miss
you and still love you, even if you
are being a big buttface head
right now.
Love R xo

Pressing send on the e-mail, I flop back to the mattress and stare back at the ceiling. "Please e-mail me back, Gray," I whisper to the dark room. My eyes become heavy and I drift off to sleep, dreaming about Arlen and the cliff.

Waking with a start, I sit upright in bed and cover my chest. My heart is racing, and I don't know why I feel like this. It feels like someone is here but when I look around my room, I don't see anyone. There's no one in here but me.

It's still dark out so it isn't until I walk into my attached bathroom I realize someone *was* in here. Someone was in my room while I was sleeping and I was none the wiser. What the fuck?

On the mirror written in my lipstick is a warning and it sends chills down my spine.

keep your fucking mouth shut!

Racing over, I pick up the hand towel and wipe away the message. Even when the mirror is clean, I can still see the message reflecting back at me. Throwing the red-stained towel into the sink, I rest my hands on the countertop and lower my head. That's when I see it. I see the discarded tube of lipstick sitting by my feet.

Bending down, I pick it up and when I realize they used and broke my favorite lipstick, that fear morphs into raging anger. "Motherfuckers," I hiss. "That was a limited edition."

Shaking my head, I drop the tube into the bin before reaching into the shower to turn the faucet on. Waiting for the water to heat, I strip off and with the room now filled with steam and the mirror fogged, I can once again see the message.

Flipping the message the bird, I turn and climb into the shower. Stepping under the spray, I drop my head back, close my eyes, and let the hot water beat down over my face.

A noise startles me and when I open my eyes, I swear I see a shadow move across my bathroom. Pulling the curtain back, I poke my head out but don't see anyone. I do however see the lipstick tube sitting on the countertop. Someone definitely was in here and they're fucking with me, and there's only one person who would have the balls to do this, Thatcher-fucking-Vanderbelt. And after I was nice and looked after his drunk ass the other night, well fuck him and fuck them. I will not take this lying down. I'm Remington-fucking-Hearst, I'm not the princess they keep referring to me as. I'm a mother-fucking-Queen and it's time to show them I won't bow to them, or anyone for that matter.

Quickly finishing my shower, I wrap my towel around me because who knows if the psycho fucker is still in my space but, thankfully, when I step back into my bedroom, it's empty.

Pulling on my favorite jeans and a black tank, I drop to the end of my bed and put on my socks and knee-high matte black boots. Grabbing my leather jacket, I slip it on and exit my room; I need to see a man about being a fuckhead.

Stalking up to the boys' floor and his room, I open the door and step in without knocking. Unsurprisingly, I find all four Lords—fucking stupid title—lazing around his room. I walk over to Thatcher, who is lying back on his bed looking sexy as fuck, and I stare down at him.

We stare at one another, neither of us uttering a word, actually no one in the room says anything. He sits up and rests his hand on my hip. My body heats at the connection and I suddenly want to throw myself at him but that feeling dissipates when he opens his mouth. "To what do we owe the pleasure, Peach?"

"Don't fucking touch me," I snarl through clenched teeth, but I make no move to remove his hand from my hip.

"I'll touch you however the fuck I want, especially when you barge into *my* room in the middle of the night. What if I was naked? Or pleasuring myself?"

My gaze drops to his crotch and images of his hand squeezing and sliding along his shaft play in my mind.

"Feel free to act out the scene currently playing in your mind," he sniggers and the assholes behind me laugh too.

"You want me to stab you in the dick? Didn't realize you were into bloodplay like that, Thatch, and neither am I, normally, but seeing you bleed and dickless is suddenly very appealing to me."

"Just fuck already," a voice from behind says.

Glancing over my shoulder, I glare at the other three, not knowing which one of them just uttered that bullshit statement.

"Hell will freeze over before that happens, again." The again is whispered because as much as that romp in the library was hot, I will not go there again. That was a one-time hate fuck, and that's all that will ever happen between his dick and my vagina ... even if the traitorous bitch is thrumming right now. I turn my attention back to Thatcher. "Stay the fuck out of my room, and you owe me a new lipstick, that was limited edition."

"The fuck you talking about?"

"Don't play dumb with me, asshole. I got your message. I'll keep my mouth shut and I only will because I have no fucking clue what you're talking about."

"What the fuck are *you* talking about?" He emphasizes the word you, repeating his statement from before.

"Did you not break into my room earlier and leave a message in my favorite lipstick on my mirror?"

"No, and that's not my style."

"Well, you clearly arranged it because you're the only asshole around here who takes pleasure in taunting me."

"I do like taunting you, Peach. I do but I assure you, that wasn't me. Besides, the only time I want to touch your lipstick is when I'm thrusting my dick down your throat and you leave lipstick stains on my dick."

The fucker reaches up and swipes his thumb over my bottom lip, I feel the pressure between my thighs, and I have to swallow back the moan wanting to break free. I hate this asshole with every fiber of my being but my body and vagina want him like a heroin addict needs her next fix.

The sound of his voice snaps me back to the present. He inspects his thumb, "Hmmmm, no lipstick, pity, but feel free to act out my fantasy."

"Fantasy is all it will ever be but regardless, stay the fuck out of my room." I turn and head toward the door, with my hand on the handle, I look over my shoulder. "I will discover what you fuckers are up to and when I do, watch the fuck out."

Opening the door, I step into the corridor and slam it shut behind me. I don't believe it wasn't him who broke in and left me that message but if it wasn't him, who the fuck was it?

The next few days pass by uneventfully and thankfully, no one reenters my room—well not that I sense or see anyway. It's Friday afternoon and I'm in the library, trying to get some studying done but everyone is talking about 'Ready or Not' tonight.

I'd be quite happy to stay in, but the girls convinced me I should come because it's 'way much fun' and 'not to be missed.' Not that I'd admit it out loud, but I am kinda excited to see what it's all about.

Alton Academy is nothing like Crestwood Prep, there were no Lords or cliques or game nights. It was your quintessential boring school academy but at least there I didn't have enemies ... just the drama associated with being a Hearst and it seems drama has followed me here too, main difference, it's tenfold here.

Refreshing my e-mail, again, I still have nothing new, well I did get one about some prince in Bumfuck, Nowhere needing my assistance to inherit a gazillion U.S. dollars. How dumb do these assholes think we are? Well, I guess some people are dumb 'cause this type of scam has been around for as long as I can remember.

Grayson hasn't replied to any of the e-mails or texts I've sent this past week and I still have no clue as to what Arlen was wishing for or who he was having an affair with. I really wish he was still here. I miss him so much and with Grayson now MIA too, I'm really alone.

Packing up my books, I'm about to stand up when a hand slams down on the table, making me jump in my seat. Lifting my gaze, I furrow my brows in confusion when I see none other than Reign Vanderbelt staring down at me. "We need to talk," he drawls.

Nodding, I gesture to the seat he's standing behind, but he shakes his head. "No, too many ears. Meet me at the cliffs in five."

Before I can agree, or refuse, he turns on his heel and storms out of the library. I stare at his retreating form and wonder if I should meet him or not. The common sense in me says 'hell no, go back to your room and get ready for tonight' but the stupid schoolgirl in me says, 'hop to it, bitch, you're gonna be late.'

Shaking my head, I stand up and grab my bag, following the path Reign took to the exit. Stepping out into the bright afternoon sun, I turn left to follow the path toward the cliff top and not right toward my room.

When I get there, I find Reign sitting on the same bench where I had my encounter with Rowan the other week. He's staring out to sea, and I notice a melancholy look on his face. The closer I get to him, I swear there are tears in his eyes.

"I can feel you staring at me," he says, breaking the silence.

"Wasn't trying to hide it," I reply, walking closer to him.

"This was his favorite spot, you know?"

"Whose?" I question, genuinely confused.

"Arlen's." That's all he says.

"I wasn't aware you knew my brother so, personally." I knew he and Arl were acquainted but this, this is much more personal than I ever thought. What am I missing when it comes to Reign and my brother?

"There's a lot you aren't aware of, Remington Hearst." *No fucking shit.*

"It's Remy," I snarl between clenched teeth.

"I know ... but he told me how much it pisses you off when people use your full first name, makes me feel ..."

"Feel what?" I ask, taking a seat next to him.

He shakes his head. "It doesn't matter what it makes me

feel. He's gone but even in death, his secrets are being revealed."

"What secrets? I'm so confused right now."

"His secrets don't just affect him." He turns to face me, and I was correct in my assumption that he was or is about to cry. "Just, be careful with what you discover. His name is already tarnished, and I hate that but it's not just him who will be tarnished if more secrets are exposed."

Before I can reply, he stands up and walks to the edge. I sit here and watch him as he whispers something and when he turns back around, a lone tear slides down his cheek. He bats it away. "He loved you so much." He smiles and walks toward me, sadness and loss radiating from him. I feel sad for him. He stops beside me and squeezes my shoulder. Lifting my hand, I cover his and squeeze back.

Pulling his free, he walks away, leaving me alone … and even more confused now.

Staring out at sea, I play our encounter just now over and over and then my eyes widen. Is Reign who Arlen was seeing? Just before he died, he confessed he was in love, but they had to keep their relationship a secret. Too many people would be against them, I presumed it was because he hadn't come out to anyone but me yet, but maybe it was because he was in love with a Vanderbelt.

Looking over my shoulder, I watch Reign sadly walk away. His shoulders hunched and even from here, I can feel the sadness radiating off him.

Looking back out at sea, I shake my head. "Ohh, Arlen, why did you do it?" And now, knowing how much and who he was in love with, I start to wonder again if he was pushed and didn't jump.

Letting out a frustrated sigh, I stand up and head back to my room. Adding to my already weird week, when I get back to my room, there's a purple box with a gold bow sitting outside my door. Bending down, I pick it up, unlock my door, and step into my room.

Dumping my bags on the floor, I walk over to the window seat and sit down. Lifting my legs up, I spin and lean back against the wooden frame and stare at the box. It's beautifully wrapped. I almost don't want to ruin the wrapping, but I want to know what it is.

Grabbing the end of the ribbon, I undo the bow. It falls away and I lift the lid and smile. Inside is my favorite lipstick, a replacement for the one my mystery mirror message man destroyed the other night. Picking the tube up, I walk into the bathroom and flip on the light. Stepping in front of the mirror, I swipe the lipstick over my lips. Grabbing a piece of toilet tissue, I blot my lips and smile at my reflection. I've felt lost these last few days without my painted lips, but now I have another unanswered question. Who the fuck replaced my lipstick?

THATCHER

It's game day and I can't fucking wait.

I've been looking forward to this day all fucking week, after dinner with our father and the clear warning to stay away from Remington, I've been on edge. The need to smash something or fuck someone—Remy—has been strong. I've found myself wanting her more, she's a drug I can't get enough of and the need to have her is addictive.

I've been watching her, imagining all the ways I could possibly torture her. The thrill of sending her over the edge has my cock rock-fucking-hard. My heart and cock are currently at war because as much as I want to fuck her, I also want to make her and her family suffer. And tonight, tonight is the night I make Remington-fucking-Hearst mine.

Her sass and fire are one hell of a turn-on and the need to fill her mouth with something other than sass has me ready to combust. I have never felt like this before, my brothers are worried about me and to be honest, I am too. I've never felt so unsure before and it's all because of Remington-fucking-Hearst. How can you hate someone with a fiery passion but at the same time want to claim them. Live inside them.

"Fuck, tonight can't come soon enough. I need some fucking pussy," Rian's voice booms as he enters my room unannounced. The rest of the boys follow behind him, each repeating somewhat of the same line he just did.

"As long as she has a mouth to use, I'm all good." Hart chuckles just as Reign comes up behind him and flicks his ear. "Ow, motherfucker. What the fuck, dude?"

"You get it?" I ask him. He nods and hands me the small bag. I replaced Remington's lipstick, the one she was pissed off over. When she found it ruined and unleashed her wrath on us, something shifted inside of me so I snuck into her room to see what was up, but apart from the discarded lipstick tube in the bin there was no trace. I pocketed it and asked Reign to track a replacement down. How he found the limited edition one again, I will never know but then again Reign Vanderbelt is a fucking genius at the best of times.

The thing that pissed me off the most is that for once, I had no part in it. I managed to find lipstick that I've missed seeing on her lips and being the nice guy that I am, I also got her a few more and some other makeup shit I know girls love.

Placing the bag I'll anonymously drop off later on atop my bedside table, I grin when I think about her reaction at receiving my gifts. My peach doesn't need to know I'm the one giving her these, but I also have an ulterior motive … maybe now I can see her lipstick-covered lips wrapped around my dick as I shove it down her throat.

Focusing on the guys—and not Remy sucking my dick—I settle back and listen to them mumble about their antics for tonight.

Saint and Reign enter together, nodding in greeting as they do.

Finally, with everyone here, I pull out some glasses and the bottle of amber liquid I stole from my father. Drinking is prohibited on school grounds but fuck them. I'm a Vanderbelt and the rules don't apply to me.

Glancing around the circle with the people who I'm closest to and would do anything for, a feeling of contentment washes over me. Each one has earned the right to be here.

"Tonight may start the same as always, but it ends with—"

"Easy pussy." Lennon chuckles, earning a glare from me.

"Do you ever think about anything else? Horny fucker," Theon states while the rest of us burst out laughing.

"Typical Len, you'd think he has a problem," Saint berates his best friend.

"Hey, I take offense to that. I'm only partially whipped by pussy." He winks.

I don't miss the way Hendrix drifts off into his own head. He catches me staring, but he quickly brushes off my concern with a small smile. A smile that doesn't reach his eyes. *What's going on with you, Brother?*

"Anyway, continuing on. Make sure the newbies know the rules." We may be assholes but we're not into forcing anyone to do anything they don't want to be a willing participant in. "No one is to touch the girls we have assigned to us, it will be their head if they do."

Murmurs and head nods break out around the circle, in an hour, sixty-fucking-minutes, I'll finally claim Remy as mine.

"What about Remy?" Hart's stare penetrates. The others look between us, they all know I've staked my claim.

"She's none of your concern, I'll deal with her."

"What if ..." he continues, but I hold my hand up to stop him.

"No what-ifs, we don't need any negativity thwarting our plan". But if I'm completely honest, I've thought about every possible 'what if' all fucking week but for some reason, I know Remy will accept it, accept us. "Have fun, boys, and don't fucking forget, 'wrap it before you tap it' because I'm too young to become an uncle." Personally, I don't want to be responsible for any unwanted pregnant chicks, I still have a life of terror and teasing to live before that happens.

With a nod and a click of glasses we take our shots. Swallowing down the bourbon, my focus turns to claiming Remy.

Before long, it's time to begin. "Masks on," Hendrix eagerly shouts.

Lifting our masks and clicking the switch to turn the neon on, it's game time. One by one we make our way out of my room. The rest of the guys wait by their doors and as we pass, each one follows us, joining us in a group. Before we head downstairs, the guys hand out a mask to each player.

Once everyone has their masks, my brothers and I stand front and center, holding our place as The Lords.

"Right, for all you newbies here, listen the fuck up. I'll only say this once," Conroy's voice booms across the grounds and even though the air is filled with excitement for the night ahead, I swear I see sweat starting to pour off them and I can't help but chuckle. "You'll each have a pick, choose any girl you want, except for the ones that will be branded. By branded I mean they'll be wearing a colored bracelet. They have already been assigned. Under no circumstances, I fucking repeat, NO FUCKING CIRCUMSTANCES, are you to pursue any of these girls. If you do, you won't like the outcome."

Taking a breath, Conroy looks around at the fresh blood. They glance between each other, some still unsure how this works.

"Remember, you can do whatever you want for twenty-four hours, but she has to say yes. If I find out anyone was forced against their will, you will suffer the consequences, and trust me, a fuck ain't worth what will become of you if you force anyone."

Everyone nods their compliance and I find myself grinning. "Masks on," I shout, my voice carrying over the nervous murmurs of the crowd.

"You can keep your identity a secret if you wish. Don't be a dick and remember if she says no, she means no," Hart bellows and then he says those magic words, "Now, go forth and have fun."

One by one, their masks click on and each one lights up neon. The dark grounds are now covered in an array of neon-colored lights. The chime of the bell alerts the girls it's time.

My heart thunders against my rib cage. Finally, I'll get her alone.

My little peach has no clue what's in store for her.

My mouth curves up at the endless possibilities, surprise shoots through me when my gaze easily finds Remington in the crowd waiting. A smile forms on my lips when I see her wearing the glow necklace, marking her as mine. She has no idea which one is me and I can't wait to come face-to-face with my little peach.

Hendrix whistles and an echo of cheers and hollers carry out as the guys head toward the girls forming a line.

Covering my mouth, I bellow, "Let the games begin!"

REMY

ALANI PULLS me excitedly along next to her as every girl in the school forms a line. "I feel like a lamb lining up to be slaughtered," I whisper-hiss to her. A part of me wants to play, but there's also a part of me who wants to hide in my room with a tub of ice cream and a spoon.

"Death by fucking, I like it." Alani bumps my shoulder and laughs.

"And what's with the fucking glow necklace?" I'm still confused by this.

"It lets the players know you have been claimed and are off-limits."

Rolling my eyes, I shake my head. Can these assholes be any more cavemanish with their claiming bullshit? It's not nineteen hundred anymore. "Why couldn't it be something cool?"

"Like what?" Alani replies, running her finger over hers with a dreamy look on her face.

"I don't know, maybe a glow in the dark T-shirt … or nothing at all, but seriously, a fucking glow stick? We're marked with something you snap to get to work. If *he* thinks he can snap me to get me to work, he has another thing coming."

"They can snap me anyway they want," Alani replies with a longing look on her face. "As long as it involves their dick and my vagina, snap away I say."

"You are such a whore."

"For them, yes."

My eyes scrunch when it clicks in my brain she said 'them' and not 'he' but before I can probe her on the 'them' aspect, across the field, neon light masks begin flickering on and then a voice I would recognize anywhere booms, "Let the games begin!"

Everyone around me, including Alani, excitedly screams and squeals and jumps up and down—fucking girls—and then they each take off running. It's chaos as girls scatter across the quad into the darkness. Thankfully it's a full moon and isn't completely dark.

Alani and I are yet to move, and I wonder if I can sneak away to my room, but no sooner do I think that than Alani grabs my hand and drags me toward the cliff top. *There goes that idea* I think as she pulls me across the grass. I can feel her excitement oozing through her and if I'm honest, it is kinda fun, but I will never admit that out loud.

"I fucking love this," she pants as we run.

"Why the hell are we running? Isn't the aim to get caught?"

"Don't be such a spoilsport, Rem. Let your hair down and have some fun. Find some random dude, or Thatch, and fuck the next twenty-four hours away. I know I plan to."

"But what if I don't want to fuck who finds me?"

"You say no."

"Really?"

"Uh-huh, no means no in this game. Anyone who breaks the rules will severely be punished by The Lords. To this date, only one person has ever suffered the consequences."

"What was the consequence?" I ask, genuinely interested and kind of amazed people obey, but then again, this game is arranged by 'The Lords' and their cronies.

"Well, for starters he no longer attends here. They really made an example out of him and beat him up pretty badly before he left Crestwood."

"Who knew they had morals?" I scoff, dropping down to the seat that has come to be my happy place at the top of the cliffs.

"They aren't as bad as you think," she snaps, dropping down next to me.

"We're a bit defensive there, Alani. Anything you want to confess?"

She shrugs at me but her face lights up.

"Girl, spill ... now."

But before she can reply, from behind us we hear the pounding of footsteps, followed by someone with a deep voice I'd recognize anywhere growling, "Peekaboo, I see you." And there's another voice, unknown, that says, "You better run, Red, "

At the sound of the second voice, Alani squeals, jumps up, and races down the path into the darkness of the woods. Her someone chases after her and I can hear her giggling like a fucking schoolgirl, leaving me alone on the cliff top.

A presence appears behind me and without even turning

around, I know it's Thatcher. The air changes when he's nearby and right now, it's vibrating like crazy. All you can hear is his deep breathing and the crashing of the waves below.

The silence enveloping us is broken when he snickers, "I think it's time you run."

Shaking my head, I continue to stare out into the darkness. Then he runs his fingertip over the back of my neck. Goosebumps break out across my skin. My breathing picks up when he slides his hand around my throat and gently squeezes. He bends down and I can feel his heated breath on my skin. His teeth latch on to my earlobe, and he sucks the skin before he whispers, "I said run, Peach."

That sparks me into action. Lifting my arm, I remove his hand from my neck and jump up. I turn and begin to run in the direction Alani went; safety in numbers and all that, right?

"I'm coming for you," he shouts as I pick up my pace and run farther into the darkness.

Even with the full moon, it's eerie out tonight and the pounding of my heart from running away from Thatch adds to the eerie feeling. I'm huffing and puffing, I'm really not cut out for running. I glance around and look for a hiding space, but I can't see shit, the moon has slipped behind a cloud, masking the night, it's pitch-black now and prime scary movie shit.

Looking back over my shoulder, I see a neon mask coming toward me. I presume he can see as much as I can … which is shit all, so I jump off the path and press myself to a tree trunk. I slip around it, hiding myself from the path. His footsteps are getting closer and closer, I hold my breath and wait for him to find me, but somehow, he doesn't know where I am. He races past and continues farther into the woods.

My eyes widen at the fact he ran straight past. Thankfully,

it gives me time to catch my breath. My breathing returns to normal as the sound of his footsteps fade into the distance. Deciding to head back to my happy place, I step out onto the path, but the crunching of a branch nearby startles me and I freeze on the spot.

Silence once again shrouds me but that eerie feeling from before returns. Not wanting to hang around, I start to head back the way I came but I come to a stop when a lone figure dressed in black steps out onto the path, blocking my way.

"Where's your mask?" I defiantly ask.

They just shrug at me.

"Who are you?"

They shake their head side to side and cover their mouth with their finger, shushing me.

"Well, this has been fun, but I say no."

They step toward me and wave their index finger side to side in a 'no, I don't think so' manner. *So much for the no rule,* I think as a bad feeling simmers within. I really hope Thatch appears behind me and whispers 'boo' but as luck would have it, he doesn't appear.

The person before me keeps walking toward me, I will my body to move but I'm frozen with fear. By the time my brain and body decide to do something, the mystery person is right in front of me. I begin to step backward away from them but they follow me, step for step.

Spinning on my heel, I turn to run away but he reaches out and grabs me by my hair. He pulls me into his body. His breathing is ragged, much like mine is now. He wraps his arms around me, holding me tightly to him. I feel his hand moving behind me. I think he's going to rape me, and my eyes begin to well with tears.

"Please don't do this," I murmur. Just as I mumble this, the moon reappears, lighting the sky up once again but with the cover of the trees, we are still shrouded in darkness. He spins me in his arms to face him. And even through the balaclava of his mask, I see nothing but contempt reflecting at me. "Please," I beg again.

He lifts his hand, I scrunch my eyes closed and flinch, but nothing happens. Opening my eyes, I notice a cap in between his teeth and then I see what he's holding, a syringe.

My eyes widen and he snickers as he lifts it and brings it toward me but before anything happens, from farther down the path, I hear Thatcher yell, "Come out, come out wherever you are, Peach."

Without thinking, I open my mouth and scream. I put everything into it and if I were auditioning for a scary movie, I'd have the lead role. I've never screamed like this before and thank fuck I do.

"Remy," Thatch yells out, "where are you?"

My attacker mumbles something and then he raises his hand and punches me in the stomach. Doubling over, I collapse to the path, and he takes off, leaving me winded and alone on the path. A few seconds later, someone appears and I know it's Thatcher.

"Remy, what the fuck?" He drops to his knees beside me. He rips off his mask and throws it to the ground. Reaching out, he pulls me into his arms and hugs me to him. He runs his hand over my body, checking for injury. Sliding my arms around him, I hang on to him for dear life. He wraps his arms around me soothingly and when I feel the comfort of his embrace, the first tear falls. Holding on to him tightly, I break down in the middle of the forest.

"Remy, babe, what happened?" he asks into my hair.

Lifting my head, I stare up at him. "He ... he ... he tried to inject me."

"Who did?" he sneers.

Shaking my head, I whisper, "I don't know."

"I ... I was so scared, Thatch. I couldn't move. I froze. I ... I just stood there. I ..."

"Whoever it was is a fucking dead man."

"He punched me when I screamed and then you were there. You saved me." Swallowing the lump in the back of my throat, I look up at him. "Fuck me, Thatch. Fuck me better."

THATCHER

"Fuck me, Thatch. Fuck me better," she murmurs.

"What?" I question, her words confusing me right now.

"Make me feel something, anything but this. Please, Thatch. Fuck me."

Taking in Remy's frightened state, I growl, lifting her into my arms. Her arms wrap around my neck and her head rests on my chest. It feels right. Fuck, why does she feel right in my arms? I should be taking advantage of her broken state but for some inexplicable reason, I can't do it.

Carrying her through the woods and toward the school, I feel her tremble the entire time. Holding her tighter, I catch the eyes of a few students lingering outside. Not paying them any attention or letting Remy down, I carry her inside and upstairs to my room. Banging the door open, I don't stop until I place her in the middle of my bed, she gasps when her bottom hits the mattress.

Turning away from her, I close the door behind me and lock it, making sure we cannot be interrupted. My brothers will not fuck this up, whatever this is.

Leaning against my door, I stare after her, relishing in the fact she's here on my bed, willing and wanton. Shocking the ever-loving shit out of me, I realize right now, my dick is unwilling to pop up and say hello. It's like her fear is affecting him.

"Thatcher," she utters my name again and sits up. She rolls over and as she leans forward on all fours, she gives me a perfect view down her shirt of her tits.

Hissing, I push off the door and go to my chest of drawers. Pulling out a pair of sweatpants and a T-shirt, I turn and toss them at her. They land just in front of her, she picks them up and laughs as she holds my clothing against her body.

"You want me to wear your clothes?" I nod, running my fingers through my hair. "I don't get it." She laughs again. "Aren't you going to fuck me?" She leans back on her legs looking every bit as confused as I feel because I should be bending her over and fucking her until she screams my name ... but I can't.

"Not tonight, Peach, get dressed. Bathroom's there." I nod toward the door.

"O-okay." She stands, grabbing my clothes and scrambles to the bathroom. Before she enters, she looks over her shoulder at me but doesn't say anything. She looks rattled and even though my plan was to rattle her myself, seeing her like this affects me in a way that shocks the shit out of me. My mouth curves up into a smile, she smiles back and then closes the door behind her.

Letting out a breath, I shake my head and walk over to my bed. I pull my phone out from my pocket, drop to the mattress, and shoot off a text to my brothers.

THATCHER

Someone attacked Remy tonight. We find them and we end them.

I expect my brothers to be occupied, but no sooner does my message send than my phone begins to buzz with responses.

HENDRIX

Fuck. Is she hurt?

SAINT

Jesus fuck, they're bold.

I chuckle when a response from Reign doesn't come through. Guess Alani has him tied up.

THATCHER

She's okay, a little shaken up. She's sleeping in my room tonight.

No interruptions.

HENDRIX

Sleeping, yeah, right!

Fucker.

Yes, sleeping. Now's not the time for that.

Reign, check security cameras. I want to know which fucker touched my girl.

SAINT

He'll be balls deep in Alani by now, our boy's becoming a man.

Middle finger emoji

I lift my head, chuckling and spot Remy standing in the doorway of the bathroom, her clothes in a pile in her arm while my clothes swim on her.

A possessiveness washes over me. Heat floods my body, and the need to taste her has my dick twitching and coming to life. Taking a deep breath to calm my racing heart, I nod toward the bed. "Jump in, I'll be out in a minute." Climbing off the bed, I watch her pull the covers back and slide under.

Jesus fuck, she's in my bed.

Closing the door to the bathroom, I take a few deep, calming breaths. This chick unnerves me in a way like never before.

Once I'm done with my nightly routine, I walk out in my briefs and don't miss Remy's gaze raking over my chest.

Sliding in beside her, I open my arms for her to lie next to me. At first, she hesitates but then she shyly nods and shimmies over next to me, lying her head on my shoulder.

"Sleep, you're safe," I murmur.

The urge to kiss her temple is strong and I can't restrain myself any longer. Turning my head slightly, I place a gentle kiss on her forehead. A hiss passes through her lips when mine touch her skin, but the kiss causes her to relax and melt into me farther.

Closing my eyes, I don't miss the softness of her or the sweetness of her scent. The last thing I hear before I drift off to sleep is a quietly whispered, "Thank you."

The next morning, I start to stir, and I feel a pleasant warmth on my cock. I'm rock-hard and when I crack my eyes open, I see my dick is resting snugly against Remy's ass. Groaning at the sensation of her against me, the little minx wriggles her ass. A soft moan slips from her lips and it drives me fucking wild. Leaning forward, I bury my nose into her hair, nuzzling her scalp.

"Careful, Peach," I warn her, "you're treading on thin ice."

My hand grips her jaw and turns her head toward me, she's biting on her lip in that sexy way chicks do and somehow, my cock hardens further.

My fingers brush over her skin causing her to shiver and rock back against me again. "You're all kinds of trouble, aren't you, Peach?"

Before she can protest her innocence, my lips crash to hers, swallowing her answer. My hand cups the back of her head, holding her just where I want her, pulling her and her lips closer. She moans as my tongue enters her mouth. She groans as I cup her breast.

Pushing her into the mattress, I lean over her, my weight crushing her into the bed, not that she seems to mind because she wraps her legs around my waist, pulling her heat into the head of my cock.

I hiss at the contact. Breaking the connection between our lips, I pull back and stare down at her.

Both of us panting and flushed.

My eyes drop to her lips, swollen and red from my attack. The sight has me wanting more. Leaning down, my lips drop to her neck. I taste her pulse as she clings to me.

"Thatcher," she pants, her breath tickling my skin. Gazing back at her, all I see is hunger. Want. Need in her eyes, and I'm positive it matches mine.

With my eyes locked on her, I pull down my briefs and quickly discard them. Tugging down the sweatpants she wears, she lifts up, allowing me to remove her—my—shirt as well.

Once she's naked beneath me, my eyes land on her tits. Her glorious tits are begging for me to suck them. Reaching out, I tweak her nipple between my thumb and forefinger before sucking her taut hard peak into my mouth. I bite down, marking her. Making her cry out in delight.

She spreads her thighs, inviting me in. Grabbing a condom from the drawer, I roll it on. Gripping my shaft, I line myself up with her entrance but I don't push inside her. I wait, teasing her slit with my tip. Up and down, I trace her pussy lips, her hands grip my forearms. "Please," she begs, and it's music to my fucking ears.

Shaking my head, I smirk at her as I slide my hand down her body, she shivers at my touch.

She's so fucking responsive.

My cock is aching with the need to be inside her but the need to taunt and tease my little peach is stronger. Her gaze reflects that same want back at me and finally, I give her, me, us, what we want. I slide into her warm, wet tightness, hissing as she wraps around me.

"Oh, God," Remy murmurs, clinging to me as I slide my dick in and out of her cunt. I take her lips in a rough, desperate kiss. My fingers dig into the soft skin at her hips. She whimpers into our kiss and it turns me on hearing her pant like that. I start to move, slowly at first, driving her just as insane as she's made me.

Goosebumps erupt over her sensitive skin as she drops her head back, letting the pleasure I'm giving her envelop her from head to toe. My hips pick up speed, thrusting in and out, faster and faster. Faster than is acceptable for someone my age, a blinding pleasure builds in my spine, I need her to come.

"Fuck," I groan.

Sliding my fingers down to her clit, I gently brush against

her sensitive bud, circling the pad of my finger around and around, bringing her closer to release. She moans under me, arching her back, needing more. Wanting more. Her fingers grip my forearms and then I feel her shudder under me.

"Oh, God. Oh, God," she pants as she reaches her peak. Her pussy walls tighten around me, squeezing the hell out of my cock and that causes me to finally explode. My teeth clench down on her shoulder as everything courses from me into her and from her into me.

My body convulses as I lie over her panting my way through my release.

"Fuck," I grunt, dropping next to her and flopping onto my back. We both lie here, breathing hard.

"Yeah," Remy murmurs.

Her blush deepens the longer we lie here, naked next to one another. "I should ..." She lifts her hand, flicking her finger toward the door.

Yeah, she should but at the same time, I want her right here with me, so I ignore her.

Removing the condom, I toss it on the floor, then grip her arm and pull her toward my chest and wrap my arm protectively around her. We lie here, cuddling like a fucking couple. The girl I'm supposed to destroy has burrowed her way deep under my skin. I know she can't stay but fuck, this is nice.

Placing a kiss on her head, we lie here in each other's arms until she pushes on my chest and pulls away from me. I let her get up and watch as she re-dresses in her clothes from last night.

Lying here, I watch her. I want her again and frustration begins to build at that.

Everything is fucked up, this can't be right. I can't feel anything for Remington Hearst.

She's my enemy. Isn't she?

REMY

ONCE I'M DRESSED, I finger wave bye to Thatch and without a word sneak out of his room, only to bump into Saint and Reign when I turn around the corner.

"Morning, Princess," Saint teases. "Good night?" He raises his eyebrows suggestively and thrusts his hips back and forth. My mind replays what Thatch and I just did, and my cheeks heat at the memory and between my legs begins to pulsate. "I take it by the blush marring your beautiful cheeks…" He runs his finger down my heated cheek and I flinch at the contact. "This fine morning that you had a veeeerrrrry good night … and morning."

My mouth opens and closes a few times. I'm lost for words, so I do the mature thing and dart around them and race down the hallway toward the stairs to take me to the girls' floor.

Lady luck is NOT on my side this morning because I run into none other than Quinn Ellis when I turn the corner toward my room. "Doing the morning run of shame are we, Remington?"

"It's Remy," I snarl at her. For the life of me I have no clue why this chick is such a bitch to me. "And yes, yes, I am." I hold my head up high. I'm not letting this bitch think she's better than me but before anything else can be said, Alani races over and wraps her arms around me.

"I just heard—"

"That she's a lousy lay," Quinn spitefully snarls, interrupting Alani.

"Uhhh, no. Hudson said Rem was attacked last night." *Hudson? I thought Alani was with Reign?*

"I ... umm ... I, I'm fine."

"You were attacked," Quinn repeats the statement, "last night?"

Nodding, I look over to her and I notice she's now pale. "Did he ... was he ..."

"Spit it out, Quinn," Alani snaps at her, clearly missing the change in Quinn's demeanor.

"Forget it," she hisses and without another word, she storms away.

"That was fucking weird," Alani says, confirming my exact thought but as I watch Quinn walk away, I get a feeling she too has met the mystery man whom I met last night. "But seriously, babe, are you okay? Why didn't you call me? And, where did you sleep last night?"

"I'm fine ... I think. I didn't call you because well, I didn't and as for where I slept, I, umm—"

"You and Thatch did it ... didn't you? You skanky ho. How

was it? How many times did you come? How big's his dick? How—"

Pressing my finger over her lips, I shut her up. "I need coffee and maybe once I'm caffeinated I will answer all of your questions."

"Sounds like a plan. Let's head into town so little ears don't hear all the big dick gossip."

"Pretty sure everyone already knows because you have a big mouth."

"All the better for blowing with." She raises her eyebrows suggestively at me. "Now, do you need to shower before we go? Or do you want to smell like sex over breakfast?"

Shaking my head, I head toward my room muttering, "I need a shower." With my hand on the door handle, I look over my shoulder. "Meet you downstairs in ten?"

"It's a date." She nods and skips—literally—back to her room to get ready for our breakfast gossip date.

Stepping into my room, I close the door behind me and lean against the wood. I take a deep breath and sigh heavily. The last twelve hours have been a total whirlwind and now, now my feelings for Thatcher are all muddied.

Pushing off the door, my eyes widen when I see a vase with a lone pink peony sitting on my dresser. That wasn't there yesterday when I left and it's the same type of flower that I've received a few times now. Walking over to it, I pick it up and bring it to my nose. Closing my eyes, I inhale, and the sweet floral scent invades my nostrils. "Who sent you?" I whisper, placing the flower back down. The longer I stare at it, the creepier the pretty flower becomes. Who is leaving these for me? It's not Thatcher because I don't see him as a flowers and chocolates kind of guy but if it's not him, then who?

Turning around, I quickly strip off my clothes and walk into the attached bathroom and right this second, I'm so grateful I have my own en suite. For the first time ever I'm thankful for Mother Dearest throwing her weight around and getting the best of the best for me.

Ten minutes later, I emerge from my room freshly showered and ready for breakfast with Alani. Walking downstairs, I cross the foyer and notice Reign loitering off to the side, hidden in plain sight. He sees me and nods in that 'come here' kind of way.

Making a detour, I stroll over to him, wondering why he's loitering. It's almost as if he was waiting for me. "Hey," I offer in greeting, putting my hands in my pockets and rocking on the heels of my feet.

"Hey, you doing okay, Princess?"

"Was, till you called me Princess."

"Don't deny it, you love it when we call you Princess."

Shaking my head, I can't hold back my smile because he's right, I do love it, but I will never admit it out loud, even though my smile just now gives away my true feelings.

"Nicknames that you love aside, are you really okay?"

"Yes. No. I don't know. It's been a full-on and weird twelve hours."

"Welcome to life at Crestwood, where every day is a new adventure."

"You got that right." I nod in agreement.

"Just now, your facial expression, it reminded me of him. He'd get this glint in his eye when he was happy, genuinely happy, and you have that glint now."

"I am happy, I haven't been happy like this in so long and it's weird to feel like this 'cause I was attacked last night."

"In more ways than one," he teases and winks at me, and my eyes widen when it clicks, I had my suspicions but right now, I'm positive Reign was Arlen's secret guy. My breath hitches and I murmur, "It was you."

"What was me?" he questions me, confused.

"You're the one he was in love with." God, why did it take me so long to figure this out?

He stares blankly at me and his face morphs from happiness into anger in the blink of an eye. He steps forward and sneers, "You don't know shit, Hearst. Shut your fucking mouth or I'll shut it for you."

We fall silent and then I see Alani coming down the stairs. He glances to where I'm looking and smiles, just like he did a moment ago when we were talking about Arlen. "What about Alani?"

"That's a story for another time."

"Just don't hurt her," I warn him.

"No chance of that happening."

"Good."

"I've never met anyone like her, and she's been there for me when I needed someone."

"She is the best ... but remember my warning." I turn to go meet her but then I spin back to him. "Are you okay?"

"We don't have time for me to answer that question, Princess, but I'm not going to go all jumpy jumpy off the cliff." His eyes widen when he realizes what he just said. "Shit, I didn't mean that."

Nodding, I purse my lips, it's on the tip of my tongue to say, "I don't think he killed himself" but I'm still not sure I can trust him. I don't think I trust anyone here, well anyone except for Alani.

"It's okay, I know what you meant. Just know, I'm here if you ever need to chat."

"You really are just like him."

"He was the best."

"Yep." He sadly nods. "He sure was."

He pushes off the wall, steps around me, and walks toward Alani. Standing here, I watch them silently have a moment and it seems like over breakfast, she has some explaining to do as well.

THATCHER

NOT EVEN TWO minutes after Remy walks out of my room, the door swings open and Saint and Hendrix enter.

"How's the Princess?" Hendrix murmurs, pulling out a small flask and taking a huge gulp.

"Really, this early?" I question him.

"It's five o'clock somewhere and after my night with Quinn, I need something strong."

"What happened with Quinn?" both Saint and I ask at the same time.

"I'm not getting into it," he simply replies, pulling out his phone and ending the conversation. "Any leads on our attacker?" he finally says, breaking the silence.

"Nope, but when I do, the fucker will pay. He tried to touch what belongs to me."

"Any clue on who you think it could be?" Saint asks, snatching the flask from Hendrix to take a gulp. He hisses after he swallows because knowing Hendrix, it's tequila, and not the cheap knock off shit.

"Fucker, get your own." Hendrix shoves him hard, snatching the flask back.

Saint raises his fist ready for a fight, but stops when Hendrix stands towering over him, he's huffing like a bull ready to charge and his teeth and fists are clenched.

"Enough," I bark. "We need to work out what the fuck is going on. Someone is walking around Crestwood forgetting who the fuck is in charge."

Gaining their attention, they both look toward the door.

"Where the fuck is Reign?" Saint murmurs.

I start to question the same thing when my door opens and in walks the man in question. He's smiling like a fucker who just got some.

"Nice of you to join us, Brother," Hendrix drawls.

"Sorry, I got caught up."

Saint snorts and takes another swig while Hendrix rolls his eyes and uses his hands to mimic a blow job.

"Caught up my ass," Hendrix chuckles, "Did she swallow?" That comment earns him a slap up the side of the head from Reign. Which earns Reign a shove from Hendrix.

"Don't go there," he warns. We're all aware of how protective Reign is of Alani but this is over the top, even for him.

"Did you check the footage?" I ask him, needing to diffuse the situation before they breakout into a WWE competition.

"Yeah, nothing. You can't see the fucker because he's wearing a black balaclava. What I can tell you is he's tall, big build, and you only get a glimpse of him before he disappears completely."

"What?" the three of us scoff in unison.

"So, there isn't any more footage of him? What about near the school grounds?" I question. My voice is laced with frustration and anger.

Reign clicks his tongue. "Nope, nothing. It's like he's a fucking ghost."

"What do we do?" Hendrix asks the question that's on all our minds.

"We find the fucker, then destroy him." They all nod in agreement. "Anything suspicious you report to me."

Hendrix salutes me before he leaves, slamming the door closed behind him.

"If that's all, I'm going to go bury myself between some thighs and not come up for air." Reign chuckles, making Saint groan out loud.

Saint lies back on my bed, staring up at the ceiling. I can see his mind is a million miles away.

"Is there anything you want to talk about?" He jumps at my voice as if he forgot for a moment he was still in my room.

"It's nothing, forget it." Brushing me off, he rushes from the room, leaving me alone.

I don't push Saint, I know he'll talk when he's ready. Besides, he's the least of my worries right now because I need to find whoever threatened Remy last night.

Exiting my room, I find myself wandering around the school looking for Remy. Why? Fuck if I know, but what I do know is after this morning, something shifted between us. Don't get me wrong, I still want to see the Hearsts suffer but maybe not at the expense of her anymore.

When there's no sight of her, I assume she's with Alani. At least together they should be safe ... should be, but with this new fucker out there, no one is safe. Not even us.

REMY

"Okay, missy, spill?" I say to Alani after the waitress leaves with our breakfast order.

"Spill what?" she nonchalantly replies, looking at her nails.

"Don't play coy with me, Ms. Thomas."

"I'm not. I really don't know what you are implying, Ms. Hearst."

"I call bullshit but just know, I am here anytime you want to spill."

"And 'Miss-I-snuck-back-to-my-room-in-the-morning' the same goes for you too."

"Touché," I reply with a nod just as the waitress returns with our coffees.

Bringing the mug to my lips, I inhale and take a sip. "Why is it that little diners like this always make the bestest coffee?"

"No freakin' clue." She lifts her mug and takes a sip. That 'ahh coffee' smile appears on her face, but it drops just as the bell over the door dings. The hairs on the back of my neck stand on end and Alani's eyes widen.

Lowering myself down, I try to hide myself from view.

"What's he doing here?" Alani sneers, staring into her coffee mug, hoping to not garner his attention. Subtly, I glance over my shoulder and it's my turn for my eyes to widen when I see who just entered, Mr. Vanderbelt.

"Who?" I nonchalantly reply, feigning I don't know who she's referring to, but the fact I'm currently pretzeling myself in half to hide away, kind of gives away that I know. There's also the fact that in the small amount of time I've known Alani, she can now read me like an open book.

"You know who I'm referring to?"

"I do not."

"The lady doth protest too much ... while hiding."

"I'm not hiding," I refute but my high-pitched tone totally gives it away I am, in fact, trying to hide. "I'm snuggling into the comfort of this booth."

She eyes me. "Babe, you are one-billion-percent full of shit because the pavement outside is more comfortable than the booths in here. If it wasn't for the coffee and the waffles, we wouldn't be here."

Dammit, she has me there. "Fine," I relent, "I got a heebie-jeebie feeling so I lowered myself down, but when I saw who it was, I couldn't be bothered lifting myself back up. I don't even know the man. Why would I be hiding from him?"

She shrugs. "No clue but he's coming this way and his gaze is locked on the back of your head like a heat-seeking asshole."

He stops by our table. I can feel his stare boring into me. I plead with Alani silently but the traitorous bitch jumps up. "Be right back." Before I can protest, she takes off, *bitch!*

Putting on my big girl panties, I lift my head and quietly whisper, "Hello."

He doesn't say anything, he just stares at me. "You look so much like your father."

My eyes widen because I wasn't aware he knew my dad. And he's right, I'm a spitting image of Dad, thankfully I got none of Mom's features or personality. "Ummm, thanks," I tell him. What else do you say to a statement like that from a stranger?

"I trust you're settling into Crestwood Prep? My sons are treating you well?"

At the mention of his sons, I think back to this morning with Thatcher. Writhing in pleasure underneath him as he fucked me like no one has fucked me before. My cheeks heat at the reminder but it quickly disappears when a deep growl comes from above me and then we silently stare at one another again.

If I thought Thatcher had a mean stare, his is nothing compared to his dad's. His dad's is downright scary.

Opening my mouth, I go to tell him it's fine when once again, he shocks me. "Are you a conniving blackmailing asshole like your brother, Arlen?"

My eyes widen at his comment, and I stare at him open-mouthed in shock and confused at his words. Arlen was a gentle soul, there's no way we're talking about the same person.

Our silent stare off is broken when his phone rings. He pulls the ringing device out of his pocket and answers with a terse, "Speak." He listens for a few seconds, mumbles, "Do I have to do every-fucking-thing," and without saying good-bye, he spins on his heel and exits the diner. Leaving me staring after his retreating form but before he exits, he looks over his shoulder at me. I can't read the expression on his face, but I do know one thing, I don't like that man.

Alani comes back. "Ohh, no, he left," she coos, dropping into her chair and grabbing her coffee.

"Thanks for leaving me with the devil himself."

"You're welcome." She blows a kiss across the booth to me. "So, what did Daddy Vanderbelt want?"

"No clue. He told me I look like my dad. Said something untrue about Arlen. Ohh, and he asked if his sons are treating me well."

"Thatcher is ... with his dick."

Rolling my eyes, I can't help but smile because she's right, that's exactly what Thatcher did this morning. Being with him in a non-quick hate fuck in the library way, this morning was everything I thought it could be and more. Who knew it would take a creepy stalker guy to thaw the iciness coming from Thatcher and have us fucking like animals.

But will it remain? Or was it just an adrenaline fuck?

But most of all, when can we do it again? Will we do it again? Or was it just a one off 'sorry you were almost attacked' fuck?

"Why do you look like your dog just died?"

"What if Thatcher only fucked me because he felt sorry someone tried to attack me?"

"Please, you two have been dancing the fucking tango since you arrived in town. It was only a matter of time before you two did the naked tango. The events that led to said fucking had nothing to do with his dick entering your vagina." Except this is the second time his dick has entered my vagina. The way he fucked me in the library was different than this morning, but still ohhh so fucking good.

Nodding, I ponder her words. Right now, I'm confused and horny, not a good combination because I'm likely to make a stupid decision since I'm thinking with my vagina.

After breakfast, Alani and I head back to school. She splits off telling me she has an assignment to complete, but I notice she heads toward the boys' wing. "Assignment my ass," I mumble.

"What about your ass?" a deep voice booms, scaring the shit out of me.

"You scared the fuck out of me," I snap.

"Sorry," he defensively replies, holding his hands up in a 'I mean no harm' kind of way.

He steps closer to me, and I find myself stepping closer to him too. There's only a hair's width of space between us. He reaches up and cups my cheek, this feels very intimate and in my peripheral, I notice others watching us. They're murmuring about Thatcher and I being together and before I know what's happening, his mouth is covering mine and my legs are wrapped around his waist.

The students whistle and holler, singing, "boom-chicca-wow-wow" as Thatcher and I make out in the entrance of the school.

"That's enough, Mr. Vanderbelt, and, Ms. Hearst," Mr. Ashford snaps, stopping next to us. Closer than is acceptable for a teacher to be to any student, even if said students are dry humping in broad daylight.

"Sorry, Mr. Ashford," I reply, but Thatcher makes no move to put me down. "Thatch, put me down and we can take this up to my room."

"Boys are not allowed in the girls' quarters, Ms. Hearst. I'm sure you are aware of the rules?"

"And I'm sure you're aware that fucking a student isn't part of the rules either," Thatcher sneers at him.

"What?" I hiss as Thatcher drops me to my feet. This must be what Alani was alluding to the other week, but surely Rowan's dad isn't fucking a student.

"I don't take kindly to threats, Mr. Vanderbelt. You'll do well to remember that before you start accusing me of something as such," he snaps.

"Then don't lecture me about mine," I hiss.

Before anything else can be said, Thatcher laces our fingers together and we exit the building. He drags me toward his car. Clicking the fob, he opens the door and growls, "In." Not wanting to enrage him, for once in my life, I do as I'm told without arguing.

He slams the door shut, rounds the hood, and climbs into the driver's seat. Without uttering a word, he starts the car, reverses out of his spot, and speeds off.

We silently drive for an hour and come to a stop at a gorgeous lake at the bottom of a mountain. "It's beautiful," I murmur.

"This is my most favorite and sacred spot." My head snaps toward him, shocked he would bring me, of all people, here. "I've never bought anyone here before, not even my brothers."

"Why me?" I question, up until twelve hours ago he hated me, and I hated him, well, I think I hated him. Surely, I'm not that good in bed he'd forget all that. He shrugs and climbs out, leaving me sitting here confused but also feeling giddy he brought me somewhere so special. Walking to the front of the car, he leans against the hood and lights a cigarette.

I join him and I lean next to him, and he throws his arm around my shoulder, pulling me into his side.

This is very romantic and not Thatcher-like at all, but I'm loving every second of it and I'll take it while I can. You can never tell which version of Thatcher will appear at any given moment.

"Why did you bring me here, Thatch?" I finally ask when the silence gets too much for me.

"Because I wanted to."

"You wanted to?" I question because his answer is confusing and non-informative.

"Yep." He flicks his cigarette away, stands up, and faces me. He steps between my legs and stares into my soul. "And now, I'm going to fuck you on the hood of my car after I feast on your cunt."

His words head straight to my clit, and I want what he's suggesting more than I need my next breath. I'm ever so grateful to be wearing a dress right now.

Gripping the hem of it, I lift it over my head, leaving me in nothing but my panties—best thing about small tits, you can get away with no bra and at times like these, it's an added bonus.

Thatcher's eyes widen when he takes in my almost naked form. Hooking my fingers in the band of my panties, I lower them down and when I'm fully naked, I hop back onto the hood, lie back and spread my legs.

Sliding my hand between my thighs, it effortlessly slides though my slit. It's kind of embarrassing how aroused I am already but from the bulge in Thatcher's jeans and the heated look in his eyes, it's having the desired effect.

Circling my clit, I stare at Thatcher. "I'm waiting," I seductively drawl out as I press a finger inside. A moan escapes my lips, and it turns into a carnal groan when Thatcher shoves his face into my pussy and begins to tongue fuck me. I go to remove my hand, but he grips my wrist and covers my hand with his. He takes control of my movements and thrusts our fingers in and out of me while his mouth focuses on my clit.

I know what I like when I pleasure myself but combine that with the suction on my clit and I'm ready to explode.

"Come for me, Peach," he demands. How he knew I was close I don't know but whatever the case, I do. My walls clench around our fingers, and I scream when he bites my clit. That's the detonation needed and I come, soaking our hands and his face with my release.

He pulls his hand out and quickly frees his cock. He tugs me to the edge of the hood and with a flick of his hips, presses his dick deep inside of me. He grips my hips and begins to fuck me. I'm going to have bruises from his grip on me, but I don't give a rat's ass. I'm lost to the pleasure once again building inside of me.

Thatcher fucks like he lives life; hard, fast, and without regret.

Sex has never felt like this before. It's never felt so intense. So perfect, it engulfs me; mind, body, and soul.

My feelings for this man are growing deeper by the minute and I'm afraid I'm in over my head, but I've reached the point of no return.

I'm falling for Thatcher Vanderbelt and that both scares and excites me because if this all implodes, I don't know if I'll be strong enough to survive the aftermath, and if we do make it, I'm not sure we'd survive each other.

THATCHER

AFTER A PHENOMENAL TIME with Remy at my special place, I drop her back at her room and head up to mine. The afternoon was amazing in every way. After fucking her on the hood of my car, we re-dressed and made our way down to the lake's edge. I had all intentions of talking. Chatting to get to know her but before I knew it, she was in my lap riding me once again.

We didn't do much talking and when the air started to chill, we returned to school. Remy fell asleep on the car ride back and as much as I wanted to talk with her about last night and everything else, I knew she needed sleep.

As it is, I fell asleep as soon as my head hit the pillow once I got back. Only to be woken hours later by a thumping on my door. "What?" I bellow and when I swing it open, I come face-to-face with two police officers. "Can I help you?"

"Thatcher Vanderbelt?" one of them questions.

"Yeah," I reply.

"I'm sorry to inform you but your father, Thornton Vanderbelt, was murdered earlier tonight. We need you to come down to the station to answer a few questions."

Dad's dead? What the fuck?

"I'm sorry, he's dead?"

"This way, please," one says, grabbing my arm tightly.

"Hey, what the fuck?" I argue, gaining the attention of the few students lingering in the hallway at this time of morning.

"Thatcher, son, do you really want us to do this in front of your peers?" one of them says and when I see the look on his face, it dawns on me—they think I did it, they think I killed my father.

Fuck.

I've been sitting in this stuffy interrogation room for I don't know how many hours now. Answering the same fucking questions over and over. Giving the same fucking answers each and every time. These fuckers are trying to trip me up, but it's hard to trip someone up when they're innocent. The evidence they say they have placing me at the scene is bull-shit. I know what they're doing, they're doing everything they can to make me stumble. First fucking time in my life I didn't do something, just so happens to be the first time I'm arrested. Well, I think I've been arrested. They haven't finger-printed me or taken my mugshot and since I've never been arrested before, I don't know if this is the norm or not. My *Law and Order* obsession isn't shedding any light for me right now.

Sitting back in this uncomfortable metal chair, I still can't believe it. My father is gone. I'm not sad about that at all, a huge part of me is glad, and truth be told, I wanna high-five the person who took him out and then punch them in the dick for getting me arrested over it. That's fucked up, right?

Then I think of Mom, she's going to be devastated. She still loves the fucker, even after what he did to her.

What *they* did to her.

The day I discovered what they had done, it changed everything for me and my brothers ...

... I arrive at the house earlier than planned but that can't be helped. I know Dad's here somewhere, but I can't deal with him right now, I can never deal with him lately but what's new? I'm a rebellious teen with no respect for authority, his words, not mine, but like he'd know. He's never around, always working. Yeah, right, working. He's hiding something, I just know it but to be honest, I don't give a flying fuck about what Thornton Vanderbelt is up to.

Heading toward the common room to wait for my brothers, my steps falter when I hear hushed murmurs coming from the library. Quietly I tuck myself against the wall and listen.

"Keep your voice down," my father's voice hisses.

Edging closer, I await the reply but instead of words, I hear the crack of a hand across someone's face followed by, "Don't tell me what to do, Thornton Vander-fucking-belt, or not. I will ruin you," the feminine voice spits at Dad. Her voice is familiar, but I can't place it.

Sneaking closer to the door, I stop against it when I hear Dad growl, that's a sound he only makes when he's teetering on the edge, and I'm guessing he was the recipient of the slap I heard.

"I'd like to see you try," he sneers, then there's hurried foot-steps followed by a scuffle. I'm leaning against the door now, about to poke my head around when the door vibrates as if

someone just hit it. The sound echoes in the almost empty room and down the hallway where I'm standing. Yep, Dad's crossed over into pissed-off-ville. "Don't test me, woman. Do you want your husband to find out you fuck me on the side? You are nothing but a conniving whore, a place for me to stick my dick when I feel like it."

What the fuck? Dad's cheating on Mom? That son of a bitch. I'm going to fucking end him.

"You think I'm scared of you, you're nothing, Thornton," she throws back at him. The door shudders again and I hear footsteps, they are heading back into the room now. Whomever he's fucking on the side has big brass lady balls, I'll give the home-wrecking bitch that, but when I discover who she is, she's a dead woman walking. "You will accept her coming here, Thornton. It's her goddamn birthright." Who's her? I wonder and with one name, uttered, I know who has torn our mother apart. "Remington has the right to attend Crestwood just like her brothers," she snaps, and my eyes widen when I realize who the woman is. My father is having an affair with Rochelle-fucking-Hearst.

"Accept it or I will make your drug-addicted, drunk whore of a wife suffer even more. Now if you'll excuse me, I have somewhere I need to be."

I hear her heels on the parquet flooring and realize she's coming this way. "Shit, I need to hide," I whisper to myself as I silently duck around the corner. Poking my head out, I watch as Rochelle stalks out of the house, her head high like her shit doesn't stink.

When I hear the front door open and close, I turn on my heel and race up to my bedroom. Closing the door quietly behind me, I lean back against it and shake my head.

He's fucking dead to me. I hope he dies a slow painful fucking death full of syphilis from the whore he's been fucking around with. And my revenge on that stuck-up cunt is being handed to me on a silver platter, sending that little bitch to my school is not going to end well for her. She better watch her back. I'm going to end Remington Hearst for what her mother's done to my family. She *ruined my mother so it's only fair I ruin her daughter. An eye for an eye.*

The door swings open snapping me back to the present and before me is a new detective. He looks me up and down with disdain. He nods at the other two to give us a minute.

He slides into the chair across from me and takes his time placing a folder in front of himself. His gaze penetrates mine, trying to intimidate me but he fails, no one intimidates me.

"In all my years, I've never seen such violence. You must have really hated your father for committing such a heinous crime?"

He smiles then says. "Or are you covering for one of your brothers. three of you are triplets right? I mean you have to have some sort of bond, something that ties you together. but don't worry we'll question them next."

Clenching my teeth and fists, I'm ready to tell him to fuck off but I don't get a chance to. The door swings open and our family lawyer, Mr. King, enters the room. He slams his brief-case next to me on the table and nods in greeting before turning to the asshole before me, who looks like he's about to shit his pants. *Go King.*

"I sure hope you're not questioning my client without his lawyer present?" he throws at Detective Asshole.

"If the kid is innocent, why does he need a lawyer?" The detective makes a strong point but when I look to Mr. King, I notice he's smirking.

He leans forward and stares at the prick. "Precisely that. He's a kid. Yes he's eighteen but that's still a kid. My question, Detective, if you think Thatcher is innocent, why did you bring him to the station to question him? Why not just ask him in his room? Or better yet, ask him where he was last night when his father was brutally murdered because I bet you haven't even checked his alibi yet, have you?"

This time it's the detective's turn to clench his teeth and seethe. "FYI, my client was with his girlfriend all afternoon yesterday and then in his room until he opened the door to your officers earlier this morning. Unfortunately for you, holding my client here any longer to question him is no longer necessary since he clearly didn't do it." Mr. King smirks at Detective Douche, "You're welcome for doing your job for you." He looks at me. "Thatcher, let's get out of here."

He grabs his briefcase and waits for me to rise. Once I'm on my feet, I follow him out of the room and to my freedom.

Stepping outside, I squint but relish the feeling of the sun beating down on me. Dropping my head back, I look to the sky and smile. After being in that dark, dank room for so many hours, the fresh air and sun on my face is bliss. I'm so fucking happy to be free.

Looking down the street, I see my brothers waiting for me and I smile when I see them.

Mr. King tells me to stay out of trouble and he will do what he can. Personally, I don't give a flying fuck he's dead, if anything, I want to high-five the guy for removing him from our lives. Maybe this will give Mom a chance to move on now.

He heads off to the left and I head over to my brothers.

When I reach them, they each hug me and then Reign asks the question I'm sure is on all of their tongues. "Is it true? Is Dad dead?"

Nodding, I sigh. "Yeah, it's true, Dad's dead.

"So, the old man really is dead?" Hendrix asks.

"As a fucking doornail," I reply, crossing my arms and leaning against Saint's car. "He was murdered," I tell them.

They all shake their heads in shock, then Saint leans in. "Who the fuck did it?" He looks around at us, each of us shrugging our shoulders. Silence envelops us and then I notice they all have the same sheepish expression on their faces.

"I didn't do it," I sneer at them. "I didn't kill the old man," I hiss. I'm pissed off they think I could do that. Sure, I'd wished him dead, we all have at different times in the past but to actually take a life, fuck no. I'm too pretty for jail and orange washes me out.

"Then who did kill the asshole?" Saint asks again, his gaze flicking between the three of us.

I know I didn't kill him, so was it one of my brothers? Nah, we aren't the only ones who hated our father. Over the years, he's pissed off ninety percent of the people in this town. The suspect list will be endless.

My gaze darts around them and Hendrix catches my gaze. The question 'did you do it' sits on the tip of my tongue but I swallow it down. I know my brothers, none of us are capable of murder.

"You fucking think one of us did it?" he questions, his tone furious.

"I don't care if one of you did, just tell me so I can protect you." I'd fucking cover for any of my brothers.

"Fuck you, Thatch," Reign spits at me, "you really think one of us is a cold-blooded killer?"

"Well, you fuckers think I did it, why can't I think the same about you guys? To be honest, I don't know what to fucking think right now. All I fucking know is for the last however many hours, I've been interrogated for killing our old man. I didn't fucking kill him, so it was either one of you three, or we have a new threat to worry about."

They all avoid my gaze, and it pisses me off. Looks like we all have secrets right now and if we're not careful, those secrets are going to come to light, and it could spell trouble for each and every one of us.

REMY

THE LAST FEW hours have been shit. Thatcher's in jail and the rumor mill is going crazy, and to top it off, I swear some underwear of mine is missing and my crazy stalker has dropped off more flowers.

Alani has gone to get us coffees and as soon as she walks away, Brennan arrives. "Is it true?" he asks me, dropping down onto the sofa next to me in the reception room. He's closer than is comfortable but he's that close, I can't get away from him.

"Is what true?"

"Did Thatcher get arrested?"

"He has been arrested, yes."

"He did it?" he all but shouts. His outburst garners the attention of the other students lingering, waiting for more gossip, and the room falls silent. "Thatcher murdered his father," he says this part louder, causing many of the students to gasp in shock and murmur amongst themselves.

"He didn't do it," I bark angrily.

He rests his hand on my knee and I'm immediately uncomfortable but from behind him, the foyer brightens from the front doors opening and then Thatcher and his brothers come into sight.

A smile appears on my face, and I shove Brennan aside. Jumping up, I race over to them and launch myself at Thatcher. He catches me in the air—thankfully—and wraps his arms around me tightly. He drops me to my feet and we stare at one another.

"Thatcher, are you okay? Are the rumors true?" Before he replies, he grips my cheeks in his hands and presses his lips to mine. It starts out soft but quickly turns heated, leaving me breathless, light-headed, and ready to fuck him in front of everyone. We earn ourselves a round of "Ohhhs," "Oh my Gods," and also a "Just fuck her already."

Breaking the kiss, he pulls back and smiles at me. That little lip lift warms my heart and it's in this moment I realize I'm falling for him. I'm falling for the boy who has taunted me since I first arrived. For the boy who has made my life a living fucking hell but the last few hours not knowing, has changed everything. I know we started off rough, very rough, but no love story is smooth sailing, hello, *Romeo and Juliet*.

"I'm fine, Peach, but what rumors are you referring to?" He slides his arms around my waist and holds me close to him.

"Where do I start? There are so many right now. The first and foremost being, that you killed your dad."

"Well, the asshole is dead."

"I'm so sorry. Did you ..." I don't finish because if he did, I don't know how I'll react, but the unknown frightens me more than the fact the man I'm currently wrapped around may have killed someone.

"Do you think I did?"

Shaking my head, I honestly tell him, "No, I don't think you did. You're an asshole but you're no killer."

"Tell my brothers that."

"What?" I hiss, my eyes snapping to the guys who are standing off to the side, chatting to their friends and cousins.

"They all think I actually did it."

"No way."

"Yes, fucking way," he snaps through clenched teeth. He stares angrily over at his brothers. "The car ride here was angsty and shit. I need a shower and some sleep."

Reaching up, I cup his face before I take his hand in mine. I lace his fingers with mine. "Come," I demand and before he can reply, I drag him toward the stairs and we start the climb to my floor.

Hand in hand, we walk toward my room. Snickers can be heard in the corridor but I ignore them. Unlocking the door, I push it open and wait for Thatcher to enter behind me. Once he's in my room, I flip the lock, turn around, and lean against it. I stare at him as he walks over to my bed, drops down onto the edge, and stares at his feet.

"You okay, baby?" I ask him, surprising myself at using the word baby and how easily it passed through my lips.

"Yes. No. I don't fucking know." He lifts his gaze to mine. "But feel free to call me baby again."

"Baby," I say. "What do you need?"

He continues to stare over at me, I can feel his gaze deep in my soul and then he utters one word that takes my breath away, "You." We stare at one another silently. He beckons me forward with his finger. "I just need you, Rem."

Nodding, I walk over and stop in front of him. He reaches

out and wraps his arms around my upper thighs and ass. He rests his head on my stomach and hugs me. He doesn't utter a word, he just holds on to me like I'm a life preserver and without me, he'll sink into the abyss.

"Thatch," I whisper, running my fingers through his hair. "Talk to me."

"I don't even know where to begin."

"Say the first thing that comes to your mind," I tell him.

"I'm glad he's dead."

"And that's okay, everyone is entitled to feel what they feel and after meeting him, I kinda don't blame you."

"Hang on a minute, when did you meet him?"

"Alani and I were having breakfast, he came over. Said some crap about my mom and just gave off creepy vibes in general."

He nods at my answer and looks intently at me. "You ... you don't think I'm a monster for being glad someone viciously stabbed him to death?" He looks up at me, sadness reflects back at me. He may think he's happy he's dead but deep down, I think there's a part of him that is upset. That sadness will eventually bubble to the surface, you can't push your feelings away, I know. I tried. When Arlen died, at first I refused to believe he was gone and then one day, it hit me like a freight train and I fell apart. Then my life was uprooted, again, and I was sent here, to the last place my brother, who I was still grieving over, was alive. But Rochelle Hearst doesn't care about things like that. All she cares about is keeping the Hearst name in a shining light. Her daughter getting arrested for drunk and disorderly after her brother's memorial was unacceptable and she punished me by sending me away.

Shaking my head, I smile down at him. "Not at all, we all grieve differently but when the person who died is a horrible asshole, there's no rule book for grieving."

"Horrible asshole doesn't even begin to cover the type of man Thornton Vanderbelt was. The suspect list will be long

and even though I'm currently sitting in the number one position, I promise you, Rem, I didn't do it. I did not kill my dad."

"I believe you, Thatch, I believe you. You don't need to
defend yourself to me."

"I wish my brothers thought that."

"They too are grieving, give them time to process." He
nuzzles himself into my belly and it's an oddly beautiful
moment. "How's your mom handling it?"

His head snaps up to mine, "Fuck, Mom. I need to go see
her."

"Then let's go."

"You wanna meet my mom?"

"Thatcher, she just lost her husband, she's going to need
all the support she can get. You're all going to need support."

He nods and stands up, causing me to shuffle backward
from his abrupt movements. He grips my cheeks in his palms
just like he did downstairs, and stares intently at me. "I ... I ...
thank you." For a second there I thought he was going to
utter the 'L' word and to be honest, I'm a little sad he didn't,
but now isn't the time to worry about that, I need to be there
for him, his brothers and his mom.

After a sexy shower with Thatcher, we dry off and then head
to see his mom. I ask about his brothers, but he's still pissed
about them accusing him of murder so just the two of us head
to his mom and dad, well, I guess just mom's place now. I
really want to junk punch them all for thinking that about
Thatcher. Sure, he's an asshole but he's definitely not a
murderer, none of them are.

After we shower, we drive to his childhood home to check
on his mom. His phone rings again and like the other times,

he lets the call ring out only for it to immediately start to ring again. This time I see Reign's name on the screen. He declines it and mumbles something about his brothers being fuckers. Gripping the steering wheel tighter, he keeps his focus on the road.

Turning into the Vanderbelt driveway, Thatcher reaches over and squeezes my hand resting on my thigh. "Thanks for coming with me."

"No need to thank me. I told you I would and the same goes for the rest of your family too."

He lifts my hand to his lips and places a kiss on my knuckles. "I'm so fucking lucky to have you in my life."

"Hell, yeah you are, I'm a catch," I throw back at him with a wink. He smiles over at me and it's breathtaking. Thatcher is hot, there's no two ways about it but when he smiles, genuinely smiles, I have no words to describe him.

Pulling up I notice his brothers' cars are here, it seems they had the same idea too. "Did you know they were here?"

He shakes his head. "No, I've been ignoring them and haven't spoken to them since they accused me of killing him earlier today."

Now it's my turn to nod and without another word, we climb out of his car and when we reach the hood, he laces his fingers with mine and then we climb the stairs. Opening the front door, we step into the foyer and my eyes widen when I take in the grandeur of this place. "Fuck me," I murmur, "this isn't at all what I expected."

"Did you expect a dark and ominous house?"

"Uhhh, yeah. The outside is all gothic and dark but inside, it's the opposite of that."

"Looks can be deceiving," he sadly murmurs, and I think he might be referring to himself as well as the house.

"Thatcher," our housekeeper, Lisette, says when she sees us. "Back again?"

Nodding, he looks uneasy at her mentioning that. "Yeah, here to check on Mom."

"You boys are so good to her. I'm sorry for your loss."

"No you're not, Lisette. Dad was a cunt—"

"Language, young man," she admonishes Thatcher and I can't help it, a snort escapes me.

"And who might you be?" she asks, turning her attention to me.

"Remy, I'm ..."

"She's my girlfriend," Thatcher informs her, surprising me with his choice of words, but his words also make me all warm and fuzzy on the inside. How did we go from hating one another, to fucking, and to now dating?

"It's lovely to meet you, Remy." She looks to Thatcher. "Your mom and brothers are in the dining room just finishing up a late lunch. Shall I fetch you a plate? It's leftover beef bourguignon."

"I'm good thanks," Thatcher tells her. She nods and then looks at me.

"I'm fine as well, thank you."

She nods and heads off farther into the house. Thatcher takes my hand again and we make our way to the dining room. Laughter can be heard coming from the room and when we step inside, all eyes look to us.

"Thatcher, honey, what are you doing here?" his mom asks, rising to her feet and walking over to us. She wraps her arms around her son, and he freezes for a moment, then he drops my hand and embraces her.

"Mom, are you okay?" he asks her.

"I'm okay," she tells him, cupping his cheek. She doesn't look like the frail woman he's previously described. Sure, her eyes are rimmed red, no doubt from crying, she was the one to find Mr. Vanderbelt after all, but she's not cowering like previously described. "And who might you be?"

"Mom, this is my girlfriend, Remy." His brothers make

smooching sounds, earning themselves the bird from Thatcher.

"It's lovely to meet you, Mrs. Vanderbelt."

"You too, Remy, and please, call me Estelle."

"Okay, Estelle. I'm sorry for your loss."

"Thank you," she replies. "Are you joining us to eat?"

"Not today, Mom, we just wanted to check on you."

"You boys are too good to me. Come, come join us while we finish up."

Estelle ushers Thatcher and me to the table and as we take our seats, I notice there's animosity between Thatcher and his brothers.

"Hey, guys," I greet them.

They each mumble a hello and offer me a head nod. Ignoring Thatcher, they go back to eating. An awkward silence falls over the table, the only sound is the scraping of cutlery on the plates and chewing, loud chewing. Thatcher is fidgeting beside me and it's unnerving to see him so non-Thatcher-like. Reaching over, I take his hand and link my fingers with his. He looks over at me and I wink at him, his lip lifts slightly.

"So," Hendrix says, breaking the silence, "if Thatcher didn't kill him, who the fuck did?"

"Hendrix," Saint scolds, punching him in the arm. "Show some respect, Mom's grieving."

All eyes move to the head of the table. Estelle is staring into space, her face blank.

"You okay, Mom?" Thatcher asks her. At the sound of his voice, she turns her gaze to his.

"I ... I don't know how I feel right now, it's hard to grieve for someone who you hated as much as you loved."

Everyone's eyes widen in shock at that revelation. Mine included because as far as I was aware, she loved Thornton unconditionally.

"You hated him?" Thatcher whispers, his voice laced with shock.

She nods. "I hated him, but I also loved him. Your father and I had a complicated relationship. He wasn't the easiest man to live with—"

"No shit," the boys all echo together.

"But underneath it all, he was still the man I fell in love with all those years ago. When you find love"—his mom looks at Thatcher and me and smiles—"you'll understand where I'm coming from. It's funny, I keep expecting him to come marching in, commanding the room like he always did but then I remember, he's gone."

"It'll take time, Mom," Thatcher comforts her.

She nods. "I know, Thatcher. I guess all we can do is remember the good times with him and find a way to move on." A silence falls over the room again. Estelle claps her hands. "Enough with the sadness, he wouldn't want us to wallow—"

"Are we talking about the same man?" Hendrix says. "He'd want the biggest and grandest funeral. A statue erected in his honor and while we're at it, a memorial holiday for him too."

"Saint Fuckwit Day," Saint suggests, "has a nice ring to it?"

"Saint," Estelle admonishes him, "watch your language. Personally, I think Saint Asshat Day has a better ring to it."

This suggestion causes everyone to laugh and for the first time since we arrived, Thatcher seems to relax. He reaches out and takes his mom's hand and squeezes. "You'll get through this, Mom. We're all here for you."

"Thank you, I appreciate that. We'll take it one day at a time."

After eating, Saint, Reign, and Hendrix say their good-byes. Thatcher and I hang back since we arrived late. Lisette brings in coffee for Estelle and me and a scotch for Thatcher. "So, Remy, tell me about yourself."

"There's not much to tell." Wrapping my hands around the mug, I take a sip and smile. This is a good coffee, a reeeeeally good coffee. "I transferred here from Alton Academy at the request of my mother."

"I take it the two of you aren't close?"

"You could say that. I'm a disappointment in her eyes. Nothing I do pleases her."

"I'm sure she doesn't feel like that."

"Trust me, Rochelle Hearst means every word that comes out of her mouth."

"You're a Hearst?" she questions me, her eyes widening at this revelation.

"Yep," I reply, letting the 'p' pop, something that would piss my mother off.

She nods. "You aren't a cheating, scheming whore like your mother, are you?"

"Mom," Thatcher growls, "Remy isn't a whore."

"Her mother certainly is."

Thatcher shoves his chair back, knocking it over in anger. He rests his fists on the table and seethes. Then his head snaps up. "Holy fucking shit," he hisses, turning to face his mother. "You ... you knew?" he questions his mom.

She nods. "Yes, Thatcher, I knew all about Rochelle and your father." She lowers her gaze and sighs. Lifting the mug to her lips, she takes a sip of her coffee and then looks to her son. "I've known about all the women your father fucked behind my back, but him and Rochelle, that one was the hardest to swallow."

She looks at me and sadly smiles at me. I sit here rapidly blinking, processing all that just came out. "My ... she ... my ... my mom slept with your dad?" I look to Thatcher for confirmation but Estelle answers for him.

"She did more than that, dear, she fell in love with him."

"What?" Thatcher and I both screech.

"Thornton and Rochelle have been sleeping with each other for years. There was a time when Rochelle and I were friends, best friends even, but when he chose me over her, our friendship ended. Years later, she thought she'd won but by that point, your father would never leave us. Without me and my family's money, he'd have nothing."

"Dad was broke?"

"Your father was, yes. Grandpa McQueen has been keeping us afloat for a few years now."

"So, why did you stay? Why not leave?"

"For you boys, I wasn't leaving you with him to get his claws into you. You boys are my everything. I'm sorry I let you all down. I should have been a better mother."

"Mom, you did what you could, especially being married to that asshole."

"He wasn't always an asshole, when I first met him, he was everything a girl dreamed of. Captain of the football team. Smart. Loving. Fun."

"Are we talking about the same man?"

"Yes, we are but one day after college and just after you were born, he started to change. He became verbally abusive, he told me I was nothing without him. He gradually got worse, and I believed every taunt he threw my way. I couldn't tell Daddy or Grandpa, I didn't want to admit to my failures. You and your brothers were all I had, and one day he threatened you boys. Said if I ever told anyone anything, he'd take you boys and run, so I stayed. I played the dutiful wife and mother while he fucked anything with tits. To cope, I drank and took pills. When he lost it all, Grandpa swooped in to help. They all blamed me for Thornton losing everything. 'Estelle's drinking did this to him' they said. Not wanting to tarnish our names, they paid for everything. Saving us from going under."

"Mom," he says, pulling her in for a hug. "I'm so sorry for everything, I should have been a better son."

"No." She shakes her head. "This is not on you. This is on me. Maybe now he's gone, I can become the woman I once was again."

"I think without him, we will all become the people we were meant to be." Thatcher pauses. "But Mom, who killed him?"

"That's something we may never know." She stares off into the distance as she says this. How she's so calm about it right now, I will never know. If Thatcher was murdered, I'd burn the world down to find who did it, but as she said, they had a complicated relationship. But why do I get the feeling she's hiding something?

REMY

THATCHER and I have just arrived back at school. Tonight was eye-opening. Very eye-opening. We enter his room and I ask him the one question that has been on my mind since I found out about my mom and his dad. "Thatcher …"

"Yeah." He turns to face me. "What's up, Peach?"

"Did … did you do all those things to me because of my mom?"

He stares at me blankly and for a moment there I think he's not going to answer, but just when I'd given up hope, his shoulders drop and he whispers, "Yeah, I did."

"Why?"

"Because I'm an asshole. I thought punishing you for your mom's actions would make me feel better."

"And did it?"

"Kinda."

"Really? How so?"

"Seeing you flustered gave me a rush like I've never felt before, but the more we pushed you and the more you pushed back, the harder I felt the need to punish you."

"That's messed up."

"What can I say? I'm a messed-up asshole but what's done is done."

If he thinks what's done is done, he's sorely mistaken and he doesn't know me at all. I'm no pushover, I will get revenge for what he's done, just not in the taunting mean way he did with me. I will bide my time and when the time is right, I will strike. Game on, Thatcher Vanderbelt, game on.

"Do I get points for the fact that along the way, my feelings changed for you? No longer did I want to punish you for her misdeeds, I wanted to punish you because it turns me the fuck on."

"You do realize punishing me for what MY mom and YOUR dad did is a dick move, right?"

"Well yeah, when you put it like that I do." He drops onto his bed, resting his elbows on his knees. From the dejected look on his face, I can tell he feels like shit, and so he should, but he also saved me from my stalker and in the last few days, he's made me feel alive and given me some of the best orgasms of my life. For the first time in a very long time, I feel happy and that's something I haven't felt since before Arlen died.

An evil thought crosses my mind, I should make him pay for that, but I think I'd rather get an orgasm or two, that way it'll be a win, win, big-O win.

"I think it's only fair I get to punish you."

He lifts his gaze to mine and fuck me sideways, this man

is stunning. His good looks almost throw me off my game, but I'm determined to win, tonight anyway.

"What did you have in mind?"

"I can think of something, Thatch." I reach out and tap his head in a slightly condescending way. "Don't you worry your pretty lil' head about that."

"Only pretty, Peach?"

Shrugging my shoulders at him I turn around and begin to unbutton my shirt. Spinning back around to face him, his eyes lock on to my chest. He bites his lip in that sexy as fuck way and my panties dampen when I see the imprint of his cock through his pants.

My hands work down the buttons on my blouse. With the opening of each button, I reveal more of my pale-pink lacy bra.

"What are you doing, Peach?"

"Nothing," I nonchalantly reply as I walk over to him and drop onto his lap, straddling his thighs. Resting my hands on his shoulders, I stare into his eyes. Leaning down, I whisper, "It's time for your punishment to begin." I bite his earlobe but rather than turning him on, I think I turn myself on.

"You can punish me like this anytime, Peach."

"We'll see, baby, we'll see."

Leaning forward, I press my lips to his when the fire alarms suddenly blare. "To be continued," I murmur against his lips.

Rebuttoning my blouse, we exit his room and hand in hand we join everyone on the driveway near the entrance. We watch the fire trucks come racing toward us and up to the school building.

Looking around the students, I notice everyone is looking at me and murmuring my name when out of nowhere, Alani throws her arms around me. "Ohh, thank God, you're safe."

"Why wouldn't I be safe?" I question her, confused.

"The fire, Rem, it started in your room."

THATCHER

"WHAT THE FUCK did you just say?" I hiss, glaring at Alani when she tells us the news about the fire.

"The fire ..." she begins, but when my brothers join us, she stops talking when Reign puts his arm around her and pulls her into his side. He leans down and whispers in her ear, causing her to giggle and smile. Confirming my suspicion something is going on between the two of them, but now's not the time to focus on Reign and his ... whatever she is.

"Focus," I snap, throwing daggers at the two of them.

"Ohh, right, yeah, so, the fire. So it, umm, it started in Remy's room."

My eyes widen again when I hear that. Anger courses through me and the next thing I know, I've forced my way into the building and I'm standing at the doorway to Remy's burned-out room.

"Son, you can't be in here, you need to go back outside," a fire marshal tells me.

Ignoring him, I step up to him. "What caused the fire?"

"I'm sorry, I can't tell you that information. If your teachers wish to tell you, then you'll be notified but unfortunately, son, you need to leave and let us do our jobs."

Spinning away from him, I look into what's left of her room, it's completely destroyed. This wasn't an accident. This was intentional and whoever did this, they won't stop until ... until, I have no clue.

What I do know is my peach is in danger and it's up to me to find out who's behind this.

"Well, what the fuck happened?" Hendrix asks when I meet back up with everyone out front.

"They wouldn't say, but there is no doubt in my mind this wasn't an accident. Whoever is trying to destroy us just made it personal by going after Rem." Turning to face her, I tell her what I saw. "Your room is destroyed, Peach. I'm so sorry."

She walks over to me and wraps her arm around my waist, resting her head on my chest. Wrapping my arms around her, I hold her close, offering her the comfort of a hug but wishing I could do more. My brothers sense what I'm thinking, and over her head we share a look that says *someone needs to pay for this*. The search for whoever murdered our father is on pause right now because finding out who's stalking my girl, who is alive and breathing, is more important. Funny thing about this, my gut is telling me one of my brothers knows something about Dad's death. They're either covering for each other, or they know who did it.

"What now?" Saint murmurs.

Looking between my brothers, I know whatever happens we have to stick together. We can't turn on each other now, so I need to put my suspicions aside and focus. "We find out who's trying to sabotage us and end them. We are still The Lords and this is our fucking school."

My brothers nod.

"We're in," my cousin says, coming toward us with the rest of our friends.

"Yeah, we've got your back, Thatch," Conroy tells me, squeezing my shoulder.

"Always, man. Tell us what you need," Lennon says.

Nodding, I realize we can't discuss it here. "We meet in the cemetery tomorrow night at midnight, this needs to end before someone else dies."

Each of them nods in agreement and then we split up.

Pulling Remy into my side, I lead us away from the rest of the student body and walk us around the side of the school. Pushing her against the side of the building, I stare deep into her eyes. "I need you safe, Peach. I need you to stay with Alani tomorrow while we handle this."

"What? No, I want to come."

"No fucking way, Peach. Whoever this is, they've made you a target, probably because of me. I'm not letting them touch you. Fucking understand?"

"Please," she begs, putting on that doe-eyed look that has the potential to bring me to my knees, but I can't risk her safety, not now.

Shaking my head, I cup her cheeks. "Not a fucking chance." Leaning forward, I press my lips to hers. Her hand travels down my chest, stopping just at the top of my trousers. She smirks at me and cups my junk. She looks sweetly at me and begins to stroke me. "Not going to change my mind, Peach."

"What if I do this?" She sinks to her knees in front of me and before I can protest, she has my already hard cock out—fucking traitor—and she wraps her lips around the tip. Hollowing her cheeks, she sucks my shaft into her mouth.

"Fucking hell," I groan, throwing my head back as she pulls back and suckles on the tip before sliding back down.

With the most amazing self-control ever, I ignore the need to fuck her face and I remove my dick from her mouth, my cock glistening with her saliva. "Not going to work," I hiss between clenched teeth, close to breaking.

"Fine." She relents and pushes on my thighs to stand, but I place my hand to her head, stopping her.

"Can't not finish, Peach, look what you did to me." I nod toward my stiff cock.

Her gaze drifts to where my cock drips with precum, waiting for her to lap it up. She lifts her gaze to mine but doesn't move and then ever so slowly, she leans forward, opens her mouth, and swallows my dick again. Inch by inch my cock slides into her mouth. My fingers curl around her hair and when her nose brushes my abs, I begin to fuck her mouth. Faster and faster, my cock slides in and out.

My cock twitches and with a guttural groan, I come. Remy swallows every last drop, making sure not to spill or miss any of my cum.

She smiles up at me, clearly pleased with herself, but I just got off so I'm not sure who's the winner right now.

Standing in the cemetery, the chill in the air picks up but the anger coursing through me is enough to keep me warm. We aren't leaving this cemetery until we come up with a plan to take this fucker down. No one messes with The Lords and lives to tell the tale.

"What if we bait the person?" Hart suggests.

"What?" Saint sneers at him, he's on edge today, really on edge.

"Right, like setting a trap?" Conroy murmurs.

"Yes, exactly, we set them up. The fucker thinks they have the upper hand, but really, it's us," Hart matter-of-factly states, pleased with himself for suggesting this grand plan.

Smiling, I nod, finally we're getting somewhere. "Any suggestions on how to trap the fucker?"

I'm met with silence. "Wow, great suggestions everyone," I snarl. Frustration creeps back in that we are once again at a roadblock with no one having any great ideas.

"Whatever we decide, it needs to be believable," Rian offers. It's not a suggestion but he's right, this person isn't a fool. They aren't going to be easily caught or fooled.

"He's right," I agree, nodding. "This person has been one step ahead of us the whole fucking time, but that's about to change." *As long as we can come up with a foolproof plan.*

My phone vibrates in my pocket, but I ignore it. We need to figure out a way to trap this fucker and we need to do it yesterday.

"Look, whatever happens we need to fucking get them. I mean, they fucking burned down Remy's room. What's next, the whole fucking school?" I snap, my frustration ready to explode.

Reign's phone starts ringing now. Groaning as he hates talking on the phone, he pulls it out and answers when he sees who's calling. Watching him, the hairs on my neck stand on end as he says hello.

"Whoa, whoa, calm down, baby, I can't understand you."

"Put her on speaker," I hiss. Reign does and the moment I hear Alani's sobs fill the silence, I know something is wrong.

"Sh ... sh ... she's gone."

"What do you mean gone?" I shout.

"I ... I ... I went to the bathroom, I was only gone for a second and when I came back to my room, she wasn't here. My room's a mess, it looks like there was a struggle and now she's not answering." She's crying harder now.

It takes a few beats for me to realize she's referring to Remy. *Remy is gone.*

"That fucker has her," I sneer.

Spinning on my heel, I bolt out of the cemetery and run back toward the school, I don't stop for anyone. The seven of them follow close behind me. By the time I make it to Alani's room, my chest is heaving. Pushing the door open, I take one look around her room and fall to my knees.

I couldn't save her.

Vaguely, I hear my name but I don't move. My head is filled with the sound of Remy's sweet, sweet voice and images of her beautiful face.

Even with the power I hold at this school, I couldn't keep her safe.

What if? Fuck, I can't even think like that.

Like a zombie rising from the dead, I move through Alani's room searching for anything to give me a clue, but I come up empty-handed.

Running my hands through my hair, I tug on the roots. "Fuck, Peach, where are you?"

REMY

Man, that was a vivid dream, I think as I slowly begin to wake up. I dreamed someone attacked me and took me from Alani's room and strapped me to a bed in a cabin by the lake, but when I go to roll over, I realize I can't move.

Cracking my eyelid open, I realize I really am strapped to a bed in a cabin. Quickly, I close my eyes and hope when I reopen them, I am just still in my dream. Peeling them open again, my breath hitches in my chest when I realize it wasn't a dream—I really AM strapped to a bed in a cabin. *Fuck!*

Closing my eyes again, I breathe deeply to calm my erratically beating heart. I need to compose myself so I can get the fuck out of here.

"I know you're awake," a deep voice says and the sound of it shudders through my body. "You're so beautiful when you sleep."

My eyes snap open and I look around, trying to find the fucker. "Fuck you, asshole, when I get out of here, I'm goi—"

"To what, huh? I hold all the fucking cards right now, and in case you need me to spell it out for you …" He steps forward and when he comes into view, I see he's wearing a black balaclava, covering his face. He's in a long-sleeve, charcoal-gray Henley and denim jeans that hang loosely off his hips. "I'm free and you, well, you're strapped to a fucking bed, just where I want you."

"For now," I hiss at him.

"Those boys have turned you into a cunt. A few weeks with me and you'll be back to the Remington I remember."

"Do I know you?"

My question obviously pisses him off because he stalks over and backhands me. My head snaps to the side and that's when I see another bed in the room. There's someone lying on their side with their back to me. A ratty blanket is pulled over them and I can't tell if they're male or female. They haven't moved and I begin to wonder if they're dead.

"They're not dead, just drugged. Fucker kept spewing shit about having my balls and making me pay. Blah blah fucking blah."

He walks over to the person and smacks them in the back of the head but again, they don't move. Whatever drug this fucker gave them has knocked them out cold. "Look who's making who pay now, asshole," he sneers with a grin.

Lifting his hand, he flicks them behind the ear, just like Grayson and Arlen used to do to me when we were younger. They still don't move and I begin to freak out at the thought of this asshole drugging me and doing who knows what to me while I'm out.

A phone rings from the other room. My captor looks at me and raises his index finger at me. If he gets close enough, I'll bite it off and spit it in his face. "I need to get that, but you make one peep and that bitch of a friend of yours will be joining you and your roomie."

He turns around and walks out of the room, slamming the door behind him, but from the force it doesn't click shut, it remains open an inch.

Leaning forward, I try to get a look into the other room, but I'm strapped down pretty well and I can't see shit. "Fuck, fuck, fuck," I chant to myself, but I stop when I hear the asshole who has me say, "I have it handled, don't get your vagina in a twist." Followed by silence. "Yeah, yeah, yeah, it's all on track. I even managed to—" But he's cut off, I really wish he had the call on speaker so I could hear what the other person is saying or know who he's talking to.

Letting out a frustrated sigh, I stare up at the gross ceiling above. It's caked in dust, cobwebs, mold, and ... and is that pizza sauce? *No, you moron, it's probably blood,* I internally scold myself. Actually, the whole place is disgusting. My inspection of the room is interrupted when assface—my name for my captor— returns. "Good girl, seems that fucker instilled *some* obedience into you after all."

"Fuck you," I hiss.

"Now now, sweet thing, don't be like that." He climbs onto the bed and straddles my hips. "You just lie there like a good little girl and when the time is right, we can be together. Just like we were meant to be."

He leans down and nuzzles into my neck. Breathing in deeply, he moans. *Did this fucker just sniff me?* He sniffs me again and licks up my neck and along my jaw. I shudder and close my eyes, clearly that was the wrong thing to do because he slaps me across the face. My cheek stings from the contact.

"Don't make me hurt you, sweetheart. You don't want to get on my bad side. Follow the rules and I'll love you like you've never been loved before. You and I can be happy together and we can rule this fucking place. We can make those Lord cunts bow down to us."

"You are fucking delusional if you think that, A. The Lords will bow down to you. B. that I will ever fucking love you, and C. I will never fuck someone like you. I don't love or fuck psychos who kidnap and drug people."

"No, you just fuck assholes who stalk and prey on sweet innocent girls."

He reaches out and grips my chin roughly between his fingers. "You will be mine, Remy. There is no other way this will end."

"He'll come for me and when he does, you are a dead fucking asshole."

My words clearly piss him off because he rears his hand back and slams his fist into my face. My vision dots and as the darkness takes me, the person on the other bed rolls over and I'm shocked to see who my roomie is.

THATCHER

It's been two days and we still have no clue who took Remy or where the fuck she is.

At this point I'm numb, downing my third gulp of the bottle I currently have in my hand. I can't even taste the alcohol, the lingering taste in my mouth is bland, if only my father could see me now. I almost want to dig up his grave to be sure he's in fact fucking dead because if he wasn't I'd think that bastard took her to spite me. He'd throw a fit knowing how drunk I am right now, but fuck him. Fuck everyone. Fuck everything.

My head's fuzzy. My vision is blurred, I feel like I might

pass out, and I'd welcome the blackout because in my dreams, my peach is safe with me here at school.

A voice pulls me back before I drift off. I mumble my annoyance but I'm too drunk to fight them off.

"Being drunk isn't going to help when we find her," Reign sneers as he tries to move me, but my dead weight makes the task impossible for him. "A little help," he hisses, and his tone causes me to chuckle, earning myself a slap to the side of my face. The crack against my cheek wakes me up a little and when I open my eyes, I see Hendrix kneeling in front of me too. He removes the bottle from my grasp.

"Hey, I wasn't done," I whine, trying to snatch the bottle back but in my inebriated state, I just clutch at air.

"You're done." Hendrix smacks my hand away and passes the bottle to Saint, who takes a sip.

"Dude, we're trying to get him sober, not get you drunk," Reign chastises him.

Saint chuckles and takes another swig.

"If," I grumble and hiccup. I'm a little more drunk than I thought if I'm drunk-upping.

"If what?" Reign asks.

"You said when we find her, I said if. If we find her."

Saint shakes his head. "It's not like you to give up so easily. I thought you loved her?"

"Saint," Hendrick scolds, "time and place, dude." He turns his gaze back to me. "Come on, bro, like seriously. I thought you'd be losing your shit right now, not drinking yourself into a stupor where you're no help to her or anyone." He pauses and runs his hands through his hair. "We can't fuck this up," Hendrix states glaring at me.

Nodding, I process his words. He's right, I need to do better. I need to pull my head out of my ass and find my girl. Pushing myself up, I stagger slightly while I stand.

"What if whoever has her ..." I stop myself, I can't fucking think about what they're possibly doing to her right now.

"Bro, we need to find answers, surely someone knows something," Hendrix murmurs.

"You're right." I nod and with that surge of adrenaline, I don't feel as drunk anymore. *I'm coming, Peach.*

Storming from my room, I make my way to the cafeteria, hell-bent on finding some goddamn answers. And some food to soak up the liquor currently swimming throughout my body.

"Listen up," I bellow at the top of my lungs, making a grand entrance as the doors fly open. The entire cafeteria comes to a stop. Rian pulls out a chair for me. Climbing up, I look around the room, making sure all eyes are on me. "I know someone knows something." Kicking some kid's tray over in frustration, his dinner flies across the room. "I want fucking answers, so anyone who knows anything about Remy's disappearance, step forward now. To sweeten the deal, I'll offer up a reward for those who are forthcoming with information that leads to us finding her, but it better fucking lead to me finding her or I'll kick your fucking ass every-fucking-day for the rest of your time here at Crestwood."

Everyone stares but no one moves.

No one speaks.

No one breathes.

Not a single fucking person comes forward.

"You have twenty-four-fucking-hours to come forward with any information. After that time, the offer is off the table, and we may just make the rest of everyone's time here at Crestwood a living fucking hell." Hendrix growls for emphasis and it causes my lip to slightly lift. "I'm not fucking playing, people," I whisper between clenched teeth, slamming my foot onto the table to show I mean business. This causes everyone to jump.

Stepping off the chair, I almost twist my ankle due to my drunkenness. My hand grips the chair I just climbed off and I hurl it across the room. It smashes into the wall with a loud thud. Anger seeps from me in waves. My breathing is harsh and violent as I take deep breaths. Some of the girls scream but all I see is her, my peach, begging for me to find her.

"T." Reign grips my shoulder, squeezing, but I ignore him. My gaze darts around the room, staring into the crowd. Someone here knows something. Without a fucking doubt in my mind someone here knows where she is.

Forcing my way through the crowd, I head outside, needing some fresh air ... and possibly more alcohol.

"Thatcher," Conroy shouts after me and follows me out.

"I need to find her," I hiss, lifting my hands above my head then fisting my hair. Groaning when Conroy's hand on my chest stops my pacing.

"We'll find her," he says, like it's so fucking easy. "After your little 'tell me where she is speech' the Dean notified the cops. No doubt you will be suspect number one since, well, you know." He doesn't need to finish that, since I'm Dad's number one suspect, no doubt I will be the number one suspect in my girlfriend's disappearance too.

"No fucking doubt." Sinking to the ground, I shake my head. "I was an asshole to her. I was so fucking angry, and now I may never see her again."

My brothers all hover around me, I can feel their unease about this whole fucked-up situation.

Reign's phone beeps, he pulls it out and when he reads, he sneers, "Fuck."

"Care to share?" Hendrix grumbles.

"Hudson found something and said we need to see it ASAP."

"Hudson? Hudson Finley?" Saint questions.

"Yes. Come on, follow me."

"Wait, since when have you and Hudson Finley been all fucking chummy?"

Reign sighs. "He's ... he's my contact."

"Wait, the other hacker? It's him?" Nodding, Reign continues walking, leaving us all behind.

"Are you fucking coming?" he bellows.

Following him, Hendrix side-eyes me as we follow behind Reign.

"Hudson Finley?" Hendrix whispers, and I raise an eyebrow at him. I shrug, I'm just as confused as my brother.

"This makes no fucking sense," Saint continues.

Reign stops in front of one of the hidden sliding doors, which leads to a secret passage that then leads to different routes throughout the inner chambers of the school.

"I guess we're following," Conroy says when Reign pops it open and climbs in.

"Where are we going?" Lennon voices. *When the fuck did he get here?*

"Hurry up," Reign groans, frustration clear in his voice as we all slowly pile into the wall.

"Fucking hell, Reign, it's as tight as a fucking pussy in here," Hart snaps, shoving Theon into the wall when he knocks into his back, who instantly shoves him back. But he's right, with all of us in this tiny space it's a tight fit.

"Keep moving," Reign snaps as he continues along the passageway.

Hendrix shakes his head, mumbling unintelligibly, and for some reason I chuckle. There's nothing funny about this but I can't control it. The farther we walk, the more I cackle.

"He's fucking lost it," someone behind me voices and that causes me to stop.

"Wanna fill us in while we take a hike?" I ask Reign who has turned to face me.

"Nope," he replies with a shake of his head.

"For fuck's sake, we're all gonna die in these fucking walls before he tells us what the fuck is going on."

Ignoring me, he turns around and we all follow him again. Reign stops when he comes to a junction, he looks down at his phone and then moves to the right. I'm about to ask him where the fuck we're going when he suddenly stops, causing me to slam into his back.

"Dude, why the fuck did you stop?" Hendrix snarls after smashing into me.

Reign looks around as if he's trying to work something out.

"This is new," he whispers, his voice laced with concern.

"What the fuck is he talking about?" Theon yells.

"Hudson said to walk until we come to the junction and then to keep going for another thirty steps and stop."

"Oh, just fucking perfect, Huddy boy sent us on a fucking scavenger hunt to kill us, fantastic choice in allies, Reign," Hart mumbles.

Then all of a sudden, another wall pops out revealing Hudson on the other side.

"'Bout fucking time, I ain't got all day," he growls as we each step into the space which is as big as a small bathroom.

A chorus of, "What the fuck" and "Holy shit" can be heard in the tiny space we're all currently sandwiched in.

"What the fuck is this?" Hendrix finally voices because mine is gone. The walls in this small space are all filled with photos, articles, and clippings from the school paper. There isn't an inch of wall not covered.

Gulping audibly, my fingers move across the wall finding a photo of Remy and me. It's taken from a distance but it's close enough you can see we're fucking. Ripping it from the wall, I place it in my pocket. Then I turn to Hudson and shove him down onto a small chair that sits in the corner.

"What the fuck is this? You do this?"

"What? Fuck no. I was wandering around down here and found this on the floor." He shoves something into my hand. "I couldn't work out where it would have come from, so I started to push on the walls and suddenly this"—he waves his arm around—"room popped up."

It's an article about the death of Arlen and how he jumped off the cliffs, taking his own life.

Reign snatches it from my hand and after he reads, he lifts his head. "He didn't fucking kill himself."

"I mean this is impressive an—" Lennon says but the dickhead stops when he sees us all glaring at him. Shaking his head, he continues, "I mean think about it, there isn't a space left, how fucking long did this take?"

"He's right," Hart agrees.

"Look, whoever did this, has to be the one who took Remy," Hudson says what I think we are all thinking.

"How do we know you're not the one who took her and are playing us? Trying to throw us off the scent?" Saint asks the obvious.

"You have to admit it's pretty suspicious you found this place and none of us knew it's been here the whole time," Reign states, and I notice Hudson looks offended at Reign's accusation.

"Because she's my friend and unlike you, assholes, I don't use chicks to make myself feel bigger." He bumps his chest into Reign's, taking a stance in his face. That action proves to me it isn't him, no one's crazy enough to take Reign on, one-on-one, especially in a tiny, cramped room like this.

"He's right, it's not his style. Hudson's one of the good ones, he knows who Remy belongs to, he doesn't want to feel my wrath." I turn my attention to the others. "Search everything, there has to be a fucking clue, an address, anything."

Once the entire place has been searched from top to bottom, we come up empty-handed. Inhaling deeply, I know we're not going to find anything and just as I'd given up hope, Saint breaks the silence when he yells, "Holy-fucking-shit."

Hendrix rips whatever Saint found from his hands and it's his turn to cuss, "That motherfucking fucker."

"What is it?" I question them.

"We know who it is," Hendrix says, with a smile that indicates someone is about to die.

"That fucking dog," Reign snaps after he looks at the proof of who did it.

"Who the fuck is it?" Hart throws his hands up in frustration.

"It's—" Reign is interrupted when a noise in the distance causes us all to freeze and then we hear footsteps, they're getting closer and closer. With no way out, we're trapped, and our element of surprise is going to be blown. Hendrix was right earlier. We're going to die down here before we get my girl back.

A bright light shines in our eyes, blinding us and a deep voice snarls, "What the fuck are you doing down here?"

REMY

I'M AWAKE AGAIN but I'm keeping my eyes closed. I don't want to open my eyes because when I do, it will reaffirm I'm still trapped in this hellhole with some fucking guy who's a raging lunatic. I was hoping Thatcher would have rescued me by now, but maybe I don't mean as much to him as I thought. Maybe once again, I was wrong about him. Wouldn't be the first time I trusted the wrong person, seems to be the one trait that follows me everywhere.

Sighing, I lie here and enjoy the serenity but then I remember what I saw before I blacked out and my eyes snap open. Turning my head toward the other bed, I hope and pray it wasn't a dream and when my eyes land on the bed opposite me, they well with tears.

It wasn't a dream.

Two eyes belonging to a person I never thought I would ever see again are staring back at me. "It's ... it's you," I blubber.

"Yeah, it's me," he says and smiles, in only the way my big brother can.

"How ... how are you here, Gray? Mom said you—"

"Mom's a lying bitch. Everything she has ever said has been a fucking lie. Wait till you see who else is here."

"What?" I question him then I whisper, "Who else is here?" But he ignores me.

"I reckon she's in cahoots with this fucker"—he head nods to the other room—"to keep us away, but we can't figure out why. Now that you're here it works into a theory I have, but he's not convinced."

"What? Who's not convinced?" I ask again.

"Mom's a liar, a bald-faced liar," he repeats. It's like he's delusional, muttering to himself how he is. "She's a fucking bitch."

"Well, yeah, but this, kidnapping her two kids? That's too far, even for her."

"You really think that?" he throws back at me.

My mouth opens and closes, but when I think about what I recently discovered about her and Thatcher's dad, I don't know what to think anymore. "Well, I hope she isn't this vindictive but tell me, Gray, who the fuck else is here?"

"Wow, you've grown a set of lady balls since I last saw you. The Remster I know and remember would be a mess in the corner crying."

"Hard to be in a corner when you're strapped to a bed," I hiss at my brother, but he's right. The old me was a pussy, the new me, well she now throws the punches and when I'm no longer strapped to this bed, I will bring down fire on the fuck face who has me, Gray, and our mystery guest. "Now, who the fuck else is here?"

He swallows deeply and from that action, I'm pretty sure he's going to blow my mind. I wonder if Mr. Vanderbelt isn't dead after all and it was all a ruse of some kind. "Why do I suddenly get the feeling it's going to implode my world?"

"Because it blew my mind when I discovered him here."

"Don't keep me waiting, who is him?"

From the doorway, a voice says, "Hey, Jellybean." My eyes widen when that voice, and nickname, register in my brain. Turning my head toward the doorway, my mouth drops open when my gaze lands on the person standing there.

"How? What? Am I dreaming?" To say I'm shocked would be the understatement of the century. Never in my wildest dreams did I think *he'd* be the one here with us.

"I'm really here, Jellybean."

"B-b-b-b-b-b-but y-y-y-y-y-y-you're d-d-d-d-d-d-d-dead," I stammer, blinking rapidly because surely, I'm hallucinating.

"Did you really think I'd jump?" With those six words, I know it's *him* and my suspicions all along were correct. I knew he didn't jump, I just knew it.

Shaking my head, the first tear falls. "No, I never believed you jumped, Arl. Not for one fucking moment." He walks over to me and that's when I notice the shackle around his ankle. He sits on the bed next to me and cups my cheek. He's touching me, my brother who's supposedly dead is sitting next to me, alive. Touching me.

The floodgates open and I cry with happiness, my brother is alive. "This really is real, right? I'm not dreaming? I haven't been drugged and fallen into some twisted psychosis?"

"If this is a dream, you have pretty messed-up ones, Sis," Grayson says from the bed opposite us.

That causes me to laugh and choke on my sobs. "Well, I have been living a nightmare recently so I guess this fits."

Then I look up at my brother, my brother, my very much alive brother. "Arl, if you didn't jump, then how are you here? Why are you here? What the fuck is going on?"

"That's a complicated and complex story, Jellybean. One I don't have time to explain but I will, soon. Right now, I just want to hug my baby sister."

"And she wants to hug her non-dead big brother."

Awkwardly, thanks to the cuffs holding me down, Arlen and I hug and it's the best fucking hug ever. "Ohhh, Arl," I cry into his neck, "I missed you sooooooo much." Opening my eyes, I look over at Grayson. "And you too, Gray."

"Ohhh, isn't this sweet," our captor singsongs from the doorway.

Arlen pulls away and immediately I miss him. He turns away from me but takes my hand in his. "You made a mistake, asshole," Arlen sneers at him.

"Yeah, how so? 'Cause from where I'm standing, dick-head, I'm free and you three are well, trapped."

"Yeah, but the odds are now three on one and if I was a betting man, I'd say you're fucked." Arlen's words light a fire within me, and I think maybe, just maybe, we will get out of here after all, but that thought quickly vanishes when all of a sudden, Arlen starts shaking and drops to the floor.

"Let's agree to disagree." His tone is sinister, and even though he still has his balaclava on, his eyes show nothing but anger at my brother, who has finally stopped shaking. Our captor just tased Arlen and before I can say anything, he pulls out another one and tases Grayson too.

He cackles maniacally and when our gazes connect, something flashes in his stare and I really begin to fear for my life, especially when he says, "Now that you're all reunited, the fun is just about to begin."

THATCHER

THAT VOICE, I recognize it but I can't place it and right now, I'm blinded from the light beaming in our faces. "You son of a bitch," I bellow.

"She's fucking mine," the voice snarls, and then the motherfucker slams the door and the loud clicking of a lock echoes through the tiny space we're now trapped in.

"I swear to fucking God, you're going to die if you touch her," I scream and bang on the door.

"I told you, Vanderbelt, she's mine and nobody is ruining that. Not even you." His voice disappears. The only sounds left are our heavy breathing and the thudding of my heart.

"Motherfucker," Hart barks, throwing his fist into the wall then hissing at the pain.

"Calm the fuck down before you break your goddamn hand," Reign growls.

"Was that?" Conroy questions just as a light bulb goes off in my head as to who that motherfucker was.

"Yeah, it was." I clench my teeth, trying my best to not lose my shit. Losing my shit won't help anyone at the moment and right now, we need to figure a way out of this fucking room.

"This whole fucking time," Hendrix sneers. He taps my shoulder and hands me what they found earlier. My eyes widen and the need to punch something builds. "I'm going to fucking kill him. That son of a bitch won't see tomorrow."

Reign bangs on the door, yelling for someone, but no one is going to hear us in here, hell we didn't even know here existed.

"Great, no service," Hudson huffs, holding his phone up trying to find a signal.

Reign kicks his boot into the door, his anger becoming uncontrollable as he kicks the wood over and over, trying to get it to budge. Each kick is harder than the previous one. His breathing is becoming labored and then I remember, he's claustrophobic and I find myself smirking, thankful Reign can't see me 'cause he'd turn his anger and frustrations onto me.

"Enough, you're going to break your goddamn foot, and I really don't want to be carrying your ass out of here," Hendrix warns him. He grunts at his brother but surprisingly, he stops his tirade against the door.

Lennon slides down the wall, taking his phone out to use as a light, each of us follow suit and slide down after him.

Hudson chuckles, shaking his head.

"What's so fucking funny, Finley?" Theon hisses.

"Never thought I'd be in such a jam that even a phone call wouldn't work."

Hart nods because Hudson's right, with no service, who the fuck knows how long it'll take for someone to find us in here.

Lennon and Hart start to speak when Reign sits up straight. "Shh, I can hear something." His voice is full of panic. Standing up, he turns his head and puts his ear to the door. His eyes widen. "In here," he bellows, "we're in here." He bangs on the door to gain the attention of no one because I didn't hear shit and then, I hear a soft voice murmur, "Reign?"

He bangs again, but louder. His fist repeatedly hits the wood but then we're met with silence, and I begin to wonder if maybe we're hallucinating that we heard someone say his name, but then we hear it again. "Reign?"

"Alani," Reign yells, "in here, open the door, please. Let us the fuck out. Please. He ... he fucking locked us in down here." It sounds like he's crying at the end, poor guy is about to pass out from fear.

"Hang on, there's a lock," she says and then everything goes silent.

"Alani?" Reign shouts, panic once again lacing his voice. His breathing is coming in fast pants. Hudson stands up and makes his way beside Reign. He rests his hand on Reign's back in a soothing manner and whispers something to him.

Before my eyes, I see my brother's shoulders drop and his breathing returns to normal. Fuck, Hudson has the magic touch.

"Alani, are you there?" Hudson voices, gripping the door handle and shaking it a few times. Not sure why he thinks he could suddenly open it.

"She left us. Just fucking great, your girl's a bitch, Reign," Lennon grumbles.

"What the fuck did you say?" Reign growls, while at the

same time Hudson hisses, "Come a-fucking-gain?" They share a look while the rest of us can't believe our ears.

Saint chuckles, shaking his head, his face full of glee. "Just great, you're both banging her, fantastic."

"Shut up, Saint," Reign barks.

A loud clanking sound comes from the other side of the door. All attention turns back to the door when suddenly, it bursts open revealing Alani with bolt cutters and a shit-eating grin on her face.

"What's up, boys?" she sasses, holding the cutters in one hand and the other resting on her cocked hip.

Reign races toward her and scoops her up into his arms. He holds her tightly to him and kisses her while the others step around them and make their way to the exit.

"Get a room." Hart laughs, slapping Reign on the back as he walks past them.

Reign puts her down and then she wraps her arms around Hudson's waist. He kisses the top of her head. Reign smiles and stares at me over their heads. I have no clue what the fuck is going on with those three, but I guess they share a girl. Fuck knows how that works. One chick is enough for me and that chick, she needs me right now.

"Let's go." Hendrix takes off before any of us can follow him.

"Wait," Alani says. "I know who has Rem. He climbed out one of the secret doors and shoved into me, knocking me to the ground in a rush and I thought that was weird. He was muttering to himself about trapping you guys, something about his sweet, sweet Remington and it all going to shit. It's—"

"Yeah, we know, it's Brennan-fucking-Dawson but I assure you, that motherfucker won't see another day," I growl at her before following after Hendrix.

We finally reach the door that leads out of here and we all

pile out, it reminds me of a tiny car and a million clowns climbing out.

Once we're all free, relief is etched on everyone's faces, everyone except Reign. "I need you to stay here," he tells Alani.

"No, I want to help."

"No," Hudson says, just as Reign says, "I'm not risking you getting hurt." He looks to Hudson. "I want you to stay here with her. Keep an eye on her. Protect her. Keep each other safe," Reign tells him.

Hudson nods and drags Alani behind him, leaving us all to look at Reign.

"Don't fucking start," he snaps, before taking off.

We all meet up on the front steps of the school. "We need to find where that fucker is holding Rem. Then we get her out. That fucker better pray he hasn't touched her."

Everyone nods.

"Sooo, what's the plan?" Rian asks. "How do we find them?" No one says anything because where the fuck do we start? We might finally know the who, but the where and why is still a mystery.

"Wait," Hart says, and everyone turns their attention to him. "Doesn't his family have a lake house? From memory, he goes with his family over the summer. And sometimes during the school year too 'cause it isn't too far from here."

Hendrix and I share a look and we both nod.

"I bet that's where he's holding her, secluded and far enough away but still close. No one would suspect him visiting his own cabin," Hendrix says.

"Wait, we're just going to go in after her?" Theon says. "All gung-ho and no plan?"

"Yeah," I deadpan. "That's my girl, I'm going to get her."

"Brennan's clearly lost a few brain cells. Do you think it's wise to just rush in? He's dangerous, fuck, what if he kills us all?" Theon voices and even though I know he's right, I just want my girl back.

"He's right," Rian agrees with a nod.

Hendrix sighs and grips the back of his neck. "They're right, T, we need a plan. A fucking good one."

Looking around at these men, I nod in agreement. I'm glad these guys are thinking clearly. "All right, fine," I hiss. "Let's come up with a rescue plan that saves the girl and takes out a fucking psycho," I say.

Reign nods and slaps my back. "Let's do this."

I just hope Remy can hold on until we get there. I hope we're not too late, and I really hope there aren't any other surprises.

REMY

AFTER HE TASED my brothers earlier, he cackled like a fucking psycho and stormed out of here. All I could do was lie here and keep an eye on them. Both are still breathing, so that's something, but both are still out cold and now I'm left alone with the raging psycho.

He comes into view and my eyes widen when I see who it is. He's no longer wearing his balaclava and I can finally see his face. I knew I recognized his voice. "Brennan?" I utter his name in disbelief. When his eyes land on mine, he smiles, and I shiver at the intensity of his gaze. Normally Brennan has a beautiful smile but right now, I see nothing beautiful about the man before me. "What the hell?" I snap, pulling at my restraints. "I thought we were friends. Why am I handcuffed to a bed? Why are my brothers here? Why am I here?" He just silently stares at me and my anger builds the longer the silence goes on until I lose it. "Give me some fucking answers, you fuckface dickhole."

"Hey, Cutie," he says by way of greeting, completely ignoring my rant and all of my questions. He walks into the room and steps over Arlen's slumped body on the floor and takes a seat next to me on the mattress. He reaches out and brushes my hair off my forehead. I flinch away from him and that was obviously the wrong thing to do because he grips my chin, his fingers painfully digging in. He lowers his face, I can feel his breath on mine. "You will treat me with respect. Seems that Vanderbelt fucker has rubbed off on you but don't worry, Cutie, you and I can be together now. No one can stop us."

"What the ever-loving fuck?"

"Don't be like that, Cutie, I know you want me. Remember that party? You were all over me that night until you disappeared with Rowan. If it was anyone else that you ditched me for, I would have been pissed, but it was a girl and I know nothing sinister or untoward would happen there." *If only you knew what happened. The kiss, my first girl kiss.* Now I'm singing in my head, "I Kissed a Girl" by Katy Perry and my lips lift slightly when I get to the 'and I liked it' part. "Are you smiling at the memory of you in my lap?" Before I can reply, he jumps up and straddles me on the bed. My eyes widen when I see the imprint of his hard cock through his pants. He wouldn't, would he?

"Brennan," I murmur, "Wwwww ... what are you doing?"

"I need you, Cutie. I need you in my life."

"I ... I am in your life."

"You are?" he asks, his face lighting up like a Christmas tree.

"Well, yeah. You're currently on top of me. Squishing me, ergo, you're in my life."

"Shit, I'm so sorry." He climbs off and drops to the floor, kicking Arlen out of the way. Arl groans and hearing that sound eases some of my worries. Brennan rests his arms on the edge of the bed, resting his chin on his forearm. He just sits there and stares at me. "You really are beautiful. You are going to make the cutest babies."

My eyes widen at the mention of babies. "Babies? I'm not ready to be a mom, I need to go to college. Get my degree. I—"

"Shhhh," he coos, pressing his finger to my lips. "I don't mean now, silly, I mean one day. After you and I become the powerhouse couple of Crestwood, we will be unstoppable. People will refer to us as Brennington or Remennan. Everyone will be in awe of you and I."

This dick really is delusional, but that delusion might actually play into my favor. I need to keep on his good side. I need to play this for all it's worth. "One day," I whisper back and nod. "Do you, umm, think you can let me up? My arms hurt and I'd really love a drink, I'm parched."

"Of course." He jumps up and leaves the room. Dammit, I was hoping he'd uncuff me first, but baby steps.

"You better have a plan, Remster," Grayson murmurs from the opposite bed, and hearing his voice once again eases some of my worry.

"I think I do," I whisper, but Brennan returns before I can elaborate.

"You do what, Cutie?" he asks as he plops back down beside me.

"I do what?" I throw back at him.

"You whispered 'I do' when I came back in. Are you practicing our wedding vows?"

"Ummm, no."

"Ohh," he dejectedly replies.

"I said, I do hope he uncuffs me, my wrists are chafing, and I can't have marred skin when we make our debut in public. What if people get the wrong idea about you? I can't have people thinking you're hurting me."

"You are so thoughtful to be thinking of me." Smiling sweetly at him, I flick my gaze to my wrist and then back to him and thankfully, he gets the hint. Standing up, he pulls a key out of his pocket and uncuffs my left wrist. "Thanks, babe," I tell him, looking up at him with what I hope are loving eyes and not the daggers I'm internally throwing at him. He smiles and reaches over to uncuff my other wrist. I go to throw my legs over the edge and sit up and that's when I realize my ankles are tied down too. How did I not realize that?

Looking to my cuffed feet and then back to him, I raise my eyebrows in a 'what about them' look. "Baby steps," he tells me and I nod in agreement.

He offers me his hand and pulls me up into a sitting position. My vision dots as I sit and I cover my head until the moment passes. Brennan hands me the water I asked for. Nodding my thanks, I take the glass from him and bring it to my lips.

Taking a sip, the cool liquid slides down my throat and a small moan slips free. Brennan's eyes widen and I notice the bulge beginning to form in his jeans. "*Shit, shit, shit,*" I internally chant to myself. He notices me staring at his crotch and a smirk appears on his face. "*Shit, shit, shit,*" I internally chant to myself again. He rests his knee on the bed and leans toward me. His eyes are closed. His lips pursed, he's going in for a kiss but I can't kiss him. I won't kiss him. In a panic, I throw the water in his face. His eyes snap open and if looks could kill, I'd be dead.

"I'm so sorry," I quickly say, reaching up to wipe at his face. "I ... I thought I saw someone behind you."

He climbs off the bed and races into the other room, but

quicker than I hoped he returns. "There's no one there, Cutie. It's just us here in our love nest."

"And my brothers," I remind him. "Speaking of them, how is Arlen still alive?"

"That's not my story to tell but I promise you, I won't hurt either of them, or you."

"Is that why you tased them?" I sneer.

"Don't take that tone with me," he venomously throws back at me. "They're alive, what more do you want?"

"I don't know, maybe to not be strapped to a bed." Silently I add *here with you* to that sentence, but I need to keep him on my side.

"In due time, Cutie. I need to head into town, when I get back, we can discuss things." He leans down and kisses me on the forehead, turns, and exits the room.

A few moments later, the front door opens, and I hear him exit. Staring at the closed door, I will it to open again and for Thatcher to be on the other side but it doesn't.

Arlen groans and I snap my head toward him. "Arl, dude, are you okay?"

"Mmmmhmpf," he groans, pushing himself up into a sitting position. He leans back against my bed, and I run my fingers through his hair. He reaches back and grabs my wrist, he spins around and when he realizes I'm sitting up, he stands and embraces me in the best hug I have ever received. "Jellybean," he whispers into my hair, "I never thought I'd see you again."

"I ... you ... you were dead, Arl. Dad said you jumped but I never believed you did." I push him back, grip his shoulders, and rest my forehead against his. "I never believed it, but how? What happened? I'm so confused."

"As I said, it's a complicated and complex story and all will be revealed in time." Why is he being sheepish? Maybe it's a horrible story and he wants to spare me the horrendous details of his ordeal over the last four months. For now, I'm going to just focus on having my brother back.

"Okay, I'll stop asking." He nods. "For now."

That causes him to smirk, "I'm glad you're safe, Jellybean."

"Safe is a loose term, Arl, don't you think? Considering where we are."

"Touché, Jellybean, touché."

"What are we going to do?" I ask the million-dollar question.

"Well, right now, I'm going to get us a drink and some food. Then, together we're going to come up with a plan to get the fuck out of here."

Nodding, I watch my brother walk into the other room. Hope blooms in my chest, maybe we will get out of here after all. This is all so fucked up and at this point in time, I have no clue how we're going to escape, but I do know one thing, Thatcher will come for me and when he does, Brennan is a dead man.

THATCHER

"I CAN'T BELIEVE it's been Brennan this whole fucking time. The fucker was right under our noses," Saint murmurs, shaking his head in disbelief.

We're in my car heading toward his family cabin. Reign is behind the wheel because I'm in no state to be handling a motor vehicle right now. It's after curfew but my peach is more important than a fucking curfew. My nerves are shot and after our run-in with him in the secret room, I'm on edge and I fear for Rem. Brennan-fucking-Dawson is obviously unhinged and come morning, he'll be six feet under.

"Let's just get there, and hope there's no other surprises,"

Reign says, keeping his eyes on the road, and I hope he's right, I don't think I can take any more surprises.

It takes a solid hour to get to the lake—close enough to be far enough away from the city ... and the perfect fucking place to stow your kidnap victim.

"Turn the headlights off," Hendrix orders Reign as we slowly creep down the road toward the cabin. It finally comes into sight and as I stare at it, I feel nothing. I don't feel my peach and it makes me wonder if we're at the wrong place.

Reign puts the car into park, and we all sit here for a moment, silently staring at the dark, seemingly unoccupied cabin.

"What do we do if he has a gun?" Saint asks.

"I'm hoping he doesn't," I say, and then I berate myself for not swinging via Mom's and grabbing one from the cabinet.

Quietly, I open my door and slowly climb out. One by one, my brothers join me just as Rian pulls in behind us. They all exit their car, quietly closing the doors and they make their way over to us.

Reign hands me a flashlight and slowly we walk toward the cabin. It's pitch-black out here, there's not one light on in any of the houses or on the road. It reminds me of a scene from *The Cabin in the Woods* and we are about to be led to our slaughter.

The closer we get to the cabin, the harder and faster my heart beats. We sneak around to the back and Hendrix jiggles the door handle but no surprises, it's locked.

"Fuck, it's locked. Are you sure this is his?" Saint argues.

"You, guys, go around the side. We'll find a way in at the front and remember, be fucking quiet," I whisper to everyone.

Everyone nods and we split up. With my brothers at my side, we climb onto the wraparound porch, one of them tries a window and it slides up. It feels too easy, a window just so happened to be open for us. Shaking off that thought, I shove my way through and climb in first.

Standing up in the living room, I look around, but all the furniture is covered in dust sheets. Saint unlocks the front door, and the others enter.

We each take a room and meet back up in the living room minutes later. Each of them shakes their head.

"It's fucking empty," Hendrix murmurs as he shines his flashlight around the empty cabin.

"Un-fucking-believable," Reign groans.

"Wait," Rian says, staring out the window.

"What?" we all hiss.

"I think we're in the wrong cabin." He pauses for emphasis, and I want to junk punch him right now, just get to the fucking point, asshole. "The cabin next door definitely has someone in it right now." He points through the window.

Stepping closer to the window, sure enough the cabin next door has a fire going, smoke billowing out the chimney, and a few lights are on. As I stare across at it, a feeling of 'she's in there' washes through me.

"Maybe that one is his and we got it wrong," Hart says behind us.

"Nah, I went over the records," Reign tells us. "This one's his. According to the county, that one has been abandoned for a few years now but recently, someone submitted an application to redevelop it. I bet it's a dummy corporation and the person behind it is Brennan."

Everyone nods as they process what Reign just said.

I'm coming, Peach, I silently say. "Let's go," I hiss. Shoving Hart out of the way, I make my way to the front door and everyone else follows me.

We quietly head toward the second cabin when the sound of a car door slams. The sound echoes throughout the quiet night air. Moving my arm across Saint to halt him, we press ourselves into the side of the cabin. Each one of us holds our breath and waits. We watch a lone figure walk up the steps of the next-door cabin.

"Motherfucker," Hendrix hisses , echoing my exact thoughts.

We watch as Brennan stomps toward the door, he swings it open and yells something unintelligible before slamming the front door behind him.

"Thatch, man, we need—" Reign whispers.

"I know, man," I bark, "I know." I don't need him to voice it because I know, without any weapons we are fucked. Brennan finding us in his lil' hidey-hole has pushed him over the edge. He's now erratic and unstable, that is not going to go well for this rescue.

Pushing off the wrong cabin, I slowly move toward the road, looking over my shoulder. "Keep down, I'll check it out." *No need for all of us to be caught.*

Everyone nods and they watch as I slink into the next yard. With a deep breath, I lift my head and peek through the window that has a slight crack open in the curtains.

I sigh when I see Remy sitting on a bed. She's bound at her feet but looks unharmed. I notice two other people in the room with her and I almost fall back when I realize who they are. "What the fuck?" I whisper-hiss.

"What?" Saint whispers quietly from behind me. He clearly doesn't understand 'wait here' means wait the fuck back where we were. May as well get everyone here so I only have to repeat myself once. Head nodding everyone, they all crouch down and sneak over to me. "Our plan just changed," I say, not that we really had a plan anyway but no longer are we rescuing one Hearst, we're rescuing three.

"What's the plan now?" Reign asks. "Is Remy okay?"

"Remy's okay," I inform them, "but it's not just her in there."

"What the fuck do you mean?" Hendrix snaps, he's on edge and ready for a fight and after what I just saw, so am I.

"Who the fuck else is in there?" Saint murmurs.

"Yeah, bro, I mean who else could possibly be in the cabin

with her? All the other girls are back at school and accounted for," Hart says.

"It's not girls, it's—" The sound of the slider above our heads squeaks and it's followed by a loud crash and a mumbled, "For fuck's sake." From the deck above someone stomps across the decking boards and to the stairs. The sound has all of us frozen, we have nowhere to hide.

We are sitting ducks about to be exposed.

Our surprise rescue is about to be blown as someone stomps their way down the side stairs.

"Fuck you, Brennan," a girl's voice hisses, breaking the silence once again, "that's the last time I help you." She jumps down the last few steps and when she rounds the corner, she lifts her gaze and pauses mid-step when she sees us all huddled together in the dark.

The clouds above part and in the moonlight, we see before us none other than Lana Dawson, Brennan's older sister. She turns, ready to run for it, but Rian reaches out and grabs her arm, twisting it behind her back. He shoves her into Theon's chest to muffle the shout about to break free from her open mouth. They both hold her and before she screams, Rian shoves his hankie into her mouth keeping her quiet. Never have I been thankful for him to be a weirdo who carries a hankie around.

Rian shoves her toward me. "Start talking," Saint growls behind me.

"You heard him," I sneer, urging her to play nicely and tell us what we want to know. "But if you scream, it'll be more than a snot-covered hankie being shoved into your mouth." Her gaze drops to my dick. "Not my dick, you sick fuck. I'll yank out every hair follicle from your head and then I'll shove the strands into your mouth before I drag you into the woods. I'll tie you to a tree—"

"And after we've had our fun," Rian sneers, "we'll leave you there and let the wolves eat you alive and that's a fucking promise. Now, be a good girl and answer our questions." Rian taps her cheek and the sound echoes around us.

Lana is wide-eyed and scared shitless right now. She nods frantically and mumbles, "Yes," around the hankie in her mouth.

Slowly, Rian removes his hankie. Theon keeps hold of her and Rian doesn't move from her back, caging her between them.

"It was all Brennan," she cries, "I swear. He ... he made me help him, told me I had no choice."

"Looks like your sides have changed," Reign says.

She nods.

"Tell us, Lana, why the fuck does Brennan have the Hearst siblings in that cabin?" I question her, proud of myself for keeping calm right now. Everyone snaps their heads toward me and even though I'm staring at our new ally, I can feel every pair of eyes on me.

"What?" Reign snaps, coming toward me. "What the fuck did you say?"

"Remington isn't the only one Brennan has in there. He also has Grayson and Arlen."

"No, that can't be right, Arlen's dead, he-he ..." Reign murmurs.

"Thatch, man, are you sure?" Hendrix questions me.

Nodding, I look over at my brothers. "It's true, I saw all three of them. Arlen Hearst is alive and he's in there with Remy and Grayson."

Everyone mumbles something but we don't have time to focus on the return of Arlen from the dead, right now we need to rescue the Hearsts and as if sensing the urgency, Hendrix gets up into Lana's face. "Thatcher asked you a question, Lana."

"He ... he's obsessed with the family," she stammers. "Says he and Remington will be a power couple and they're meant to be together. It's his rightful place."

"Sorry to break it to your brother, but Remy's my girl, and there is no way he's taking her from me," I inform her.

"Keep her here," I order Rian and Theon. "I'm going to get my girl."

And without thinking, my legs carry me around the cabin toward the front door. Climbing the steps, I stare at the piece of wood separating me from my peach and with everything I have, I slam my shoulder into it. The wood splinters but it's still closed. Taking a deep breath, I put all my force into me and try again. This time, the door flies open and bounces off the wall.

Slamming it back, I step inside the cabin and look around. Someone growls my name but before I find Rem, something slams into my side and I collapse to the floor.

REMY

ARLEN'S and my great plan is to escape. By any and all means but our plan, well, it's kinda shit. He and I are no MacGyver, we weren't able to use a hair tie, a dead bug, and a twig to escape. I call bullshit that MacGyver could do all that anyway. Aside from us not being able to MacGyver our way out, not long after Brennan left earlier that chick, Lana, arrived with food.

As much as I want to stab her with a rusty fork—if I had one—she brought burgers and fries and they smelled a-mah-zing. She can't be all that bad, she has good junk food taste. It's a shame that good taste doesn't extend to her drink choice. She handed me a Dr. Pepper, a Dr.-fucking-Pepper. I'd rather drink curdled milk than that shit.

While I nibbled on my burger, I watched her in the other room. She happily ate her burger, sipped on her shitty drink, and played on her phone. She and Brennan seem close, but I don't know their connection. Other than being fucking psychos I can't work them out. They're always chatting in hushed voices and giggling. They seem close but cracks are appearing in their relationship. I don't think she's too happy with him at the moment and maybe we can use that to our advantage, but how?

I've just finished my burger when the front door to the cabin flies open, slamming into the wall from the force and causing me to jump in fright, which sucks donkey dick because the cuffs cut into my ankles causing me to wince. Leaning forward, I look into the other room and see an enraged Brennan. He paces back and forth, tugging at his hair. A murderous look is etched on his face, he's clearly agitated, obviously something happened while he was out.

My thoughts are confirmed when he starts muttering, "Fuck, fuck, fucking fuck," over and over to himself.

Looking over at my brothers, they both have worried looks on their faces. As does Lana and seeing her worried too, causes a pit of despair to form in my stomach. That burger and shitty drink is close to making a reappearance.

Lana grabs Brennan by the shoulders, trying to calm him down but it seems to have the opposite affect and in a fit of rage, he slaps her across the face. The crack of his hand colliding with her cheek echoes around the cabin. Instinctively, I cup my cheek. She flips him off and walks out of view. I hear a door slide open and then close. Followed by a crash and an angry, "For fuck's sake." She stomps across the deck while Brennan remains in the other room, throwing a stool across the room in anger.

"Someone's a little pissed," Grayson nonchalantly says.

"Stating the obvious there, Brother," Arlen deadpans.

Something catches Brennan's attention, causing him to mutter his "Fuck, fuck, fuck," again. Shaking his head, he bends down, picks up the stool he just threw and holds it like a weapon above his head as he walks toward the front door of the cabin.

Something crashes into the front door, causing Brennan to bare his teeth in a sneer. The wood cracks but the door doesn't open. A growl can be heard on the other side and then suddenly the door flies open, and I smile, Thatcher is here. "Thatcher," I sing out as he steps into the cabin but it's too late. Brennan uses the chair as a bat and rams it into Thatcher's side. He falls out of view and lands with a thud. "Thatcher," I cry out again, my eyes welling with tears.

The sound of my voice causes Brennan to turn his attention to me and if I thought he was angry before, I was wrong, he's really angry now. His face is purply red and there's a vein in his forehead pulsating. "You," he snarls and points at me. He storms my way like a raging bull. With each step he takes toward me, that vein pulsates and fear courses through my veins.

Arlen steps in front of me, covering me like a hero would. One minute Brennan is storming toward me, and Arlen is in front of me, guarding me. And the next, they're both on the floor with another body on top of them. The gate crasher lifts their head and smiles over at me. "Reign," I whisper with a smile.

"Hey, Princess," he replies with a smile.

Someone beneath him grunts, and when he looks at the body below him, his eyes widen to the size of dinner plates when he sees who he's on top of.

REIGN

"YOU MIND GETTING OFF ME?" Arlen says from below me. The sound of his voice vibrates over my body but I don't move. I rapidly blink and stare down at Arlen, an alive and breathing Arlen.

Arlen-fucking-Hearst is here.

Reaching out, I pinch his cheek to make sure I'm not hallucinating. He smacks my hand away. "Ouch, you fucker," Arlen sneers, "what'd you pinch me for?"

"You're ... you're meant to be dead."

"Surprise," Arlen says, waving his hands at me.

Reaching out, I cup the cheek I just pinched and run my

finger along his jawline. "You're really here," I whisper. He smiles back at me and it's a smile I've dreamed about for months. Reaching down with my other hand, I lower my head and slam my lips against his. My tongue pushes into his mouth and I kiss him with everything I have. He covers my hands and kisses me back.

A throat clears from behind us, and I quickly pull back, pushing myself off Arlen. Readjusting my dick, I reach out a hand to help him up and that's when I see Brennan on the floor.

Walking over to him, I grip his hair in my fist and pull him up into a standing position. "You have some explaining to do, Dawson."

"Fuck you, faggot," he sneers in my face, and it was the wrong thing to say. Rearing my head back, with as much might as I can conjure, I slam my head forward, headbutting him. My forehead connects with his nose and an audible crack can be heard, followed by Brennan crying like a pussy.

"You broke my nose."

"Wait till Thatch regains consciousness, you'll have more than just a broken nose. Now, where are the fucking keys?"

"Eat shit, you fucking cunt."

"In the drawer to the left of the sink," Lana says from the other room.

Brennan's eyes widen and he scrunches his face up. "You fucking bitch," he sneers at his sister. "Why are you helping them? Why the fuck are you not helping me?"

She storms into the room, shoves me to the side and gets into her brother's face. "It's over, Bren. You've been caught and to be honest, you've turned into a fucking psycho douchehole. You told me doing this would help our family, but all it's done is turn you into a kidnapper and me an accessory. I refuse to go down with you."

"I don't see anyone else here, do you?" I ask the room.

"Nope, all I see is the Hearst siblings, us, and that douche-hole," Saint says.

"Same," Hendrix says, returning with the keys, swinging them around his index finger. He walks over to Remy and uncuffs her first. Then he does the same to Grayson and finally, he undoes the lock on Arlen's chain.

The three Hearst siblings, all embrace in the middle of the room and seeing them all together again, causes me to smile. This is all a total mindfuck, Arlen is alive. Grayson and Remy are here. What the fuck did the Hearsts do to the Dawson family to warrant a faked death and two kidnappings?

Brennan isn't so happy at the reunion and from the corner of my eyes, I see him lunge forward and try to grab Remy, but I reach out and grab him by the upper arm. I slam my fist into his face, and he falls onto the bed Grayson was on. Quicker than *The Flash*, Grayson straddles Brennan's chest and he has the cuffs that were on him attached to Brennan's wrist. "Oops, that might be a little tight," he teases Brennan as he spins around to attach the cuff to his ankles too. In the process of restraining Brennan, he earns himself a growl. "Ohhh no, not a growl," he playfully taunts. Before he climbs off him, he slaps Brennan on the cheek, the sound vibrating through the room. He then climbs off the bed, pulls Remy into his side, and kisses her temple in a brotherly way. "So, what's the plan now?"

Before any of us can reply, Thatcher storms into the bedroom. "Where the fuck is that asshole?" He's fuming right now, I don't think I have ever seen him this fired up before. "He's going to d—" But he doesn't finish his threat because his eyes find Remy and like a scene from a sappy romantic movie, he and Remy throw themselves at one another. He winces but pushes through the pain because he once again has his peach in his arms.

The two of them kiss one another like long-lost lovers. Then they declare their undying love blah blah fucking blah.

"Get a fucking room you two," Saint teases.

Shaking my head, I exit the room and walk into the living area, I drop down onto the sofa. "So, what do we do now?"

"Lana needs to leave," Hendrix says. "And then we need to call the police and let them deal with Brennan." He looks to Arlen and Grayson. "Guess they'll deal with you too, I'm not sure what the procedure for coming back from the dead is."

"You and me both," Arlen says with a shrug.

Looking at him, it's hard to compute he's alive, guess Remy was right, there is more to her brother's death in that there was no death, but why?

"Speaking of that, what the fuck, man? How did you end up here?"

"I'd like to know that too," Thatcher hisses from the doorway. Remy is tucked closely under his arm. I don't think I've ever seen her smile so brightly.

"Can we wait till the cops get here?" he asks. "I don't really want to have to repeat myself."

"Of course," Remy softly says, smiling at her brother. While Thatcher barks, "Tell us now."

"Thatcher," Remy hisses and smacks him in the stomach, causing him to flinch and groan in agony. "Shit, sorry, forgot you took a hit."

Once again the two of them suck face and once again Saint tells them to get a room. Leaving them alone, I pull my phone out and call the police. Within half an hour, the place is swarming with police and paramedics. Brennan is taken to the station to be processed. The Hearst siblings are taken aside and questioned by the local detective who investigated Arlen's death and Grayson's and my kidnapping. Thatcher is taken to the hospital to be checked over and the rest of us are ordered back to school.

A few hours later, we're all in my room. Thatcher has just returned from the hospital, thankfully Brennan didn't do any major damage, but he will be sore for a few days. Remy,

Arlen, and Grayson are still at the station, awaiting Rochelle to arrive.

We're passing a bottle of tequila around. Hendrix takes a swig and then he looks at me and I know what's coming as soon as I see him open his mouth. "Anyone else want to know why Reign and Arlen sucked face back there?" All eyes turn to me but before I can answer, he asks the other questions I knew would follow. "Are you gay? What about girls?"

"My sexuality is a story for another time," I tell him. Snatching the bottle from his hands, I take another swig.

"Will there be tequila?" Saint questions, causing me to laugh and snort tequila through my nose. Trust him to make a joke regarding something serious but it also eases my apprehension over telling them.

"No doubt there will be." I pause. "But I just wanna say, I'm still me ... I just—"

"No need to explain, bro," Thatcher says, squeezing the back of my neck in that 'it's all good' kind of way. "Just know, we're here when you're ready to talk."

Nodding, I take another mouthful and pass the bottle to him. Leaning back, the rest of them start talking about the events of the night, the focus no longer on me. I look around at my brothers and friends and I notice that we're still us, that kiss they witnessed hasn't changed a thing. I don't know why I'm so scared to share my secret with them because deep down I know they'll accept it, and me, but before I confess all, I need to figure a few things out.

THATCHER

THE LAST TWELVE hours have been a fucking roller coaster, but one thing became abundantly clear, I unequivocally love Remington Hearst with all my heart, and I will do so until my last dying breath. How my feelings for her have changed. Don't get me wrong, I still want to strangle her with my bare hands at times, but now, I want to do it with my cock buried deep inside her and my fingers wrapped around that pretty little neck of hers.

I let her spend tonight with her brothers, they all need this and I'm not that much of an asshole to ruin them being back in her life again. I know how much they mean to her because if the same thing happened to my brothers, I'd want to spend every minute with them once we were reunited.

"Hey, Thatcher," a deep voice drawls and when I look up, I'm surprised to see Grayson approaching me.

"Hey! I thought you were with Remy?" I ask him.

"Yeah, I am, she and Arlen are picking a movie. I just wanted a word first," he says, kicking his shoe like he's not sure where to start. I cross my arms over my chest and stare at him, waiting for him to speak.

"Look, I can see how much my sister means to you, and I wouldn't be her big brother if I didn't give you the talk," he warns, making us both chuckle because he and I both know, no matter what he says, Remy is mine and I'm not letting her go, not for anyone and certainly not for him.

"Look, I know we have a past but for the sake of Rem, I'd like to keep it there, where it belongs." I nod at him, in total agreement. "But just know, if my sister hurts because of you, I'll end you, Vanderbelt, no questions asked, nothing. I'll just end you. Got it?" He means business, it'd be too easy to fuck with him right now but if I had a sister and she was dating someone like me, I'd totally give the same speech so I get where he's coming from.

Holding out my hand for him, I wait for him to take it. At first, he looks down at my outstretched hand and after a few breaths, he reaches out and shakes it.

"I wouldn't expect anything else from her big brother, but I don't plan on hurting Remy. She's amazing and now that she's mine, I'll do everything in my power to make that girl smile every day for as long as she'll have me," I honestly tell him.

Grayson nods and then I ask the one question that has been lingering in my mind since we found the Hearst brothers in that cabin. "Do we know if your mother is involved in this shit show?" I ask him. That woman better pray she had nothing to do with Brennan becoming obsessed with my peach.

Grayson shrugs. "I couldn't tell you, but knowing our mother I wouldn't put it past her if she had some sort of hand in all of this."

"Really, you think?" I ask.

"Like I said, our mother is a raging bitch on the best of days, and after she realized she'd never have your dad, she went crazy with jealousy and rage and everything in between," he says and suddenly things click into place.

"You ... you don't think your mother had something to do with my father's death?"

It has to be her, right? Who else would it fucking be?

"It's highly possible." He pauses. "Look, I wouldn't put it past her, but I really can't see her killing the guy she loved, even if he was never going to leave your mom—" I go to interrupt him but he raises his hand. "But how many people did your old man piss off? There's only a handful of people who liked him and my mom just happened to be one of them." I sigh because Grayson's right, my dad had a swarm of enemies, a fucking harem of mistresses, and a gaggle of pissed-off husbands. Then he says, "What about your mom?" That question shocks the shit out of me.

"My mother wouldn't hurt a goddamn fly," I sneer, ready to deck the fucker for even considering my mother. "You think she's capable of murder?" I snap roughly, clenching and unclenching my fist.

"I don't know, man, I don't really know the woman, but I do know people do weird shit when their pride is fucked over."

"Yeah, but I know my mom didn't do it. She stayed with my father, even after your slut of a mother ruined our family."

"Okay, well then, I guess we're back at no fucking clue." His phone beeps. Pulling it out, he smiles reading the message. "It's Remy, telling me to hurry up." He looks to me. "Thanks for the chat, we'll talk soon, Vanderbelt." And with that, he turns and leaves.

Once he's out of sight, I spin around and head up to my room. My mind is reeling with the endless possibilities on who could have killed my father. However, after chatting with Grayson just now, Rochelle Hearst is firmly on top of my suspect list, but also on that list now is Mom. Is my mother really capable of committing murder? Love and hate, make people do crazy things. Then there's also my brothers, what about them? Saint's been going through something lately and he's derailing as quickly as an avalanche. Hendrix has always been a loose cannon, and Reign, well he's the nicest out of us but I know after everything that's happened this year, he's got his own demons. But murder, fuck. As much as we hated the fucker, none of us are killers, that much I'm sure of.

Since Remy is occupied with her brothers, I decide some snooping is in order. I need fucking answers and after my chat with Grayson just now, I have a feeling I know exactly where I'll find them.

Turning back around, I head toward the exit. The heavy doors click closed behind me and I head straight for my car.

Revving the engine, I don't look back as I zoom through the school gates, driving toward the one place I'm sure I'll find what I'm searching for.

Pulling up in front of the fountain, I see my father's ridiculous car still parked where he left it. It's the ugliest piece of machinery I have ever seen but it suited the asshole. I wonder what will happen to it. Mom could sell it or send it to the scrap yard. I chuckle at that thought, he'd be rolling over in his grave if that happened, but the fucker deserves it after what he did to her and us.

Opening the front door, I let myself in and Lisette is in the foyer, my presence startles her, and she gasps at seeing me.

"Thatcher," she whispers, "you startled me."

"Sorry, Lisette," I tell her and when I apologize to her, I actually mean it. Lisette has been a constant in our life and someone I trust implicitly. She's always had Mom and our backs.

"Your mother is resting," she tells me, smiling that Mom is looking after herself finally ... only took our father being murdered for that to happen but whatever, she's finally the Mom I remember.

"It's okay, I'm just here to grab something." The lie slips from my tongue so easily and thankfully, Lisette just nods and smiles, leaving me to walk through the house and upstairs to my father's office.

Pushing the door open, the smell of his cologne hits me as soon as I enter but I feel nothing. Not an ounce of sadness washes over me that he's gone, I really am an asshole.

Closing the door behind me, not wanting my mother to know I'm here, I make my way over to his desk. It's as pristine as ever and I shake my head at the ridiculous facade he always kept.

Rummaging through his desk drawers, I open each one, going through every last piece of paper. Nothing of interest jumps out at me, that is until I catch sight of his will. Deciding to take a look, I sit back in his chair and open the folder.

My brothers and I each inherit a hefty amount from his life insurance, not enough to become men of luxury but enough to help us get on with life. Our mother also gets a lump sum but knowing Mom, she'll give it all to Grandpa McQueen to pay him back since he's been keeping us afloat recently. What surprises me the most though, is what I find inside a random envelope. There are two checks, one made out to Rochelle Hearst for eight million dollars, and a blank one for three million.

"What the fuck?" I murmur. Why the fuck did Dad pay that cheating cunt eight mil? And who is the other one for? What the fuck does it mean? I notice neither are signed and now he's dead, they won't be cashed. I'd love to mail that whore her unsigned eight mil check and be there when she realizes it's unsigned.

My eyes read over them again and again. What am I missing?

I'm barely holding it together. My anger is getting the better of me, but if this is here, there has to be a reason why somewhere in this cabinet.

Throwing the will and envelope on the desk, I return to the drawers but the last one is locked. Shocking me, the key is easy to find under a fake compartment in the top drawer. Clever Father, real clever; not. I roll my eyes as I take the key out. Dropping to my knees, I slip it into the lock and turn.

The click of the lock is deafening, and my heart races as I open the drawer. The first thing I see is a folder marked, "Hearst" staring back at me. The name catches my eye immediately.

Picking it up, I open it and file after file on all the Hearst family members falls out. The biggest is Arlen and the focus is on his death. Looks like Dad didn't think it was suicide either, but why?

Shaking my head, I continue flicking through the papers again but this time, I come across another note stuck to a family photo of the Hearsts at Arlen's funeral.

The handwriting is unfamiliar, but what I read makes my stomach roll.

Father really pissed someone off because this note is demanding him to end things and give them what they're entitled to. I knew he was a despicable human being, but seeing the evidence of what he and Rochelle had planned for Remy makes me glad that Father is already dead because after discovering this, I'd kill him myself. The silver lining though, I can still make her suffer. I knew I hated that bitch, and the fact they were going to sell off the Hearst siblings, including the woman I love, is unfathomable, but it makes me wonder what else is Rochelle Hearst capable of? Murder maybe?

"You really shouldn't have found that."

A voice from the doorway says, startling me and I drop the paper, it floats to the floor and slides under the desk. When I look up, my eyes widen when I see who's there. "You?" I gasp in shock.

"Surprise," they utter as they step into the room, closing the door behind them. Leaning back against the wood, they stare over at me. "You remind me so much of your father."

"My father was a cunt and I'm far from a cunt, but I can unequivocally say, your daughter is nothing like you."

She shakes her head, ignoring my taunt. "You've ruined everything, Thatcher."

"You mean the fact that now your children are safe and no longer in your clutches, you have no one to sell off to the highest bidder?"

"That was a setback, but I have a new plan now."

"And what might that be?"

"You." Before I can process her word, she pulls a taser out of her purse and pulls the trigger. My body shakes uncontrollably as fifty thousand volts enter my body.

Dropping to the floor, I look up and stare at Remy's mother's sinister smirk before something collides with my head. My vision dots and just before I black out, I hear her murmur, "I'm going to make so much money off of you, Thatcher Vanderbelt, so much fucking money."

HENDRIX

"FOR FUCK'S SAKE, Thatch, answer your damn fucking phone," I grumble for the tenth time today. Thatcher still isn't answering his phone and it's starting to piss me off. Usually, I'd accept he'd be balls deep in his girl, even if it is a school day, but since his girl is currently sitting at her desk across from me and just as worried about him, something's up.

"Has he answered yet?" Saint asks as he slides into his seat next to me.

"No," I hiss, shaking my head in frustration.

"Shit," he sneers.

Where the fuck are you, Brother?

"Don't you guys have that weird triplet thing?" Lennon asks, breaking the silence that fell over us.

"What?" I snap at him, confused as to why us being triplets is anything of importance right now.

"You're triplets, right?" I nod. "Don't you guys usually have that telepathic connection thing?" he asks, and I stare blankly at him. My blank expression annoys him, and he throws his hands up in frustration. I feel that frustration because, yes, Thatcher, Saint, and I are triplets, but we don't have that super strong psychic bond thing and right now, a super strong psychic bond thing would be real fucking handy.

"You can feel something, can't you?" Saint asks as if he can read my mind right now.

I nod because Lennon's half right, I feel something is wrong, but I can't pinpoint what. I do know sitting here in history isn't going to find him. "Fuck this," I hiss as I stand up, walk between the desks, ready to leave the classroom when Mrs. Reed, stands up and rests her hands on her desk. "Sit down, Mr. Vanderbelt, class isn't over."

Stopping in front of her desk, I glare at the woman and without a word, she sits back down. Smiling at her, I walk out of class with Saint close behind me.

Turning to face my brother, I stare at him. "What are you doing?"

"Helping," he states matter-of-factly.

"Saint," I growl.

"Hendrix," he hisses back at me and stares at me in a way that lets me know he's not going anywhere. He's a stubborn asshole when he wants to be and right now, that stubbornness is waving its tassel covered tits at me.

"I'm going for a drive."

"Good, I'm coming too."

"Fine," I hiss through clenched teeth.

He falls into step beside me as we make our way down the corridor toward the exit.

"How about we start at home?" he suggests.

"Fine," I snap.

Pulling through the gates, we head up the driveway toward home, not that it's been that for a long time. My phone pings with multiple messages as we reach the circular driveway. I know it's Quinn but I'm not ready to deal with her right now. One drama at a time.

"You going to get that?" Saint asks when it pings again, but I ignore him and point, Thatcher's car is sitting next to Father's. Shaking my head, I can't believe the fucker's been here the whole time.

Pulling up behind his car, without a word to Saint, we exit my car and storm into the house.

"Oh, boys," Lisette coos as we enter. Alfred stands to the side and shakes his head at our lack of reaction to Lisette. Ignoring them both, I stalk toward the stairs, taking them two at a time, and head up to our old rooms but stop when I glance into our father's office and see a hand resting on his desk.

Saint and I share a look. He shrugs and we walk over to the door, I lift my hand and push the down open. Mom's sitting in the chair behind the desk, a folder is in her hands and she's just staring at it. Tears stream down her cheeks.

"Mom?" Saint says.

She doesn't move, just stares down at the folder clasped in her hands.

We both enter and make our way over to Mom. Kneeling down next to her, she finally looks at me, surprised to see me.

"Where did you come from?"

"The door," I reply and my smart-ass response causes her lips to lift into a sad grin. "What's going on? Why are you in here crying?"

"The door was ajar and when I came in, I noticed there

were files open on your father's desk. I ... I came over and I started to read." She swallows deeply and I have never seen Mom look so broken.

"What is it?" I ask her.

She shuffles a few papers around and then hands me a file, but I notice she has an envelope clutched in her hand. Saint comes up behind me and I open it. We begin to read over what's in my hands and it's not until we get to the very last page that I understand what has Mom frozen.

I'm looking at birth records for a set of twins, birth certificates, and adoption papers. The first birth certificate is for a girl. It lists her first name as Risa and her date of birth, but everything else is blank. The second certificate is also blank, except for the first name and date of birth but it's a name I'd recognize anywhere.

Shuffling those to the back, I look at the adoption papers next. There are two sets, one is mostly blacked out, except for the name Risa. The second is for Rian, our cousin. This confirms his adoption to Dad's sister and her husband.

Throwing the file on the desk, I hiss, "What the fuck is this for? Is he adopted?"

Mom shakes her head and sniffs. "I have no clue, but it seems your father has more secrets that involve his sister, your cousin, and a child named Risa. Every time I think I've discovered all his secrets, more pop up."

"What other secrets?" Saint asks, leaning against the shelf behind the desk, crossing his arms.

"There are too many to unleash, but you boys don't need to worry about them. He's dead now and they all died with him."

"Well, not all of them," I throw out and then I ask the question I'm not sure I want the answer to, "Do you think we have a sister out there? And that Rian is our brother and not our cousin?"

"Don't be fucking stupid," Saint snarls.

"That there," I tap the file on the desk, "alludes otherwise."

"It could be fake," Saint offers.

"And why would Dad have a fake file like that? That makes no sense."

"Nothing with him ever does make sense," Mom adds. Then she stands and looks to Saint and me. "What are you boys doing here anyway? Shouldn't you be at school? Are Reign and Thatcher here too?" Just as my mom asks, Lisette enters the room with a tray of drinks.

"Thanks, Lisette," Mom says, smiling at her and I love seeing her look relaxed.

"Ummm, Reign's at school but Thatcher, we, umm, can't find him."

"He was here last night," Lisette says as she pours Mom a cup of tea. "That boy scared the bejesus out of me."

"Is he still here?" I ask her.

She shakes her head. "Sorry, I'm not sure."

"Do you know where he went?"

Again, she shakes her head. "Sorry, Hendrix, I don't. I was doing the final checks before heading off to bed when he raced upstairs. He looked like he was on a mission."

Turning around, I exit the office and head to Thatch's bedroom but he's not in there. Returning to the office, I pass Alfred along the way and then I step back into the room.

"Anything?" Saint asks, but I shake my head. "Fuck," he hisses.

As I walk back over to them, I notice a piece of paper poking out from under the desk. Bending down, I pick it up and begin to read. "Fuck me," I whisper.

"What is it?" Saint asks.

"Another doozy of a secret, but this one involves Rochelle Hearst too."

Mom rolls her eyes and looks at the paper. "Even with the death of your father, that slut is still in my life, but I can guarantee you one thing, that bitch isn't getting a cent from your father's estate. That check is unsigned, therefore it's null and void." Mom grasps her fingers over the envelope tightly. Saint mouths 'what check?' but I shake my head because I know nothing of any checks. "I wish I never have to see that woman again."

"Mom, your son is dating her daughter, that might be a little hard."

"I can try, but thankfully her daughter isn't anything like her. Remington is a lovely girl, and I can see she's good for Thatcher and as a mom, that's all I want. I want my sons to be happy and in love, like I once was." Mom gets this goofy look on her face and for a moment there, she looks happy. "Now, what's the next secret your father has been keeping?"

Closing my eyes, I take a deep breath. "It seems he and Rochelle are into human trafficking. They were going to sell Rem and Grayson."

"What about Arlen?"

"There's no mention of him, but I guess his return from the dead would put him into the 'to be trafficked' column too."

"My God," Mom scoffs. "I wish he was still alive so I could kill him again."

Saint's and my eyes widen.

"Again?" I question.

"You know what I mean," Mom nonchalantly says. "Whoever killed him did us all a favor. The world is a better place without him in it."

Watching Mom just now, I process her words and she's not wrong, the world is definitely better off without him being in it, but her words just now *"kill him again"* have me suspecting her as being the killer but surely if it was her, she'd have come forward when Thatcher was arrested, right?

My phone begins to ring and when I pull it out, it's an unknown number. Usually, I ignore them because it's a telemarketer or someone claiming to be from the IRS telling me I'm going to be arrested for tax fraud or some shit. But my Spidey senses are telling me I need to answer so I do but before I can say anything, the person calling beats me to it. "I need you."

"Thatcher? What the fuck, man?"

"I don't know where the fuck I am, but I need you to find me."

"Of course, what can you tell me?"

"I'm in some underground fight club. I had to knock a guard out to get his phone. Thank fuck I know your number by heart."

"The fuck?"

"Focus," he barks. "You need to get me out of here or I'm going to die. This is a to-the-death fight."

"Fuck," I hiss again, "just keep your head down, don't go all Thatcher-like and get yourself killed."

"Trust me, I'll be a Boy-fucking-Scout. Find Rochelle, she's the one who took me."

"That fucking cunt." Before we can say anything else, there's a commotion on the other end of the line. "Thatcher?" I shout, but the call disconnects. "Fuck," I sneer. Looking up at Mom and Saint, I see worry etched on their faces. "It's not good."

REMY

WHEN HENDRIX and Saint raced out of history, I wanted to follow them, but I knew I'd just slow them down so I stayed. I can't tell you what Mrs. Reed taught us today because all I can focus on is Thatcher is missing and Mom is blowing up my phone, wanting to catch up and bitching that Grayson, Arlen, and I left the hospital before she arrived.

They both think Mom's involved in everything, but as much as she's the bitch of all bitches, there's no way she'd have us kidnapped or fake Arlen's death, right?

"What's got you thinking so hard, Sis?" Grayson asks, dropping onto the sofa next to me. We're currently staying in a house they found on Airbnb since my room at school isn't big enough for the three of us, ohh, and Brennan set it on fire.

"Do you really think Mom is involved?"

"I don't know what to think, but the fact the three of us ended up in that place and Brennan was working with a woman, who else could it be?"

"There are two and a half billion women in the world, and you think it's Mom?"

He shrugs at me as my phone begins to ring again but this time, it's Hendrix. "Did you find him?" I breathlessly shout into the phone.

"No, but we need your help."

"Anything," I tell him and I mean it.

"Can you come to the house?"

"Your mom's house?"

"Yeah. Saint and I are here. Reign is on his way, and ummm, bring your brothers, this involves them too."

"Ooookay," I reply, "we'll leave as soon as Arl gets out of the shower."

"See you then." With that he hangs up.

Grayson is already up and banging on the bathroom door demanding Arlen to hurry up.

Thirty minutes later, we're pulling into the Vanderbelts' driveway and when I see Thatcher's car here, I get excited. As soon as Grayson comes to a stop, I open the door and race toward the house. Taking the front stairs two at a time, I push the door open and shout, "Thatcher? Thatch, where are you?"

Reign steps into the entryway from the living room and when I see the look on his face, I know he's not here. "He's not here, is he?" I dejectedly ask.

Reign shakes his head and my heart breaks.

My legs giveaway and I fall to my knees, the emotion I've been holding in lets go. Tears cascade down my cheeks, splashing on the marble tiles below.

Covering my face with my hands, I break down and sob.

Arms wrap around me and then a soft, soothing voice whispers, "He'll be fine." Turning my head, I see Thatcher's mom staring at me. "My son is a fighter, and he will do everything he can to get back to you."

"What if he doesn't?"

"We have to think positive, now, come into the living room, we are going to need your help in getting him back."

"You know who has him?"

"We have an idea," Hendrix says, "and we're going to need you and your brothers to get him back."

My eyes widen. "My mom has him, doesn't she?" He nods. Shaking my head, I push up to my feet and I stare at him. "Let's go get Thatcher."

THATCHER

My ribs are possibly broken, and the pain is killing me. The asshole guard crash tackled me after discovering I knocked out his colleague and called Hendrix, but thankfully, I smashed the phone, and they have no clue who I called.

Sliding down the wall, I kick my feet out in front of me, holding my side as I do. Fuck, this sucks. I really fucking hope they find me soon because I really do not want to have to fight to the death. I thought underground fight till the death things only happened in movies, clearly I was wrong.

Sweat beads on my forehead as the pain becomes too

much. There's no way I can win in this condition, I need to figure a way out, just in case my brothers don't come through.

The sound of heels click and echo through the underground cavern. The footsteps come closer and closer. Not wanting to be at a disadvantage when that bitch arrives, I grit my teeth and push myself up. Leaning against the cinder block wall, I stand and wait.

A moment later, Rochelle comes into view smiling like she's won. She unlocks my cage and steps in. "Thatcher Vanderbelt, what an honor to have you in my little club, do you like it?" she gloats, spreading her arms wide, proud of her hellhole.

"Not particularly, the room service is bleak at best and there's a god-awful stench, but that might be because you just entered the room," I throw at her. Her face scrunches into a scowl. Clearly, she was expecting me to be a blubbering mess, but she's severely underestimated me. She quickly schools her features and laughs, actually she fucking cackles like the fucking witch bitch she is. "I'll be glad when that smart mouth of yours gets what it deserves, your father may have been too weak to end you and your brothers, but I'm not. I'll end the Vanderbelt line"—she lifts her hand and lowers each finger while singsonging—"one by fucking one." She looks over her shoulder and then growls to one of her henchmen, "Get him ready."

The guard from before and another comes into view and they each nod at her like the pussy-whipped fuckers they are. Rochelle turns her attention back to me and smiles a sinister smile. "Enjoy your final minutes, Thatcher, I'll be sure to console my daughter when you're gone."

Her words snap something inside of me and I race toward her. The need to strangle the life from her at the mention of Remy has me raging. Her men catch me before I reach her. They slam me back into the wall I was just leaning against and I drop to the floor, causing a searing pain to shoot through me. My ribs burn even more now. I take a deep breath through clenched teeth, urging myself not to pass out from the pain.

A hand grabs me and roughly forces me up onto my feet. "Let's go," he hisses. Pushing me out of my cell, he directs me down a corridor to my ill-waited fate.

As soon as I enter the arena, if you'd call it that, I know this is it. For an underground fight-till-the-death thing, it's much more elaborate than I thought. There's a raised dome like you'd see in WWE. On one side is a platform with throne-like chairs, presumably for the VIPs. On the other three sides, it's standing room only. I take in the room and realize I'm fucked, totally fucked and not in the good Remy's pussy clenching my dick kind of fucked. I'm fucked in the I'm done for kind of way. There's no way in hell I can fight till the death and win, not in this condition. Hell, I don't think I could even if my ribs weren't broken.

I'm shoved again and that feeling of 'they won't find me in time' washes through me again. We enter a waiting room of sorts, and every head turns my way. There are ten other guys who stand between me and my freedom. I'm pushed farther into the room and each one of these assholes sizes me up and sneers, trying to intimidate me.

When it comes down to it, it's them or me and if I was in a better headspace, I'd be doing exactly the same thing in return.

"You've got ten minutes," one of the guards tells the room, everyone nods and starts jumping about, clearly these guys are happy to be here. Before the asshole leaves, he focuses on me, drawing the attention of the other guys too. "And, pretty boy, you're up first. You're gonna make me a whole lotta cash tonight." And with that parting remark, he exits, slamming the door shut behind him, the deafening click of the lock echoes through the room.

Holding my side to try and ease up the pain, I slowly make my way toward a bench in the middle of the room. FYI, holding my side doesn't do shit, it still hurts like a motherfucker.

Taking a seat, I suck in a deep breath and wince each time I move. I'm pretty sure something is broken but very soon I'll be dead, so it doesn't really matter.

Lowering my head, I close my eyes and think of Remy. Thank fuck it's me here and not her, no one should have to live through this, well, maybe Rochelle and my father should but that's kind of moot since he's dead and she's running this shit show. I can feel all their eyes on me, but right now I don't care, I close mine and focus on the memories of Remy and what could have been. "I'm sorry, Peach," I mumble to myself.

"Who's Peach?" a voice says across from me.

Opening my eyes, I'm surprised to see four guys standing in front of me, towering over me. The atmosphere is suddenly filled with anger and it reaffirms I'm not making it out of here alive. I swallow, praying Hendrix will make it here on time.

"My girl," I say, smiling when I think of her.

"You're hurt," another states.

"I'll be fine," I tell him.

It's his turn to scoff.

The door creaks open and the guard stands there. He lifts his hand and points a finger at me. "Let's go, pretty boy."

Bright lights blind me as I step into the dome. Waiting for me inside the cage is a guy, he's shirtless and pacing back and forth. Blood coats his skin and I'm pretty sure it's fresh. There are puddles of red liquid sitting in pools on the dome matting.

Speakers above crackle to life and then Rochelle's shrill voice bellows across the dome. "You know the rules, keep going until there's only one of you breathing." She looks at me and then sinisterly says, "May the best man win."

The guy takes a fight stance so I take mine, wincing as I lift my hands. This is going to hurt like a motherfucking bitch, but I'm not going down without a fight. Sure, I haven't had any training, but I know how to throw a punch. Plus, I haven't had enough time with my peach yet and if I can win, it'd stick it to her mother and that's a victory I'd die for.

A whistle blows and in the blink of an eye, the guy advances toward me. Somehow, I manage to dodge him so he doesn't take me down, but he forces me backward, I gasp for breath, and he takes the chance and his fist hits my stomach. Bending over, I hiss, "Motherfucker." A growl slips from my lips as I stand up straight. He takes another swing and clips my jaw, knocking me down onto my ass.

He leaps toward me again, his fist flying toward my face but by some fucking miracle, I move my head and his fist slams into the mat below. Another growl slips through his lips, and then he shocks me and whispers, "I'm sorry, it's you or me, dude, and I don't feel like dying today." In a one-two punch combo, one fist collides with my cheek and the other flies into my ribs.

The wind is knocked from me. My body freezes and I lie here, staring up at the guy straddling me, at the guy who is going to end my life. "Do it," I whisper-hiss.

He pulls his arm back, ready to unleash his fury when a loud bang echoes around us. He pauses with his fist midair, and I take the opportunity and knock him off me. Pulling out my best Jackie Chan moves, I somehow manage to kick him in the groin and scramble away from him.

I'm struggling for air.

I can't breathe.

My vision is fuzzy, I think when he punched my chest, my rib punctured my lung. I hold my chest, doing my best not to pass out and then I hear it. A voice I'd recognize anywhere purrs, "Thatcher."

Turning my head, I see a blond blur coming toward me but before it reaches me, my eyes close and everything goes dark.

REMY

"HE HAS TO MAKE IT," I cry, "he has too."

"He's a tough asshole," Reign assures me, "he'll be fine." But from the look on his face, he doesn't even believe it and if he doesn't, how am I supposed to?

"Reign is right," Estelle agrees, dropping into the plastic seat beside me. She reaches over and takes my hand. "Thatcher is strong, he'll get through this."

Nodding, I smile but we all know it's a forced one. How can I smile when the man I love is in surgery after my psycho mother kidnapped him and entered him into a fight-till-the-death match?

Leaning back in my chair, I sigh and close my eyes, exhaustion is setting in. Thatcher has been in surgery for over three hours now. He has a punctured lung, several broken ribs, and a concussion. It could be worse and had we not gotten there when we did, he could be dead.

The police have just left and will come back once he's awake to get his statement, but regardless of what he says, mother has been arrested and she can no longer hurt anyone.

After an anonymous call was made to the local authorities, after we got Thatcher out of there, the FBI and local cops raided the warehouse where the illegal fight club was being held. They found something even more sinister deep down underground. On the lower levels, they discovered cages of kidnapped women and children, ready to be sold to the highest bidder and trafficked.

My mother really is a monster and if she wasn't locked away, I would kill her myself. How my own mother could do something like that, I will never know. Orange will be her color choice for the foreseeable future and when this goes to trial, I will be in the front row, cheering the prosecution on. Wishing with everything I have she gets locked away for life. It's times like these I wish the death penalty was still on the table.

The doctor walks in and removes his surgery cap, he's stone-faced, and I don't know if it's good news or not. "Mrs. Vanderbelt," he says and Estelle, myself, and the boys all jump up and walk over to him.

"How's my son?" Estelle asks, her voice wavering. Reaching out I take her hand in mine and squeeze, we stare at the doctor, waiting for him to speak.

"Thatcher is in recovery—"

"Thank God," Estelle shouts and we all hug one another tightly.

"The surgery went well," the doctor continues, "we've

repaired his lung and as soon as he regains consciousness, we'll transfer him to a private room."

"Can we see him?" I ask.

"Once he's in his room, family will be able to visit with him."

"Ohhh," I dejectedly sigh, nodding.

"She's family," Estelle informs the doctor, squeezing my hand again. "We'll all be going to see him."

He nods but you can tell he knows I'm not family per se. "A nurse will be back when you can visit."

"Thank you, Doctor." Estelle drops my hand and offers hers to the doctor. He shakes and then leaves the waiting area. She turns to me and pulls me in for a hug. "Told you he'd be okay."

"No one likes an 'I told you so,' Mom," Saint says, shaking his head and smiling. "But in saying that, Thatch would totally be gloating if it was one of us in there and we just found out that all was okay."

We all laugh because it's true, Thatcher is arrogant at the best of times but when he's right, everyone knows about it.

Thatcher has been transferred to a private room but was still quite groggy from the surgery and he soon fell back to sleep. Pulling the chair closer to his bed, I carefully take his hand in mine, not wanting to bump the IV ports.

Placing a kiss on his knuckles, I hold his hand on the bed and rest my head on his upper arm. It's not the most comfortable position to be in but I need to be near him.

A gruff, "Hey," echoes from above me and I immediately lift my head. A smile appears on my face when I see Thatcher's gorgeous eyes looking alert, staring down at me.

"Hey," I repeat, "how you feeling?"

"Like I was in a fight with Mike Tyson."

"Too soon, Thatch, too soon."

"Are you okay?"

"Me?" I scoff, "I'm fine. I wasn't kidnapped or nearly beaten to death in an underground fight club."

"Peach, I'm fine. Seriously. It was thoughts of you that kept me going while I was in your mother's clutches."

"She can never hurt us again," I tell him. "She's currently sitting in jail and the list of her charges are the size of your e—"

"Dick," he interrupts, "you were going to say enormous dick, right?"

"I think the drugs are messing with your head. Did you forget you also asked the surgeon for gender reassignment surgery before you went in? You are now the proud owner of a vagina."

"Nice try but for the record, the only vagina I own is yours. Now come here and gimme a kiss, I did nearly die, after all."

"That I can do." Pushing up from the seat, I lean down and press my lips against Thatcher's for a quick kiss, but that isn't enough for him, he slides his hand around the back of my neck and pulls me down into him for the kiss of all kisses. His tongue pushes into my mouth, tangling with mine. The moment is interrupted when there's a knock on the door. "I'm here for your sponge bath," a deep voice says from the doorway.

Pulling away from Thatcher, I look over my shoulder and see Rian standing there. I feel Thatcher flinch and when I look at him, he smiles but it's his 'I'm hiding something' smile.

"Dude, what's up?" Thatcher says to Rian.

"Not much, how you feeling? Heard you auditioned for *Fight Club* 2 but they passed 'cause you weren't tough enough."

"I'm tougher than you, asshole."

"Wow, they must have you on some good drugs, you're delusional." Rolling my eyes, I shake my head at the two of them and when I catch Thatcher's eye, I definitely know something's up.

"Rem, babe, you mind getting me a Coke ... maybe with some whiskey in it?"

"Coke I can do, whiskey and meds, not a good combo." Leaning down, I press another kiss to his lips and then whisper, "Everything okay?"

He nods. "I'll tell you later."

With another quick kiss, I leave Thatcher and Rian alone, wondering what he could possibly need to chat to him about.

THATCHER

WATCHING Rian say bye to Remy, a sinking feeling develops in my gut. How do I tell my cousin he has a twin sister? And he's adopted? ... And maybe my brother too? Dad having those files can only mean that, right?

He looks to me with not a care in the world and it guts me I'm about to implode his world. "So, Remy's mother, huh, who would have thought that?"

"Everyone, she's a delusional bitch," I sneer, still pissed at the she-devil for all that she's done. I don't think I'll ever forget what she did to me or what she was going to do to

Rem. Forcing myself to sit up a little, I wince when the pain hits.

"You really had us all worried there for a second, man," Rian says, toying with his boot on the floor.

Inhaling deeply, I take a breath, hold it, and close my eyes.

"Thatch, you okay, man? Do you need me to get the nurse?" he says, pointing his thumb over his shoulder toward the door.

"No, I'm fine. I ... um ... ahh, we need to talk," I stammer, gripping the back of my neck anxiously.

"Talk? About what?" he asks, dropping into the seat Remy has been sitting in.

"Look, I don't know how to tell you this, so I'll just come out with it."

Rian eyes me cautiously, waiting. The silence, well apart from the heart rate monitor beeping beside me, is deafening. He nods in that 'come on' kind of way.

Nodding, I lick my lips. "Okay, so, when I went snooping in my father's office, I found something."

Rian chuckles. "Something? Care to elaborate? But if it's dino porn, you can keep that shit to yourself. This one time—"

"Rian, focus," I snap.

"Right, sorry. Continue."

I swallow, hating every fucking second of being the one to tell Rian this secret. How my father and his parents could keep this secret from him, I will never know.

"You're adopted," I say in one quick breath, the words flowing into one but from the expression on his face, he heard me.

"Adopted?" he screeches. "Yeah right, nice joke, man." He laughs and slaps the mattress beside me but stops suddenly when he notices I'm not laughing. He looks off into the distance. A stoic expression washes over him. His mouth opens and closes but nothing comes out. I've shocked him mute.

"Rian, man, I'm sorry. I found the papers just before everything went to shit. I didn't want it to come out like this, but you have the right to know."

Rian chews on his bottom lip while staring into space.

"Ri?" I holler. Gaining his attention, he looks at me before a frown mars his face.

"So, I'm adopted, lots of kids are. Doesn't mean anything, right?" He shrugs.

"No, it doesn't, you're family, Ri, and you always will be," I reaffirm, but my cousin knows me too well, he can read my expression clearly.

"Why do I feel like there's more?"

"Because we're Vanderbelts and there's always something else." I exhale, hating having to tell him this next part. I think telling him this is worse than the adoption revelation. I hesitate, worried about his reaction. "You have a sister," I murmur softly.

"What?" he hisses, his gaze locked on mine.

"You have a twin sister," I add.

Rian jumps up and starts to pace back and forth across the small hospital room, muttering to himself about being adopted and having a sister. I fucking hate seeing him like this and if I know my cousin like I do, right now his head is filling with all the wrong ideas.

"Wanna talk about it?"

"Talk?" he snaps. "Talk about what, Thatcher? That my parents aren't my fucking parents? That my entire life has been a lie?" he shouts and seeing him like this is killing me ... and I still have to tell him I think my dad is his dad.

"I ... I need some fucking air." He spins on his heel ready to leave, but I need to tell him this next bit.

"There's more?" I spit out.

My words stop him in his tracks. He spins to face me. "What fucking more could there be?"

"There are two more things, actually."

"Fuck me," he dejectedly hisses. Walking back over to the bed, he drops back into the seat. "Okay, shoot?"

"Your sister, she ... she was sold."

"Sold, what the fuck do you mean?"

"Risa was sold to the highest bidder."

"Risa?" he whispers her name, and a look of bewilderment crosses his face. "Her name is Risa?" I nod. "Okay, well I need to find her, but you said there were two things."

Nodding, I bite my lip. "I ... I think my dad might be your bio dad."

He just sits there. Silently staring at me. He blinks occasionally but he doesn't utter a word. "Ri, are you okay?" I ask, knowing right now, he's far from okay.

He lets out a burst of air, sliding off the chair and onto the floor. He lifts his gaze and our eyes lock. I see hurt, devastation, betrayal, and longing in his eyes.

"And my mom? My real one?" he asks, his voice scratchy.

"We'll track her down," I tell him, even though I have no fucking clue how to do that.

The door opens and Remy enters, seeing Rian on the floor she looks over at me then back at him.

"Why does life suck?" Rian says out loud. I'm sure he's not actually asking us, I think it's just rhetorical. A fact.

"Rian, are you okay?" Remy asks, walking around the bed and sitting beside me.

I take her hand in mine while we both watch Rian as he shimmies around and leans against the bedside table. He spreads his legs out in front of him, letting out a deep breath.

This time the silence isn't deafening.

Finally, he lifts his gaze to Remy and me. "How ... how do I live a life that's a lie? My entire life's a fucking joke. I'm not even a Vanderbelt. I ... I'm a nobody," he says.

"You are a Vanderbelt, Rian. The blood running through your veins doesn't change," I say, my voice breaks at the end, "you ARE a Vanderbelt." Rian misses it but my girl, she picks up on it. Remy stares at me and once again, nothing but silence fills the room.

This secret needs to stay within this room because once this gets out, who knows what else it will unleash upon us.

Crestwood is beginning to fall, and I have a feeling this is just the tip of the iceberg, and I'm afraid it's going to drag us all down with it.

REMY

... four weeks later

A LOT HAS HAPPENED in the last four weeks and tonight, we are going to let our hair down and forget all the shit and celebrate we're still alive. I kinda feel bad celebrating since my mother is dead. Ohh yeah, I should mention that. Mother was killed in prison last week, she clearly pissed the wrong person off inside because one afternoon someone strangled her with a pair of panties while she was on the toilet.

I'm the worst daughter in the world because I felt nothing when Grayson told me, but then again, she did have me kidnapped by Brennan with the intention to sell me off to the highest bidder. We still have no clue what she planned to do with my brothers but whatever the plan, it went astray when Thatcher and the boys rescued us. I'm guessing she took him and made him participate in a high stakes fight-till-the-death thing to make up for the loss of my income. Thankfully, we all got to each other in time and there was no death involved. My man was beaten severely by a man who was just trying to protect himself.

Thatcher spent seven days in the hospital after his ordeal and the day before he was released, I did something I never thought I would do one afternoon after school when I went to visit him ...

... my heart is racing as I walk toward Thatcher's hospital room, at least if I have a heart attack, I'm in the right place. My hands are clammy and my pussy, she's throbbing like no tomorrow. I'm surprised those around me can't hear the pulsing drum of my clit.

Stopping outside his room, I take a deep breath, push down on the door handle, and enter his room.

"Hey," he nonchalantly says in greeting.

"Hey," I reply back, leaning against the closed door. Reaching behind me, I flick the lock.

"What's going on?"

"Shhhh," I whisper, covering my lips with my index finger. "I'm here to make things all better," I seductively tell him as I begin to unbutton the coat I'm wearing.

One by one, the buttons pop open and then I drop my coat to the floor. Leaving me in my Mary Jane school shoes, knee-high socks, and a sexy nurse outfit that hugs my curves and shows off the girls, and from the heated look on Thatcher's face right now, I've got the sexy part down pat.

"Fuck me, babe. You're a vision."

Not uttering a word, I stand here and trace over the swell of my breasts with my fingertips, circling my nipple through the flimsy material. I'm so turned on right now and apart from my finger tracing over my skin, there has been no touching. "I'm here to give you your medicine."

"Mmmmhmpf," Thatch replies, throwing the sheet off and showing me his tented boxers. He cups his dick and begins to stroke himself.

Licking my lips, I focus on his hand moving back and forth over his shaft. "As your nurse, I'm here to administer anything you need."

"Well, it just so happens that right now, I need your mouth on my dick and then once I've come down that pretty little throat of yours, you're going to ride my dick so I can play with those sexy as fuck tits of yours."

"Lucky for you, I have just the prescription to cater to your needs and wants."

"Well, what are you waiting for?"

He pulls his dick out and offers it to me. Walking over to the bed, I lean down and press my lips to his. My tongue pushes into his mouth as I reach down and grip his cock. Together we work our hands up and down his shaft. "Babe, fair warning, I'm going to come extremely fast. It's been far too long."

"Well, lucky for you, I can go all night long."

With that said, I climb up onto the bed and throw my leg over him. Sliding down his body, I circle my hips as I pass his cock, earning myself a hiss. That sound has my already wet panties soaking further.

With my eyes locked on him, I open my mouth and swirl my tongue around the tip, licking the head before hollowing my cheeks and taking him deep into my mouth. Bobbing my head up and down, I suck on his dick like a starved woman. FYI Thatcher-flavored lollipops would be a bestseller.

Thatcher wasn't wrong with how quick he'd come because way sooner than I expected, he comes with a groan and I drink down every last drop of his essence.

Lifting off him, he apologizes but I press my finger to his lips. "Uh-uh, I'm not done yet."

Alternating between licking and kissing, I make my way up his abs. I place a lingering kiss over the bandage on his upper chest before licking along his collarbone, up his neck, along his jawline, and up to his lips.

We lie here kissing one another until I feel his once again hard dick pressing into my belly. Lifting myself up, I push my panties to the side and slowly slide down his dick. Both of us groan in pleasure once I'm fully seated on him.

With our eyes locked on one another, I begin to gyrate my hips in circles before I ride him. Thatcher reaches up and cups my breasts, squeezing them in his palms. My head drops back, and I give myself over to the sensations building deep within.

Freeing my boobs, he tweaks my nipples in that way he knows I love and before long, that tingly feeling develops low in my belly. "I'm close," I whisper.

Thatcher reaches down and presses on my clit through my panties and that's the detonation I need. My pussy clenches down on him and I explode. A tsunami of pleasure crashes through my body and I bite down on my lips to stop myself from screaming, we are in a hospital after all. My release sets Thatcher off and he too comes, spilling his seed deep inside of me.

Opening my eyes, I stare down at him, breathing heavily from administering Thatcher's, and my, medicine. "It's tough work being a nurse," I pant.

"I better be the only patient you give medicine to like that."

Nonchalantly I shrug my shoulders at him, earning myself a growl.

"Ease up, caveman. You know you're the only one for me, well except for if Nick Bateman comes through that door. He does and it'll be like Thatcher who?"

"Nick Bateman, whoever the hell he is, is a dead man if he walks through that door. You are mine, Remington Hearst, mine."

"And you're mine, Thatcher Vanderbelt."

Climbing off Thatcher, I clean myself up and then climb into bed next to him. We fall asleep watching television, happy and content with each other ...

"What you thinking about, Peach?" the man I was just reminiscing about asks me, sliding his hands around my waist from behind.

"The day I played sexy nurse for you in the hospital."

"That was a good day, a veeeery good day. Maybe you should give me some medicine now."

"Sorry, dude, you have to wait till later. We need to get to this party."

"Do we have to?" he whines like a baby.

"Yes, yes we do. Rian needs a night to let loose with his friends and stop focusing on finding his sister."

"I hate I imploded his world like I did."

"You had to, Thatch. I just wish your aunt and uncle would give him answers. Them not willing to discuss things makes me think there's way more to the story."

"Of course there is, they're fucking Vanderbelts. Nothing is ever simple with us."

"Tell me about it. You do remember how we started, right?"

"Yes, yes I do," he replies with a smirk that sets my insides ablaze, "but you know what?"

"What?"

"I wouldn't change a thing because I got the girl." He lowers his head and presses his lips to mine and kisses me. The kiss leaves me light-headed but then again, I'm always light-headed around him. We may have started off hating one another but there's a fine line between love and hate, and we've managed to push through the hate and develop a love I will fight till the end of time for.

REMY

THE PARTY last night was just what the students at Crestwood Prep needed and like most parties at Crestwood, it started with the usual Lords 'we rule all' bullshit game but this time, I was on The Lords' side. And I have to admit, it's so much more fun being with them, just don't tell them I said that.

I'm walking back from lunch with Alani and that girl has no idea I know what she got up to last night. I found out sooooo many secrets last night, luckily for everyone, I'm good at keeping my mouth shut.

My phone rings and I smile when I see Arlen's name on the screen. "Hey, hey, big brother."

"Hey, hey, little sister. What's shaking?"

"Not much, just had lunch with Alani and now I'm headed to the library to work on my history paper. It's due Monday."

"And let me guess, it's already finished but you being you, will be reading it for the millionth time to make sure it's perfect."

"Maaaaaaybe."

"No maybe about it, Jellybean, but anyway, I was wondering if you want to get dinner with Grayson and me one night this week?"

"Sure, can I bring Thatch?"

"Not this time. I ... I have something I want to tell you guys."

"Is it about you know who?"

"No, I've decided what I want to do now that I'm back from the dead."

"I'm so happy for you, Arl. And yes, I'll be there with bells on."

"Please wear more than bells, you don't really have the bits I like to ogle ... and you're my sister, that's just gross."

"I missed you and your weirdness, Arl. Text me the deets and I'll be there."

"Sweet, see you then."

Hanging up from my brother, I go to head up to my room but the person I've been wanting to chat to is alone in the reception room, so I walk over and plonk down next to him, "what's up Re-EIGN?"

"Not much, and you Rem-E?"

"Same," I reply with a shrug and then I decide to go for it. "I know," I tell him.

"You know what?" I give him 'the look' and his eyes widen. "How?"

"I've had an idea for a while now but when you guys found us at the cabin, it confirmed my suspicion. But what really confirmed it and added a whole other layer of 'now it really makes sense' was when I, umm, ahh, saw you last night."

His eyes widen. "Please don't tell anyone. I ... I still have a few things to work out but I'm, well, we're going to confess all soon."

"Look, it's not my secret to tell but, Reign, don't hide who you really are. You are an amazing guy and I want you to be happy. Actually, I want you all to be happy."

"I am happy, Rem, it's just ..."

"I get it but just know, I'm here for you if you ever need someone to chat to. So is Arlen."

"I know, I've already spoken to him." He looks sheepish at revealing this to me. It's as if he feels like he's betraying everyone by talking to him.

"You have?" I ask him, shocked at this revelation.

"Yeah, he was my best friend, no, he was more than a best friend and I'll always love him, Rem, but ..."

"But you love—"

"Yeah. I do." He nods and gets that goofy in love look on his face. "Again, please don't say anything because I haven't said it yet."

"Your secret-ssss are safe with me but for what it's worth, I'm happy for you guys." And I mean that, it's like since I found love, I want everyone around me to find love too. I really hope Reign gets his happily ever after too, however unconventional it might be.

The End!

That's the end of Remy and Thatcher, we hope you enjoyed their story. Yes, there are still a few unanswered questions ... like who killed Thornton? Where's Rian's sister? What secrets is Reign hiding? But don't fret, you'll get some answers in the next Lords of Crestwood book, coming out next month.

Want to find out what happens next? Well, you can in Reign, book 2 in the Lords of Crestwood Prep series.

REIGN

This is our school, our kingdom.
My brother's and I rule, we are The Lords.
My secrets have always been just that mine. But my biggest secret is about to be exposed.
I'm in love with two people—Alani Thomas and Hudson Finley.
They love me and I love them.
I thought it was game over now that everyone was out in the open, turns out, it wasn't.
There's a new secret.
Nothing is as it seems and my end game, isn't as clear as I thought.

SPOTIFY PLAYLIST

Sweet But Pyscho - Ava Max
Bad Liar - Imagine Dragons
8 Letters - Why Don't We
Im A Mess - Bebe Rexha
Tequila - Dan+ Shay
Freaking Me Out - Ava Max
Queens Don't - Raelynn
Woman Like Me - Little Mix feat Nicki Minaj
Better - Britney Spears
Ruin My Life - Zara Larsson
Tribulation - Matt Maeson
Give 'Em Hell - Robbie Nevill
Blank Space - I Previal
Titanium - David Guetta feat Sia
Look What You Made Me Do - Taylor Swift
Guys Dont Like Me - It Boys!
Teeth - 5 Seconds Of Summer
Savage Love - Jason Smith feat Devon Derulo
You Broke Me First - Conor Maynard
There You Are - ZAYN
Small Doses - Bebe Rexha
Sweet Little Lies - Bülow
Like That - Bea Miller
Prisoner - Miley Cyrus feat Dua Lipa
Queen - Loren Gray
Train Wreck - James Arthur
Thick Skin - Leona Lewis
This Love - Camila Cabello
Flames - MOD SUN feat Avril Lavigne
What Other People Say - Sam Fischer feat Demi Lovato
Hard For Me - Charley
Healing - Riley Clemmons

Liar - Camila Cabello
Kill This Love - BLACKPINK
Sabotage - Bebe Rexha
The Heart What It Wants - Selena Gomez
You Don't Own Me - SAYGRACE feat G-Eazy
Sit Still, Look Pretty - Daya
Alarm - Anne-Marie
You Ruin Me - The Veronicas
Let It Go - Sofia Karlberg
You Set My World On Fire - Loving Caliber feat Selestine
Somebody To Die For - Hurts
Of These Chains - Red
Sweet Sacrifice - Evanescence
Born Without A Heart - Faouzia
Warrior - Beth Crowley
Kiss My (Uh Oh) - Anne-Marie feat Little Mix
Heavy Is The Crown - Daughtry
Secret - The Pieces
Hit Me With Your Best Shot - ADONA
Stuck Inside My Head - Riley Clemmons
Princess Dont Cry - CARYS
Games - Demi Lovato
Rapunzel - Emlyn
Tears Of Gold - Faouzia
Butterflies - Zendaya
The Audacity - Emlyn

This playlist can be found on Spotify.

ABOUT TARA LEE

Tara Lee is an Australian author who writes spicy romance, and men to swoon over. She comes from Hobart, Tasmania where she lives with her husband and two children.

When she's not a stay at home mum wrangling her two small children or fighting the voices in her head to be quiet she's getting up before the sun rises as a qualified baker.

Tara is a Pisces who survives on energy drinks, chocolate frappes and busting moves at Jazzicise for some me time.

ALSO BY TARA LEE

All of these books are available on Amazon.

ABOUT DL GALLIE

DL Gallie is from Queensland, Australia, but she's lived in many different places all over the world, including the UK and Canada. She currently resides in Central Queensland with her husband and two munchkins. She and her husband have been  together since she was sixteen, and although they drive each other crazy at times, she couldn't imagine her life without him.

Shortly after her son was born, DL began reading again. With encouragement from her husband, she picked up the pen and started writing, and now the voices in her head won't shut up.

DL enjoys listening to music, drinking white wine in the summer, red wine in the winter, and beer all year round. She's also never been known to turn down a cocktail, especially a margarita.

ALSO BY DL GALLIE

STAND ALONES

Antecedent

Doc Steel

Oops

Off the Books

Fractured:A driven world novel

Deck…the Balls

Secrets and Sunrises

Always in the Cards

Out of Nowhere

Love Me Like You Do

Never Let Me Go

Seven Nights

Seven Kisses

After the Ashes

PUCKING NOVELS

I Pucking Hate That I Love You

A Pucking Good Christmas

...and a few pucking more

FALLING NOVELS

These men make it hard not to fall for them

Falling for Dr. Kelly

Falling for Dr. Knight

Falling for Agent Cox

Falling for Agent Cruz

Falling:The Complete Collection

THE UNEXPECTED SERIES

When it comes to love, expect the unexpected

The Unexpected Gift

The Unexpected Letter

The Unexpected Package

The Unexpected Connection

The Unexpected series: The Complete Collection

THE CASTAWAY GROVE COLLECTION

Love has arrived in the Grove

Oasis

Unequivocal Love

Five Words

Broken Rules

…and a few more to come.

The Castaway Grove Collection, Vol 1

THE LIQUOR CABINET SERIES

Liquor has never been so disturbingly saucy

Malt Me (Book 1)

Tequila Healing (Book 2)

Wine Not (Book 3)

The Final Shot (Book 4)

The Liquor Cabinet: Series boxset